C00 16776240

EDINBURGH CITY LIBRARIES

D0297610

	WH	GN	CU	BN		MB
	$\frac{5}{00}$	$\frac{4}{01}$	$\frac{10}{01}$	✓	$\frac{10}{02}$	$\frac{04}{03}$

MAY 2

20

-2 JUN

THE KING OF THE BARBAREENS

Also available in this series:

Fred Archer	THE DISTANT SCENE
	THE SECRETS OF BREDON HILL
H. E. Bates	FLYING BOMBS OVER ENGLAND
Brenda Bullock	A POCKET WITH A HOLE
William Cooper	FROM EARLY LIFE
Kathleen Dayus	HER PEOPLE
Denis Farrier	COUNTRY VET
Lady Fortescue	BEAUTY FOR ASHES
	RETURN TO "SUNSET HOUSE"
Mollie Harris	A KIND OF MAGIC
	ANOTHER KIND OF MAGIC
Elspeth Huxley	GALLIPOT EYES
Rachel Knappett	A PULLET ON THE MIDDEN
Brian P. Martin	TALES OF TIME AND TIDE
	TALES OF THE OLD COUNTRYMEN
Victoria Massey	ONE CHILD'S WAR
Frank Moore	THE HORSES KNEW THE WAY
and John Hynam	
John Moore	PORTRAIT OF ELMBURY
	BRENSHAM VILLAGE
Phyllis Nicholson	COUNTRY BOUQUET
Valerie Porter	TALES OF THE OLD COUNTRY VETS
Geoffrey Robinson	HEDINGHAM HARVEST
Sheila Stewart	LIFTING THE LATCH
Jean Stone	
and Louise Brodie	TALES OF THE OLD GARDENERS
Edward Storey	FEN BOY FIRST
	IN FEN COUNTRY HEAVEN
	WINTER FENS
Joyce Storey	JOYCE'S WAR
Nancy Thompson	AT THEIR DEPARTING
Marrie Walsh	AN IRISH COUNTRY CHILDHOOD
Roderick Wilkinson	MEMORIES OF MARYHILL

THE KING
OF THE
BARBAREENS

Janet Hitchman

LARGE PRINT

Oxford, England

Copyright © Janet Hitchman, 1960

First published in Great Britain 1960
by Putnam

Published in Large Print 1998 by ISIS Publishing Ltd,
7 Centremead, Osney Mead, Oxford OX2 0ES.

We are delighted to be publishing our ISIS edition of this classic
book. Whilst every effort has been made to trace the owner of
the work without success, we would be pleased to hear from the
Author or her heirs.

All rights reserved

The moral right of the author has been asserted

British Library Cataloguing in Publication Data
Hitchman, Janet, 1916-
   The King of the Barbareens. – Large print ed.
   1. Hitchman, Janet, 1916- 2. Orphans – England – East
Anglia – Biography 3. Large type books
   I. Title
   362.7'32

ISBN 0-7531-5053-0

EDINBURGH CITY LIBRARIES

AC
C0016776240

CN HV

14·95 | 151 | 887
22/3/00 | G7

Printed and bound by MPG Books Ltd, Bodmin, Cornwall

FOR RACHAEL

CHAPTER
ONE

Oh will you surrender, oh will you surrender
The King of the Barbareens?
We *won't* surrender, we *won't* surrender
The King of the Barbareens.
I'll tell the King, I'll tell the King,
The King of the Barbareens.
You can tell the King, you can tell the King,
The King of the Barbareens.

Harry was King of the Barbareens, sitting on the bank
making a pop-gun, and Maudie was the messenger. The
rest of us, six or seven, perhaps more, holding hands in a
long line, surged back and forth, yelling our defiance.
Maudie, fat and delighted, took the message back, "They
o'nt surrender, oh King, oh King." Harry closed his pen-
knife, put that in his left pocket, and the unfinished
pop-gun in his right, then rose in majesty as befits a
barbarian King. "Then I'll come arter them, with a one, a
two and a three." Hands dropped now, everyone for
himself, the shrieking rabble rushed for the well, which
was "home". But Harry caught me first, and plumped me
on the bank beside him. "Now you belong to me, you're
a barbareen." While the line formed up again, and once

more Maudie sallied out, "Oh will you surrender, oh will you surrender," I wondered what a barbareen really was. The game would go on, until Harry had caught everyone, and the last one left would be the new King.

Then I was four years old, and the "King of the Barbareens" was a nice game to play; and perhaps Harry would give me the pop-gun when he had finished it.

Now I am forty, and I know that the game remembered some long-dead barbarian king. Perhaps the children of the Iceni played this game, and it lingered in Boadicea's Norfolk: long after other parts of England had turned it into "French and English", "Cowboys and Indians", and now "Martians and Earthmen". However the game originated, its call to surrender, and its defiance has become to me symbolical, for all my life I have had to fight the barbarians within me, and without.

How far back can human memory reach? A scientist once told me that with the aid of drugs pre-natal memories could be brought to the surface. Without drugs I can remember sitting in a large arm-chair, and remembering the day I was born. I have forgotten now what it was that I remembered, but I can remember remembering it. The chair was the world, black and cold to the calves of my legs. There was more of it beyond my feet, which were wearing white button boots, and when I stretched out my arms I could not touch the side of the chair; the back rose behind me like a wall. I know that my dress was blue, and that I wore a silver bracelet. Before the chair there was the cot. I looked through the bars at a black apron pocket, with a key hanging from it. Above and below the pocket was a mist, and from somewhere in the mist came voices.

Another memory I have is of being carried through a darkened street. I know, without knowing how I know, that the street was in war-time Yarmouth, and that I was wearing a pink knitted suit. Nothing happened, I was just being carried along in the dark.

These are small and tenuous things, but they are the only clues I have to my beginnings. I was born, according to my birth certificate, on 5 July 1916, at Holly Road, Oulton Broad. I was named Elsie May Fields and was the daughter of Margaret May Ames, formerly Mayhew, a seamstress. Columns 4 and 6 which should contain details of a father are blank, but pencilled on the back of the certificate are the words "Frederick Burrows, deceased 27.9.1916". My mother, always referred to by anyone who knew her as "my poor mother", has no part in my memories, so I presume she also died when I was very young. This is all I started with, and throughout the years I have only been able to add the tiniest details to the picture. When I was a child I was naturally curious about my parentage, and asked repeatedly for information. I was always told, "We have no records", and now, of course, it is too late. The people who might have known are dead, and what records there were have been pulped. This latter fact I learnt quite recently when I applied to the Ministry of Pensions. Knowing that great fat file, which had contained reports of all my misdemeanours, my small achievements, and detailed medical history, was now in all probability being served out as bus tickets, made me feel that I had lost my only relation. But vague relatives did fade in and out of the first three years of my life. There were two girls, who came and spent a day with me, and were never seen again. One I was told was my stepsister, and one my "own real" sister. One was dark and wore a reefer coat, the other had long auburn curls, and was dressed in green. She gave me a bright new penny, when the elderly gentleman who had brought them came to fetch them home again. Afterwards I argued because I wanted the dark one to be my "own real" sister, but it seems it was the other way round. "Own real", or step, that was the last I saw or heard of them.

On the day the war ended I was pushed out by a bigger girl to see the soldiers. The push-chair was made of wood and carpet, and had tiny metal wheels. It was meant to fold up when not in use but it didn't seem to know when that was, for I was always getting my fingers pinched in the collapsing arm-rests. Safety straps for babies were not invented then, so I was fastened in with a large shawl which went once round my neck, crossed over my chest and was tied in a knot at the back of the chair. Thus gagged and bound, whatever fate befell, the push-chair and I took it together. Today we watched the soldiers doing incomprehensible things with guns, and I chewed the teat off my dummy, and left the stopper and ring hanging on a piece of tape, to be chewed up another day. After the soldiers had gone, the girl turned for home, surrounded by more shadowy children glimpsed through the holes in the crochet shawl. She tipped the push-chair back and skipped along singing, "The war is over, the war is over." The shadowy children shrieked and shouted, while I with my boots higher than my head could only see the pale grey sky and feel afraid. Someone said, "Put har down, Marjorie. Du you'll hev har spew har dinner up."

4

The chair came down again on to its front wheels, and the children were quieter. Marjorie chanted, "The eleventh hour of the eleventh day of the eleventh month," and a boy's voice said, "Elsie won't remember the war; she's only two and a bit."

All this time I was living with Mr and Mrs Sparkes at the end of the "loke". Whenever we met anyone who said "Another of your grandchildren, Mrs Sparkes?" Gran would make an "o" of her mouth, draw in her breath sharply and say "No, no relation of mine. *None whatever*." The house was at the end of a row, nearest the well. It had a "backus" where we lived in summer and where the cooking and washing was done. This led into the "front" room, papered in bright scarlet satin ribbon stripes. A hard horsehair sofa stood beneath a large photograph of Aunt Alice. There was of course other furniture but it is not clear in my mind. Lace curtains covered the window, and potted plants stood before it. In the same wall as the window was the front door, permanently locked and covered with a baize curtain. On the mantlepiece were two framed pictures of me, as a very tiny baby, and later with long black curls. This must have been the only time in my life when I had long hair, or perhaps I have made a mistake and the photograph wasn't of me at all. The stairs, enclosed in a kind of cupboard, led from beside the fireplace straight into the only bedroom. The cottage was of the type known as an "up-and-a-downer", that is having only two rooms one above the other. The "backus" was no doubt a later addition. Gran and Granfer slept in the large double bed, and in the corner was my cot. I believe there was also a single bed in another corner, at any rate there wasn't much room on the floor, one had always to move about sideways like a crab. The cot must have been very old, for I was constantly falling through the bottom, and Granfa would have to thread cord through the frame, tying it in intricate seaman's knots; then there would be a hunt for stiff cardboard and brown paper to make a base for the folded blankets that served instead of a mattress. I never wore night clothes and went to bed wrapped in a piece of flannel or an old vest of Gran's.

The garden seemed enormous and fell away quite suddenly, as if it were on a cliff-top. I never dared go to the edge to see what really happened to it. Granfa put up a swing for me and I seem to have spent days and days just swinging up and down. If I went high enough I could see the river and the cattle half buried in the long rushes on the other side. Far beyond the chasm into which the garden fell was the high embanked railway track, and little toy trains went up to Norwich and down to Yarmouth. Once in the pink sunset we watched an airship threading in and out of the clouds like a weaver's shuttle, and as the train went along Granfa said, "I reckon them up there'll be the death o' you old chaps." At the other end of the row of houses lived Mrs Edwards and her two daughters: one was Marjorie who took me out and played with me. I remember kicking her so hard one day that she cried, and to see her cry made me afraid of what I had done and I howled like a banshee. Mrs Edwards rushed out with a shovel, and in some magical way dug up the top soil and revealed a rich vein of wet golden sand. Then she gave us flower-pots and broken cooking spoons so that we could make sand pies. Mrs Edwards was considered very "fast" by Gran because she smoked, but to me she was very kind and always seemed to be laughing, squint-eyed through her cloud of cigarette smoke.

Granfa spent a great deal of his time knitting. He made me "garnseys" in intricate patterns, and in wool so strong that they stood up by themselves. He knitted stockings for Gran, and socks for himself and me, and once he produced a muff in rainbow-shaded wool, which I treasured for years. I had it until I was twelve, when I unravelled it to make egg cosies for an adored Guide Captain.

I was three when I went to school, in a new green garnsey, and a pleated skirt that had been Marjorie's, a round velvet hat and a moleskin dolman of Gran's. Down the front edges the dolman had a pattern in tiny beads which were fun to pull off. School was nothing but confusion. Gran always said I was "Elsie Burrows": but the teacher called me "Edith Ames", so that I never knew when she was speaking to me, and she must have thought me stupid. We were given cards, full of holes with long coloured boot laces attached. My lace was yellow, and we threaded them in and out of the holes to make patterns. I had never seen anything like this before and it delighted me, especially as I thought it was a present. At the end of the session the teacher took it away again and I cried for it all the way home. Marjorie explained to Gran who tried to comfort me by promising to buy one in Norwich, "all for my own self"; but of course she didn't, not knowing what to buy. Ever after that I ensured myself against disappointment by asking whenever I was offered anything, "is it mine to keep for my really own?"; and even now I always make sure that any small children I deal with understand what has been given them and what lent.

I don't think I went to school very long. It was such a tiring walk four times a day, and made the going very hard for Marjorie, who could not have been more than ten or twelve, and who took the task of looking after me very seriously indeed. I am afraid I was not so grateful to her as I should have been. There was a discussion around the well. All the wives agreed it was better I should be at school than getting into mischief in the loke, but the journey was too long and the push-chair now worn out. Mrs Ringer offered her stick cart, but Marjorie flatly refused to push that to school, and besides what would Mrs Ringer do when she went wooding if she had no cart? I listened, caring nothing for the outcome of their talk, spitting large frothy spits into Gran's clean water, so that she had to empty the bucket and draw again. Granfa decided to wire up the gate so that I couldn't get into the loke to annoy the neighbours. It was a big iron gate, and I was so thin I could get through the rails He lowered himself stiffly on to his knees one afternoon, with a roll of wire which he laboriously threaded up and down, up and down, making a zig-zag mesh which he thought would be impenetrable. I watched him for a while, as he puffed and grunted and shuffled on his rheumaticky joints, then went down the garden and crawled through a gap in the hedge. I arrived on the other side of the gate and danced like a dervish in front of the tormented old man. His face was scarlet from his exertions. "How did you git *out*," he bellowed in unbelief as I ran yahooing up the loke.

Anyone who fondly believes that children are not *soaked* in original sin has entirely forgotten themselves.

Now and again we had a visitation from Aunt Alice. She was Gran's daughter, now married to Uncle Herbert, and with a baby called Gwennie. But — she had been a nurse. My memory of Aunt Alice is that she disapproved. On the days that she came she would scrub the house, Gran, Granfa and me, disapproving all the time. When she had gone we would sit in our cleanliness, not saying much — just being glad the wind had stopped blowing.

Once when Aunt Alice was really wanted she wasn't there. I had a pain in my head, and a great swelling behind my ear. Gran put hot fomentations on it and called the neighbours in for advice. They all agreed, "there's nothing else you can do, Mrs Sparkes — except perhaps the doctor". Gran shouted above my moans and shrieks, "If my Alice were here, she'd know how to fare." This went on for a day or two and everyone agreed there was nothing for it now but the doctor. Granfa wrapped me up in every available covering and wheezed and tottered his way to the doctor's. He sat panting in the waiting-room, with me a moaning bundle on his lap, prophesying between gasps both his and my imminent deaths. The doctor, hearing the commotion, left the patient in his surgery and came into the waiting-room. He took one look at me and said I must go to hospital straight away. Granfa didn't know what to do so he gave a little boy a halfpenny to go and fetch Gran. She came in a fluster, with her best bonnet a little askew, and the hooks and eyes not matching on her cape.

"She's got what they call a mastoid," Granfa told her. "The bones in her ears is tuberculous."

"That's her poor mother agin," said Gran. "She'll go the same way."

The doctor came out again and gave me some white powder in a teaspoon, and a glass of water.

"We won't lose our little maid will we, doctor?" asked Granfa. "Don't tell us that."

"Not if we can get her to hospital in Yarmouth right away," answered the doctor. I have no memory of the appearance of the doctor, only of his voice, his hands and his wrists covered by the cuffs of a khaki shirt.

Gran and Granfa exchanged lost and helpless looks, and Gran was near to tears as she asked, "How do such as *we* get to Yarmouth?"

How we, or rather I, eventually reached Yarmouth I don't know. To me Yarmouth is a horror compounded of agonizing dressings, burnt porridge, boiled fish and liquorice powder. Although this period was a short while ago, the treatment of small children in hospitals, compared with present-day methods, was almost barbaric. We were more nuisance than even grown-up patients and were heartily disliked by everyone. Only children who had been in hospital for a long time were allowed visitors, and these were the only ones who had toys, which their friends brought in. The hospital itself provided nothing at all for the children's amusement. To cry was sinful, and to need a bedpan at any other than stated times was a crime. For a time I was delirious and semi-conscious, screened from the rest of the ward, so I wasn't able to make much trouble. In the bed next to mine was a little boy who had lost his leg in an accident with a steam roller; when I heard him crying I knew that it would soon be my turn for dressings. Nowadays medical opinion does not consider it necessary to keep tearing bandages from open wounds and poke around them with probes and swabs. Nor is it considered immoral to use anaesthetics to deaden any kind of pain.

In spite of this and the constant misery of the appalling food, I did recover a little. This brought no joy to the nurses, poor slave-driven girls, for I became the naughtiest child they ever had to deal with. I have never been one of those people who go to sleep easily, and in the long evenings when all the other children were quiet I would fill in the time by unwinding my bandages and tying knots along their complete length. Another time I reached up to the temperature chart and with a wet finger made a nasty smear of each neatly rounded red point. When I became seized with an urgent desire to climb out of the window, which was three floors up, I was moved to a cot in the centre of the ward, where the nurses congratulated themselves I couldn't get out and couldn't reach anything. It was a long night, but the cot was fitted with lots of brass knobs. On a similar cot not long ago I counted four large and thirty-two small ones. When the night nurse foresook her fire behind the screen to investigate the clinking noise they were *all* in neat rows on my blanket being soldiers. The next night I was bandaged down to the mattress, and threatened that something dreadful would happen if I misbehaved.

Not long after, something dreadful did happen. Dreadful, that is, to me. To the overworked nurses it was just a routine job. I was wrapped around in blankets, and jollied along that I was going to the seaside. I wasn't very bright, but I demanded my boots for this excursion. The nurse nearly burst herself with laughing, but assured me my boots were waiting in the hall. She fetched a wheel chair, and still reassuring me about the seaside — wheeled me to the operating theatre. While I kicked and screamed on the table one nurse strapped down my legs, and another held my hands. A man hovered around with something that looked like a tea-strainer and this he finally clamped over my face, and I went drowning into unconsciousness. I came to on my way back to the ward, quite sure that my head had been sawn off, and that I was dead, but I was only minus my tonsils and adenoids.

My ability to annoy matron, sisters and nurses seemed to be boundless. Just before Christmas I somehow contracted rheumatic fever, causing a great deal of trouble to everyone. The nurses wanted to decorate the ward and the children were possessed with gaiety, so I was moved into a side ward. The sister came to look at me. "I doubt if she'll get through the night," she said, "but it'll be better really, she doesn't belong to anyone and would only be a burden all her life."

The side ward was cold and quiet, untroubled by the rustle of crêpe paper. Framed exactly in the window was the tower of St Nicholas Church, and I came to know every stone of it so well that for years I could recognize uncaptioned pictures of it. Once I woke, and the sky behind the tower was dark blue, shot through with stars. Someone had told me that stars were holes in the sky, that the light of heaven shone through, and that angels could look through these holes and tell God what we were doing. I believed it of course, and this night it all seemed so near that I turned my head away from the window. Through the bars of the cot I could see the cook dozing in the chair. I know it was the cook, but I can't think why she should have been there, unless she was the only person available or willing on Christmas Eve to watch by the dying. From somewhere came a wailing sound of carol singing which hurt my head; I partly pulled myself up in the cot and said "Hi, what's that row?" The cook opened her eyes, and leapt to her feet saying, "Glory, glory hallelujah, there's one in the eye for Sister Johnson." Whether this Sister Johnson was the one who had foretold my imminent end, or the one in charge of the carol singers I don't know.

Eventually I was taken in an ambulance from Yarmouth General Hospital to the Isolation Hospital. I can't remember much that happened there, except standing in long grass picking buttercups, while a nurse taught me the poem "Buttercups and Daisies". Life was quieter there, and people kinder. Finally I was fetched and delivered, not as I had thought to Gran, but back to the General Hospital. The fuss I made on that occasion must have entered into the hospital's history. A gala day did come, however, when Aunt Alice arrived, with a bundle of clothes — and boots.

With understandable joy the nurses dressed me and led me to Aunt Alice in the passage. She held out her hand to me, but I was not to be caught again.

"Where do I go?" I demanded.

"Why, home of course."

"For always?"

"Yes, of course; come on or we'll miss the train."

"If I git out of here, you on't bring me back? Du I on't come now."

"You won't come back," she promised. "You're going home to Gran's for good."

I took her hand then, and went with her. Perhaps I should explain that useful Norfolk word "du". It can mean anything and makes for great economy in speech. In this case I meant "If you are going to bring me back again, I'd rather stay here until I can go for good."

One of my favourite stories is of the mother who was told that her small son had fallen down and probably hurt himself. Her reply was "Du, he'd a shruck." Meaning, "I don't think he has hurt himself, otherwise he would have shrieked." This economy of the spoken word among Norfolkmen is attributed to the cold east winds. The more you open your mouth, it is held, the more cold air you take in.

I had been away a long time and the cottage was very small after the vast wards of the hospital. I always seemed to be bumping myself against the furniture, and I was afraid to go out of doors. As I didn't "fare to settle" as Gran said, she sent me for a holiday to one of her daughters in Kessingland. The house was full of children but only Hector had emerged from the shadows. He held my hand at the edge of the sea while the waves sucked the world away from my feet. When I fell he picked me up, and taking off my wet overall he put his bright jersey in its place, and spread the overall out to dry. "You'll have to keep your bloomers on," he said, "but if you lie on your belly and stick your bum in the air, they'll dry all right." So Hector gathered shells, stones and seaweed and we made a fairy's garden while my bloomers dried in the sun.

14

A walrus came up the beach one day at Kessingland. Or did it? I have always known what a walrus was and seen it in my mind flopping up the beach, shaking the spray from its whiskers. Maybe there is an aged man at Kessingland who remembers the summer of 1920. The summer of the walrus. Or perhaps Hector, grown to kindly middle age, is still there and remembers. Another time a small aeroplane came down and bounced along the water's edge. It seemed to be made entirely of wire and paper. Everyone else ran close to look at it, except me. The whirling propeller frightened me and I hid, as the ostrich doesn't, in a hole in the sand.

I ended my stay at Kessingland by falling against a sharp-edged chair and cutting my head so badly that it had to be stitched up. "There's nothing, nothing but trouble," grumbled Hector's mother, "wherever that child is."

Looking back to infancy the days are nearly always sunny, but St Valentine came in the winter. He would knock loudly on the never-used front door, and Gran would cry, "Run, Elsie, run out the back and catch him." I never caught St Valentine however hard I ran, though I'd sometimes see Granfa disappear round the corner. I never connected him with the saint, nor with the paper bag full of buns and sweets, but I would not have dreamed of eating any without first offering them to Gran and Granfa. This natural courtesy for some reason always touched Gran and she would sigh and look at Granfa and murmur, "What's to become of the little mawther, Sam, once we are gone?" I suppose it was a bit odd, that in spite of being extremely bad-tempered, and when in a temper insufferably insolent, I was still a very well-mannered child. I never had to be reminded to say "please" and "thank you"; nor did I eat from my knife, or let my nose run, as all my contemporaries did. My politeness, even to other children, was frequently remarked on, but it caused me no trouble at all.

One day I crawled from under the table and said to Gran, "Did we once live in a bigger house than this? With yellow walls?" Gran stopped dead in her tracks and looked curiously at me. "Why — yes," she said at last, "we lived in a fine big house, and there was yellow wallpaper on one of the rooms. We had a lot more money then." I must have had a sudden flash of memory like the one in the arm-chair but the memory itself has gone.

I was becoming too much for Gran. The District Nurse told her so when she came to dress my ear and do up Gran's hair. Gran had a bad arm, and couldn't reach up to plait her long white hair and pin it in a bun. "I won't part with her," she told the nurse. "I promised her poor mother when she lay a-dying that while I lived the child should stay with me." The nurse made a noise which is usually written, "Tut-tut".

That evening Gran told Granfa what the nurse had said. He poured himself a glass of stout, put it on the floor by his chair and took up his knitting. When he reached for the stout I was drinking it, and he thought maybe the nurse was right. "*Not* while I live, Sam," declared Gran. She was trying, with her stiff rheumatic hands to thread a darning needle, and just as the wool was nearly through I pulled it away. "But I'll flay the skin off your backside if you don't mend your ways," she yelled.

She nearly did too. A young soldier came to visit one day and left his swagger stick behind. Gran found it very useful as a cane. One of my less likeable habits was to take off my knickers and refuse to put them on again. Gran would chase me, pants in one hand and cane in the other, right down the loke and up the hill. It would usually end in my falling down, for I seemed to have a genius for getting tangled with my own feet. After one of these chases I slipped on the loose flints and scraped practically all the skin from one side of my face. I should of course have died of tetanus, for Gran had only three remedies for ills. A mustard plaster for aches, hot fomentations for lumps and vaseline for everything else. Oddly enough the only lasting effect of this accident is one very small scar.

All my days seem now to be a catalogue of misdeeds. I ate the boiled nettles intended for the rabbits, and wedged my knee between two palings so that Granfa had to saw me out. More and more the peace of the loke was shattered by my yells, and the swagger stick worked overtime. The neighbours complained and said I'd be better in the Union, but "Not while I stand upright outside my coffin," said Gran. "She'll mind in time. I'll have that devil out of her yet." She took me to see a gentleman called Mr Corbyn, who lectured me on the advantages of being good. He asked me how I came by the bruises on my legs, but I pulled my skirt over my knees, grinned at him and said nothing.

Gran's arm didn't get better, and my ear still needed attention, so the nurse came in once or twice a week. One day while combing my hair she was horrified to find it was "alive", so she cut it all off, to my delight, for now I looked like a boy. Gran protested that I must have picked up the nits from someone else. "Not one, not a single one of my children ever had a dirty head, did they now, Sam?" she declared.

Granfa shook his head, too distressed to speak. "She go here, there and everywhere, she won't keep by me, nor mind what I say. I can't tie the child up like a dorg. Now there's this disgrace!"

I could not understand why they were so upset nor what terrible thing I had done to bring shame upon them. For days afterwards Gran would scarcely let me outside the door, and would follow me down the garden to the closet to see that I didn't stray on the way back.

Perhaps it was the creatures that finally parted me from Gran. No doubt officialdom had been working in the background. Officialdom strong enough to break a vow she considered binding, whatever the trial and torment and even disgrace, involved.

"I shall regret it, Sam," she said at breakfast, "I shall regret it till my dying day."

"It's no use regretting," said Granfa. "It has to be."

"What I shall say to her poor mother when we meet on the other side I just don't know."

Miss Browne suddenly appeared before me as I was idly playing with the well-handle. I had been warned to "keep tidy", for I had on my best skirt and a new garnsey specially made by Granfa. My velvet hat had been garnished with a sailor ribbon, which bore the prophetic legend "H.M.S. Indestructible". Then I couldn't read it, but I had the ribbon long after the hat had ended its days in a pond. I should have called the lady Miss Browne even if it had not been her name, for she was dressed entirely in that colour.

"Come along, Elsie," she said. "It's time to go."

In one hand she had the brown tin hat-box — full of my worldly possessions. I took her other hand and walked with her to the station. Leaving the loke, and the well, which was for ever to me the piece where Jacob met his Rachel, and where Jesus talked with the woman of Samaria, we went up the hill, away from the river, where not long before someone had caught an eel and laid it on the grass. I told Miss Browne about the eel, and how we had watched it until sundown because eels never die till sunset. I showed her the field where we had come across the dead horse, in a pit, its legs so crossed and tangled it seemed to have many more than four. I said it was asleep, but one of the boys jumped into the pit and walked along its back to prove it was dead. I still said it was asleep. I told her, too, that there were herons in the churchyard, and, remembering my own confusion, made it quite plain to her, that they were herons which were birds, not herrings which were fish.

I knew that the white letters on the blue enamelled board spelled Reedham. I was not quite five years old, and as the final board slid past the accelerating train it was the last I saw of Reedham, or any of its people.

CHAPTER
TWO

It was a hot day and Miss Browne must have been very tired by the time we reached the offices of the Ministry of Pensions in the Cathedral Close. Perhaps that was why she could not tell me anything about the stone lions on either side of the doorway. She assured me they were not real and did not bite, so I traced my fingers round their stone manes and offered them my hand to eat, but tea was calling Miss Browne, who had grown out of lion-wonder. Recently I tried to find these beasts again; I came to know them very well, but either I looked in the wrong place or they have been moved. The whole Close looks different now and the Cathedral no longer threatens to fall on top of one, so perhaps some of the houses have been cleared away.

We went to an office where several people sat at desks and one man was using a typewriter. The clatter, the movement of the carriage and the "ping" of the bell fascinated me and my eyes never left the machine; to the embarrassment of the operator, who after twice pulling out and tearing up letters, pushed the machine away from him and went out of the room.

Two women, both dressed in black, were shown in. One

glanced at me. "Is *that* the child?" she asked, horror in her voice and face.

"Yes, Mrs Everett," replied Miss Browne and added somewhat defensively, "we told you she had been ill and neglected."

The woman I was to know as Aunt Ada recovered herself. "I wasn't expecting a child so small, and with bandages. I thought she would be a school child."

"The ear trouble should clear up soon with proper care and feeding; and she'll be old enough for school after the summer holidays."

"Well, I've given my word to Mr Tooke, so I shan't take it back, and I'll do my best for the poor mite."

I expect the phrase "a little girl" to Aunt Ada conjured something pretty and dainty, with golden curls perhaps, and blue eyes. Too old to play with dolls in her childless late middle age, she had sought something to fill the gap and had, without deserving it, got me. The hair that poked through my bandages was black, and my eyes like the shoe-button orbs of a home-made toy animal. My mouth was much too big and my nose turned up in a yellowish-green tinged face. My limbs and body had no more substance than a scarecrow. I would have made an admirable demonstration skeleton in a medical school, for every one of my 220-odd bones could be counted from without.

I was to live four years with Aunt Ada, but I don't think she ever got over her first shock at seeing me; and I never forgot the look with which she betrayed that shock. The woman with her was her sister, Aunt Minnie, who lived in Bury Street, Norwich, and there we went for tea after Aunt Ada had signed the papers.

We went to Brooke by horse bus, and were met at the King's Head by Uncle George. He was, I believe, Aunt Ada's brother-in-law, and in appearance he resembled George Lansbury, except that he grew his beard a bit longer round the chin. To me he became an Imperial Standard for justice and tolerance. The wisdom of Solomon paled before Uncle George's, for I never asked him a question he couldn't answer. He was a very quiet man, hardly ever raising his voice, and on the rare occasions he did, the effect was terrifying.

In the back kitchen Aunt Ada washed me and gave me supper while she unpacked the tin box.

"When do we go home again?" I asked.

"You are home, my dear," said Unde George. "This is your home now."

"Not my real home. I live with Granny Sparkes."

"Ah, poor dear, she can't keep you no more. She's ailin'."

"She'll have me back though, when she's better. She'll keep me till her dyin' day. I know that."

"One day I'll borrow a trap and we'll go over to see her."

"You don't need to borrow a trap. She'll come and get me."

"Maybe, maybe."

It was a long time before my first waking words ceased to be "Is it today my Granny Sparkes is coming?" It must have been galling for Aunt Ada, for she really did her best for me, and became reasonably fond of me. With her I was better fed and clothed, and although I received quite a few smacks I was never beaten.

I also had the tender love and strong protection of Uncle George, and later on this was leavened by the jollity of Uncle Ted. Yet I still hankered for the familiar, if rough life with Gran, and although I could not put it into words, or even formulate the idea, I knew I was betrayed. Nothing could have been more certain than Gran's "Not until my dying day", and had she died I would probably have accepted the situation. If reasons and explanations had been given me I might have understood. Perhaps they were, and I did not understand, but I doubt it. No one thought of giving explanations to small orphans, any more than to market-bound pigs.

Aunt Ada had emptied the box and all my things lay on the table. A fluted mug decorated with roses, a much-handled Christmas card and a pop-gun. Two jerseys, some socks, a scarf and a muff, all Granfa's handiwork. A skirt, a pair of knickers and a chemise. That was all.

"Look, George," commanded Aunt Ada.

Uncle George surveyed the articles, then gazed into the deep blue depths of the tin.

"No brush and comb," he said at last.

"And no nightdress." I could see she was shocked, though I didn't know what a nightdress was. In hospital we had worn calico garments, open down the back and called "slops".

"Perhaps the Jays —" suggested Uncle George.

"Never!" The Jays were a family who lived next door but one. There were identical twin girls called Kathleen and Eileen, and a boy Geoffrey. Although Aunt Ada was very friendly with them she had a pathological hatred of borrowing.

Uncle George made another suggestion.

"Something of yours then, or an old shirt of mine. There's that flannel one what shrunk."

So it was in Uncle George's flannel shirt that I was eventually put to bed, in the large double bed in the back room. I was terrified! Never before had I slept in anything but a cot and as I sank into the deep feather mattress I was sure I would drown. I said so to Aunt Ada.

"You can't drown out of water, that's a sure thing."

She was very definite about it, but I wasn't so certain. She told me to say my prayers.

"Gentle Jesus meek and mild,
Look upon a little child.
Pity me a cup of tea,
Suffer me to come to thee. Amen."

"Is that all you say?"

"Yes."

"It's 'pity my simplicity' not a 'cup of tea'."

"No, it's 'pity me a cup of tea'"; and no matter what Aunt Ada said then or later, "a cup of tea" it always was. A cup of tea was something tangible, people were always asking for one and being thankful when they'd had it, but "simplicity" meant nothing to me at all.

Aunt Ada shared the double bed with me at first, but I fidgeted so much that she had to get a mattress and make me up a bed on the floor. Uncle George didn't like this and didn't think the "Pensions" would approve.

"Well, let them provide a bed," snapped Aunt Ada.

The "Pensions" loomed like fate behind Aunt Ada. She

24

was always so fearful that something might happen to me for which they would hold her responsible, that she hardly dared let me out of her sight. I might get run over, drowned in the mere, stolen by bad men or catch fleas. I could get struck by lightning, tossed by bulls or be lost and starve to death. Of all these things and many more Aunt Ada was afraid, and she dared not take any risks for fear of the terror that might descend upon her from the Ministry of Pensions. All these fears were communicated to me until I became a jitter of nerves, frightened even of my own shadow. The Ministry paid, I think, twelve shillings a week for my keep and gave a quarterly clothing allowance. Considering that she not only had to cope with me, but the visitations of the Ministry's inspectors and doctors as well, Aunt Ada thought this sum very inadequate. She had lost her husband, whom she always referred to as her "dear one", not long after their marriage. When I went to live with her she must have been in her late fifties, but she would frequently read his letters, gaze upon his photograph, and brush the last suit he had worn, one of khaki-coloured corduroy. I never saw her shed tears for him, and his photograph was not displayed, but kept in the bureau drawer. The last time I saw her she was eighty-five and she still spoke of her "dear one".

After Gran's "up-and-a-downer" Aunt Ada's house at Brooke seemed very large. It was the end one of a row of four with a garden at the front, side and rear. I knew every foot of this garden, or rather the paths around it, for I rarely played anywhere else. At Reedham I had burrowed my way through every obstacle Granfa had put up and sometimes wandered for miles; but now, imbued with

Aunt Ada's fears, I would feel unsafe as soon as I was outside the gate. The house had two bedrooms upstairs, one leading from the other, and downstairs a front room, living-room and back kitchen. In the summer we did not use the front room at all. As soon as spring came Aunt Ada would paper the walls, dye the curtains and polish the grate, which was then filled with coloured paper shavings. Except to water the potted plants or to receive important visitors the "front" was forbidden ground until the autumn. This did not worry me, for I always preferred the pink distempered living-room which caught and held the sunshine.

My first days were spent getting used to the house and its furniture, and its steps in unexpected places. I had to learn to pick up my feet over the high threshold between the living-room and kitchen, otherwise I fell and always bumped my head against something. A lot of the time I spent at the gate, peering through the palings, for I was not tall enough to see over the top — waiting, waiting for Gran to come. Later, when I knew she would not come I would watch for the mail van to pass. This was one of the few motor vehicles to come through the village and as it had a golden crown painted on the sides, I was quite sure the king was inside. The Post Office was not far down the road, and although I would sometimes unlatch the gate and lean out as far as I dared I never managed to catch a glimpse of His Majesty.

I was suddenly aware of another occupant of the house. He had been there all the time, of course, and I had seen him, but I didn't realize he lived there. He was a young man, Mr Mason, and I became conscious of him one

26

Sunday morning, when I saw him shaving in the back kitchen, his braces hanging down over his best blue trousers. I went to Aunt Ada in the pantry. "Is that man your husband?" I asked.

She was so shocked that for a moment she couldn't speak.

"Don't ever say a thing like that again," she stormed in an angry whisper. "Mr Mason's engaged to be married to a young lady."

Time and again I was to worry her with the things I said, and it ended with me becoming so self-conscious about saying the wrong thing, that it became difficult for anyone, other than those in the house, to get a word out of me, so I gained the reputation of being very shy. Born bad-tempered, I was given to screaming fits when I couldn't get my own way, and Aunt Ada was unwise enough to let me see that the screaming worried her. She would call over to the next-door neighbour to apologize for the noise, and to assure her that she hadn't laid a finger on me. Mrs Greenacre, who was stone deaf, would come to the fence and smile benignly at me. Some people who are deaf have loud speaking voices, but Mrs Greenacre could hardly be heard, she would mouth all the words but only now and again could one be distinguished. Aunt Ada would yell her apologies and explanations, and Mrs Greenacre would smile, mouth "Oh dear" and sometimes shake her head. Between her back garden and the next was a wall, with a little sliding door like a serving hatch cut into it. At the height of the noise this would slide back and Mrs Craske would poke her head through to join the conversation. I don't remember ever seeing the whole of Mrs Craske, but

I had lots of conversations with her round, snowy-crowned head. She and Aunt Ada would bounce back conversation and Mrs Greenacre would swing from one to the other like a tennis umpire, gradually giving it up and fading indoors. In spite of these conversations, Aunt Ada for some reason disliked Mrs Craske intensely. She advised Aunt Ada to take no notice of my tantrums, and assured her I would outgrow them, while another neighbour, Mrs Nobbs, advised locking me in the wood shed. All this attention only served to make me worse. My habits also were not attractive. I was never a serious bedwetter, but during the day I would put off going to the lavatory until the last moment. When there, I would get into such a muddle with my knickers, which buttoned on to a bodice, that they usually ended up rather damp. I bit my nails, and this positively infuriated Aunt Ada. She tried all kinds of remedies — mustard, bitter aloes, cotton gloves and slaps — but the habit is uncured to this day. I do not defend this habit, but I am at a loss to see why some people take an almost moral stand about it. It harms no one except the nail biter, and is cheaper than smoking. Apart from my nails I also chewed up collars, handkerchiefs, bits of string and newspapers; it's a wonder I wasn't poisoned by printer's ink. The few toys I had were soon in pieces. Granfa had made me a stout little wheelbarrow which had been sent on after me. It was painted bright red, with black handles. One day Uncle George came down the garden to find it in all its component parts. It wasn't broken, I had with my bare hands prized out every nail. He could not believe his eyes, and he took the pieces in to Aunt Ada, who was equally flabbergasted. The barrow was never put

28

together again, but was brought out periodically to show astonished neighbours and inspectors.

Quite often during these first few months Aunt Ada would take her troubles to Mr Tooke. He was a clerk in the Ministry of Pensions office, a kind quiet man, with a small toothbrush moustache, and with one of his fingers missing. I used to like going to his house to play with his naughty, red-haired little boy, Denny. Denny was about a year younger than I, but he had an even greater capacity for mischief, and while the grown-ups discussed my sins, he would be leading me into more, for which I always had to take the full blame. We once, I remember, dug up the garden gate-post, and another time stripped the kitchen of most of its wall-paper. When Mrs Tooke and Aunt Ada came to the door we were nearly buried in long swathes of pink paper roses. Mrs Tooke roared with laughter, and had to sit down, and tap her chest while she wheezed, "No, Mrs Everett, never mind, Mrs Everett" to Aunt Ada, who was belabouring my behind. Denny rushed for refuge behind his mother's chair, and in doing so knocked down his father's war medals, which hung in a frame on the wall. This stilled Aunt Ada's hand and Mrs Tooke's laughter, who almost whispered, "Pick 'em up, Denny; put 'em on the nail again." It was as if an act of sacrilege had been committed.

Mr Tooke would always listen patiently to Aunt Ada and sympathize with her, promising to tell his superiors next day that she couldn't possibly put up with me a week longer. Morning would bring repentance and she would send Uncle George over early with a message that nothing should be said just yet.

Life was not all irritation and bad temper though. With better feeding my health improved and my ear healed up so that I could be free of bandages. I was left slightly deaf on one side and subject to noises in the head, particularly at times of stress. Clothes too were improved after a visit from Miss Hayhurst, a Ministry of Pensions inspector. We eventually knew each other very well, but her first visit filled both Aunt Ada and me with alarm. She was very tall and somewhat severe-looking, and with a true Norfolk habit of getting straight to the point, which many people find disconcerting. She arrived unexpectedly in mid-morning to find me sitting on Aunt Ada's lap wearing nothing but a chemise.

"Not outside on a beautiful morning like this?" she exclaimed. The beautiful morning was brittle with frost, which was why Aunt Ada had allowed me to stay in bed until the room had warmed up.

Aunt Ada muttered something about me being "poorly". No doubt she felt a little guilty about pandering to me.

"Fresh air — best thing." Miss Hayhurst had a habit of speaking telegraphese. "Clothes," she went on.

Aunt Ada displayed my wardrobe, and while Miss Hayhurst turned over the garments and made notes, she dressed me. To my shame she complained of the wet knickers.

"No wonder," Miss Hayburst gingerly spread out the button-on garments from which no amount of Aunt Ada's scrubbing had been able to remove the stains.

"Old-fashioned," announced Miss Hayhurst. "All right with nursemaids. Outgrown," she wrote on her pad. We

30

waited somewhat fearfully for her next pronouncement. It was "Toothbrush."

"No, no, there wasn't a toothbrush — a flannel" — as if the latter would compensate for the former.

"Toothbrush essential — straight away — also powder. Send in account." With a sudden smile like a flash of electricity, she went.

As if the hounds of hell were after her, Aunt Ada rushed me up to the shop for the toothbrush and tooth powder, grumbling all the way. The shop was kept by Mrs Cutbush, who was also a recipient of her troubles. One day after a long recital Mrs Cutbush ventured to say that perhaps Aunt Ada was too old to take on so young a child. So offended was Aunt Ada by this suggestion that she transferred her custom to the other shop.

The clothing orders came a day or two after Miss Hayhurst's visit. Aunt Ada, who had expected cash, was worried by the forms and passed them over to Uncle George. Putting on his steel-rimmed spectacles, he studied them carefully. "As I see it, Ada," he said after reading them twice, "you take this here one to Bond's, they fit the child out with what it says here and send the bill to the Ministry. This here one you take to the boot shop and they do likewise."

"Thass a rum way to go shopping," grumbled Aunt Ada. "I never shop at Bond's. You know I always deal with Frank Price's in Magdalen Street."

"I expect they get a discount or something at Bond's," said Mr Mason, who having but lately been at the wars was more familiar with the ways of the world.

"Ah, I reckon they do," agreed Uncle George.

"Best take Minnie with you. She'll know what to do."

So off we went to catch the horse bus at the King's Head. While we were waiting a strange wild woman came up and began talking to us. Aunt Ada edged away from her, being a terribly afraid of catching fleas. The woman talked on and on very loudly, and I in embarrassment turned my attention to the shop window. Suddenly she stopped, by now there were several other people there, and Aunt Ada took my hand and moved over to speak to someone else. The woman caught her arm. "Don't lose that child, missis," she whispered. "She's going a long, long way. She'll be heard of, you'll see."

Aunt Ada didn't forget this prophecy, but she never saw it fulfilled.

Aunt Minnie came with us to Bond's, where they were glad to find the assistants knew all about the Ministry's vouchers.

I returned home with a fine new outfit, including elastic-waisted bloomers, and there were no more accidents.

Although Aunt Ada and all my other foster-mothers found the Ministry of Pensions inspectors a trial, and we children were apt to make fun of them, a word of thanks and appreciation is due to them. They were mostly well-bred, recently franchised ladies, and many of them had suffered personal tragedies in the war. Denied children of their own they gave their lives unselfishly, and for very little money, to the service of other people's. Many of these children were like me — illegitimate, sickly and difficult. Child psychology was in its infancy, and they could only learn by trial and error. The country had never been faced before by such a flood of orphans.

Foster-mothers were not easy to find, and were an awkward race, most of them taking the children for the money or for unpaid domestic labour. Ladies like Miss Hayhurst and Miss Cozens-Hardy had often to stand up to viragos who pelted them with insults and not infrequently offered personal violence. Public transport was very limited and many journeys had to be made on foot through hot, dusty country lanes, or across bleak fenlands. Cars were not yet supplied to welfare officers, and only those who were wealthy could afford to run them. Many gave their services quite voluntarily. All war orphans, and the country as a whole, owe a great deal to these gallant women who carried on a two-fronted crusade — against the devil in the graceless children, and against the thick-skulled, unimaginative myrmidons of the "Head Office". These were permanent civil servants drafted in a hurry from other departments and who only knew one thing about children, viz: that some were girls and some were boys.

After the summer holidays I went to school, and was thoroughly happy there. The first day Aunt Ada took me up and explained my circumstances to the teacher. Her name I think was Miss Emney and I thought she was the most beautiful being in the world. Angels still in my imagination wear Miss Emney's face. I think our liking must have been mutual for she seemed to find me extremely amusing. I was also, it transpired, a very quick learner, and I picked up writing, reading and arithmetic like lightning. Miss Emney would round off my letters with her red pencil and say, "Now if you leave the gate open like that, all the little pigs will get out"; and thus my o's and a's and so on grew in perfection.

Miss Emney wore open-necked shirt-type blouses, usually pink or beige, and the *décolletée* was filled in by that very pretty forerunner of the brassière — the camisole. Many ladies found the camisole a useful repository for handkerchiefs and other small articles. Miss Emney often kept letters in hers, which could be seen when she leaned over to mark one's book. It was whispered that they were *love* letters, for she was engaged to be married.

I soon outstripped my classmates in practically every subject, including handwork. Poetry I could learn after hearing it read once only. I can see now the exercise book full of neat sums and Miss Emney's gay red R. beside each one; and with all the tables up to seven times written out from memory.

Quite recently I read *The Only Child*, by James Kirkup, and found that like him, and I expect like most other intelligent children of our generation, I took pleasure in reading anything. We read the same things, Brooke Bond Tea packets, Camp Coffee bottles, H.P. Sauce and Lyle's Treacle tins. That lion bothered me too, because I knew that bees made honey, whereas sugar beet made treacle, and I couldn't see the connection.

But my wonderful new-found knowledge was all to be lost again, and for several years I had to struggle to relearn painfully all that had once come so easily. I didn't lose my ability to remember the spoken word, but I completely forgot how to read and write, and to do sums. Arithmetic never came back with any ease and I would weep with vexation knowing how easily I had once learned the tables. At five and a half I was considered the brightest of children, "sharp" is the Norfolk expression; but at eight I was backward, almost subnormally so — and all because I caught whooping-cough.

Of all the diseases, which like hobgoblins lie in wait for small children, I think this is the worst. It goes on and on for weeks, sometimes months. Its spasms are terrifying both to the sufferer and the nurse, and it destroys sleep for the entire household. After every one of my coughing fits I was quite certain I was going to die, and I almost did. Once in a delirium I saw my mother looking at me through the window, and called to Aunt Ada to come and see her. As I say, I never knew my mother, nor had I seen a photograph of her, but this head, bobbing about like a balloon on the window-sill, certainly belonged to her. I was angry with Aunt Ada, who said there was no one there, and my insistence that there was, and not only that, the sky was full of angels and music, filled her with alarm. She went to the top of the stairs and called, "George, George, the child is going; bring the brandy."

I could tell she was upset, and I, who seemed to be living on two planes at once, kept saying, "Never mind, never mind."

Uncle George came up with a bottle and spooned pure fire down my throat, saying, "If that don't do nothing else, that'll help her to sleep." It did, and I expect it saved my life.

All through the dreary winter I coughed and whooped. People called with little presents; the doctor brought fearsome medical catalogues for cutting out, Mr Tooke came with sweets and the clergyman scraps and pretty floral texts. They all shook their heads and doubted I would see the spring. Everyone was kind and for the first time in my life I was being spoiled. Sometimes Aunt Ada would carry me downstairs and sit nursing me for hours, while she read to me, or told me stories about her many brothers and sisters. Sometimes she made up stories about the pictures on the wall. There was one of an old seaman rowing in a small boat with a little girl at his knee. Another of a lady at a spinning wheel, and a copy of the famous picture of two little girls asleep in a railway carriage.

Much to everyone's surprise, when spring began to glimmer I was still alive, though still coughing. On sunshiny days Aunt Ada would wrap me up like an Eskimo and let me into the garden with strict instructions not to "bop down" or to stand still for long. Everything, even eating, was a great effort, and when people stopped at the gate to speak to me I would smile, but not answer in case opening my mouth would bring on a coughing fit.

The great Dr Christopherson arrived one day to examine me. He has but recently died, and was one of the foremost specialists in the country. I expect his importance was impressed upon me, but I am afraid I took a great dislike to him, and although I saw him at frequent intervals until I left Norfolk at thirteen, I never really conquered this dislike. I was probably put off by the aura of greatness surrounding him, or it may have been his appearance. He seemed very tall and wore I think rimless glasses of the type we associate with Americans. His countenance was lean and aesthetic, but the whole thing was incongruously topped by a mop of curly hair. Strangely enough,

36

someone who knew him at the end of his life has told me he was in fact a very small man.

As it appeared that I was not going to die immediately, people stopped spoiling me. I do not mean that they deliberately withdrew their kindness. I don't suppose they noticed any difference in their own attitude towards me, but I did, and showed my resentment by reverting to my former bad temper and irritability. Aunt Ada lost no time in giving the doctor a catalogue of my sins.

"Well, let's have her undressed," he ordered. When I stood before him in just my bloomers, my hands fidgeting with the elastic because there was nothing else to do with them, he said "off with those", and I was left stark and ashamed in my socks.

He turned his attention to the discarded clothes. A flannel vest, calico chemise, a pair each of linings and bloomers, a wadded red flannel bodice, a flannel petticoat, a cotton ditto, a skirt, jersey and print overall, ten garments in all.

"I don't wonder she's irritable," was his comment; "she's wearing enough clothes for three children."

"But we aren't to the end of May yet," said Aunt Ada.

"Stuff and nonsense," snorted the lordly doctor; "there's more clothes there than an Eskimo wears."

The upshot of this visit was that the bodice linings and petticoats were discarded, and Aunt Ada's outrage soothed by the promise that I should go to a sanatorium. When I inquired what a sanatorium was and learned it was something like a hospital, my memories of Yarmouth filled me with foreboding. Before I could go there I had to be vaccinated, a more painful process then than it is now. Dr

Basden came, on a motor-bike with his equipment. He was a much-loved character in the Brooke area, with his great moustache and peaked cap. His cheerful manner alone was reputed to be able to raise the dead. He was also an excellent and painstaking practitioner, although how he made a living in a predominantly working-class area I can't think. Agricultural workers were not at first included in the old panel system. Most of them paid into clubs such as the Shepherds, Buffaloes or Foresters. In country districts people still talk of being "on the club" when they are receiving National Sickness Benefit. When he came to vaccinate me the doctor promised me a penny if I didn't cry, and I got it though tears were restrained with difficulty.

The dreaded day arrived when Aunt Ada had to take me to the sanatorium at Holt. I was by that time nearly seven and I had not been to school or submitted to any sort of discipline since before I was six. I have never been so completely miserable as I was during the next ten months. I went, it is true, with fear and apprehension, but I went wanting love and willing to give it. I came out knowing hatred as a concrete thing, and cruelty an established fact.

I believe this sanatorium still exists and like other institutions has no doubt vastly improved. I do not know what official reputation it had in my day; it was no doubt subject to inspections and had to keep to certain regulations, but to me it was hell. I have a feeling it was named after Queen Mary, which was no compliment to that gracious lady. The building itself was situated practically in a pine wood; and had a central block with two wards, one above the other, leading off on either side. There were three wards for boys and one for girls; thus the girls were very much in the minority. Being used to small cottage rooms with low ceilings, I felt lost and unprotected in the high, many-windowed wards and corridors. The only place where I felt safe was in the room occupied by the seamstress and her treadle machine. Whenever I could I would steal away there, to thread needles for her and sort out buttons. Sometimes she gave me snippets of material, and I pulled the threads apart one by one, utterly content with my work of destruction. The resulting piles of threads were put into an old pillow-case to be mixed with flock for repairing mattresses and pillows. Quite recently I read a report by someone who had visited Broadmoor Institution, where the women spend much of their time picking rags to pieces in a similar manner. The author of the report deplored this occupation and hoped something more satisfying and rewarding would be found for the women to do. As a small child I found unpicking extremely satisfying, and as many of the Broadmoor women probably have the mental attributes of a six-year-old, I should think they do too. So many people who deal with animals, children and the mentally handicapped use their own intelligence as a yardstick. This quite often leads to failure, disappointment and waste of money. For success in these fields it is essential to discard one's own mind and use that of the animal, child or deficient. Many of the old-time matrons of children's homes, and former school teachers, were successful because they had this ability, even though they were untrained and not particularly clever.

The outrage began as soon as Aunt Ada had left. All my clothes were taken away, my hair cut as short as possible, then I was bathed and put to bed. I had never been in a full-sized bath before, and I was so frightened of drowning that I refused to get in. Thereupon the nurse picked me up and plonked me down in water which was too hot for my liking. I said so, and was rewarded by a stinging slap on the behind and the order to "sit down if I didn't want another". I was too frightened even to cry, fear rose up in bubbles from my stomach and roared in my ears so that I could not hear. I dared not look at anything and could only see the white walls of the bath and the nurse's steel-cold hands as she scrubbed at me with a rough flannel and red carbolic soap. Out of the bath she propelled me to the wash basin, and pushing my head down and holding it there in the vice of her hand she washed what was left of my hair, finishing it off with cold water, a horror I was to face every week for nearly a year. There was no end to terror, for next I had to meet the water-closet, a modern amenity which, if I had en-countered at Yarmouth, I had forgotten about. With a certainty that this was a well and that the nurse was going to sluice me down it, I was quite unable to perform. This fear lasted long, and was played upon by the staff and other children, so that the matron had to admit defeat, and a chamber-pot was placed in the lavatory for my exclusive use. Soon I was alone in a bed which seemed miles from the floor, with a hard mattress and even harder pillow. Every time I moved the thick rubber mackintosh sent cold waves through the sheet. Though it was a hot summer day I was frozen. Unmoving, oppressed with a feeling of guilt as if I had committed some enormous sin, I lay the whole afternoon — and no one came to look or speak to me. Then the other girls came back from the afternoon's walk. There was no playroom, so leisure time was spent outside in fine weather, or in the wards. As the days passed I grew to know the routine and the rules, and I never acquiesced with either. A bell rang for rising at seven, but it took the combined efforts of nearly all the girls and the nurse to get me out of bed. The floors were polished and uncarpeted, so it was a rule that socks had to be put on first before standing on the floor. At first I could never find my socks, and as I always lost my temper (and I still do) when I couldn't find anything the morning began with a scene. After a while it dawned on me that the other girls were hiding my socks, because it amused them to see me in a temper, and they got vicarious pleasure from the shakes and slaps I had from the nurse. Then I hid the socks myself, and later went to bed with them still on, so that trouble was overcome. The food in this place, in common with most of the institutions at that time, was disgusting. The general hospital speciality, burnt lumpy porridge, was served up daily, but nothing would make me eat it. Forcible feeding was tried but the only time any of this muck was got down me I promptly sicked it up again all over the matron's apron. It was then presented to me at every meal for two days, but I won, and I was beginning to learn that if I persisted long enough I would probably always win. I was allowed to have bread and milk.

After breakfast the chairs and tables were pushed aside and we stood in rows, while the bigger boys rolled lengths of stair matting at our feet; on these we would kneel for prayers. The post was brought in. Those who could read were given their letters — the others were read aloud there and then by the matron, causing acute embarrassment to the recipients. Even though I suspect the matron abridged a good many of these letters, to those of us who had none it was a long time to stand still without fidgeting. Parcels were also publicly dissected, all foodstuffs being removed. What happened to all the cakes and so on we never knew, for they didn't appear on the tables, and the rumour was that the matron ate them all herself. As she was extremely fat I was very willing to believe this. Although Uncle George and Aunt Ada did write and send me parcels I had none of them, nor were my letters read. Occasionally I would be given a message that "Mrs Everett hoped I was being a good girl". I only knew Aunt Ada as such, and was not interested in the hopes of "Mrs Everett". After this long-drawn-out morning ceremony we went to school in a little wooden building in the middle of the woods. What happy hours I had were spent there. We were not taught anything academic, but the teacher, Miss Healy, was lively and amusing. She read us stories, taught us songs and poems and we did raffia work or drew with pastels on brown paper. Outside in the wood we could see the red squirrels and we once caught a glimpse of what was reputed to be a bear. It was I expect a badger, but the staff encouraged the legend of bears to deter would-be runaways. We all wore a kind of uniform, the girls had scarlet dresses and pinafores, and the boys navy knickers and jerseys. The smaller boys wore bright blue smocks as well. Our clothes were changed weekly and we did not always get the same ones back, we just got clean ones which more or less fitted. I hated having any kind of personal contact with anyone, and the thought of wearing someone else's clothes always worried me, though as an orphan I was fated to do so. This fastidiousness about clothes and food was to cause me trouble at every institution I lived in. I had a special reason at the sanatorium for disliking other people's clothes for some of the girls had haemorrhages and however well the dresses and pinafores were washed the stains never quite disappeared. One of the matron's favourite punishments for the small boys was to dress them in girls' clothes and put them at the girls' table for meals. What lasting effect this had on the little boys I cannot imagine. If our modern psychologists are right it must have been very damaging indeed.

One of the younger nurses thought the converse should hold, so that when I misbehaved once, she put me into a blue smock. I was highly delighted, feeling no shame at all, and joyful to find that the smock had a pocket in which to put the pieces of rag we were given for handkerchiefs. We had no pockets in our clothes, so for the most part we had to hold those wretched things in our hands. Matron, no doubt noticing how pleased I was, ordered the smock to be removed. We were given no outer garments at all, and even in deep snow and frost we went to school and for walks bare-headed and coatless. Some of the girls had calico bags to tie round their waists under their pinafores. In these bags were kept sputum bottles and the sight of them always nauseated me. There were a few children who were so ill they spent their time permanently in wooden huts in the garden. During sleepless nights when the owls hooted not far from the window and matron's great lurcher dog prowled around I would think of those children alone in their huts, and pray that this awful fate would not overtake me. Tuberculosis was in those days considered extremely infectious and no visitors were ever allowed, so that once a patient was there he was cut off entirely from the outside world. Whether these conditions were responsible for the attitude of most of the staff towards us I don't know, but they seemed to look upon us, not so much as children needing care and affection, as criminals who must at all cost be repressed. For a long time I thought I had been sent there, not to recover from a serious illness, but as a punishment for being naughty.

It is not in the nature of children to be in a permanent state of melancholy and I often had my moments of high spirits and fits of the giggles. Apart from the daily battles with food and clothes one of the nurses had picked me out for her special spite. She was Welsh, and not I think very good at her job. It may be that she suffered on this account from Matron's wrath, and revenged herself by making my life miserable. By this time I knew when I was doing anything wrong, and knew too that punishment would follow. Sometimes I thought I wouldn't be found out, at other times I thought it was worth the risk. Although when punishment did come I would rail against it, I knew that it was deserved, and young as I was I could see the justice of it. With this woman, I will call her Nurse Jones, it was different. She it was who handled me on the first day. She could not see me without pushing or slapping me, and anything that went wrong would according to her be my fault. I once heard Matron's voice raised in anger at Nurse Jones for neglecting some job or other and finishing up with, "It is not Elsie Burrows's duty to change the sheets." It puzzled me at the time, but now I can sympathize a little with the matron, who must have been tired of hearing my sins used as an excuse for Nurse Jones's shortcomings. This definite and active hatred held for me by this nurse, who was probably still a girl in her teens, was quite beyond my comprehension. She was perhaps lonely and far from home, overworked and underpaid, all things which I could not be expected to understand. At first I bore her no more ill will than I did the other members of the staff, and I would try very hard to please her. Then I came to fear her, and finally to loathe her with an intensity that had I been older would have been dangerous. This change of feeling came about after an incident in the sewing-room. I had taken with me to the sanatorium a little teddy bear about six inches long. It had for many years been a kind of fetish, going everywhere with me. It was small enough to go into a pocket, but now I had no pockets it spent most of its time tucked in the top of my bloomers. It was now rather flabby and the sawdust was leaking through a hole in one of the seams. I took it to the sewing-room to see if Miss Taylor would put some more stuffing in and stitch it up. Nurse Jones was there, sitting most un-nurse-like on the fireguard.

"What do you want?" she barked at me.

Ignoring her I said, "Please, Miss Taylor, can you mend my Teddy?"

"Miss Taylor hasn't any time for that rubbish," cut in Nurse Jones before the seamstress could answer, and snatching the bear from me she flung it on the fire. "Get out," she ordered. Hardly able to take in what had happened I went, and as I closed the door I heard Miss Taylor say, "That wasn't necessary," and Nurse Jones's reply, "I can't bear that kid. It was a filthy thing anyway; full of germs." Now I made no attempt to understand or placate this woman — the war was on. I found numerous ways of annoying her and getting her into trouble, and in the end I think I made life as miserable for her as she did for me. I frequently had to spend days in bed, but when Nurse Jones was on duty I was allowed no toys at all. Whenever I heard her in the corridor, for she squeaked and rustled like a frosted tree, I would hide whatever I had under the mattress, and watch her balefully as she swept and dusted, noting exactly the corners she had missed. When Sister or Matron came round to inspect I would stare fixedly at this spot and sure enough they would follow my eyes and see the fluff or crumbs, or the undusted window-ledge. Back Nurse Jones would be sent, crashing with her mop and bashing the beds against the wall. One day I found that the coloured wool used for hemming the blankets was quite easy to pull off once you had found the right thread. We had three blankets and Sister found me playing cat's cradles with the wool from each of them.

"What on earth possessed you to do that?" she stormed.

I muttered something about having nothing to play with because Nurse Jones had put the toys away. In such small ways I was able to pay off some of the score, and this absorbing hatred probably stopped me fretting for Aunt

Ada and Uncle George, and helped me to put up with strict sanatorium routine.

My chief trouble was talking. Talking at the table, where silence was the rule; whispering during prayers and singing to myself during the "rest" hour after dinner, when we had all to lie on our beds. It was the custom of the older ones in the wards to send persistent chatterers to the dining-hall during this period. I was sent down one day and sat on the floor with my back against the wall. Against the opposite wall was a little boy who had also been turned out. He had fair curls and the face of an angel. For a while we sat and looked at each other. Suddenly he whispered, "Here, if you show me yours, I'll show you mine."

"Your what?" I whispered back.

He showed me what with a giggle. "Now you show me yours." I was deeply shocked, but as he was such a pretty little boy, I quickly raised my skirt for a second and dropped it again, well over my knees.

"No, properly," said the boy. I was saved from further exposure by the bell ending the rest hour and I promptly forgot the incident. A few nights later I was hauled out of bed before the Matron and accused of doing "rude things" in front of this boy. Stoutly I defended myself. "But I didn't do anything, it was him."

"Nonsense," retorted Matron, "a dear little boy like that wouldn't dream of such a thing." She promptly bent me over a chair and belaboured my long-suffering behind with a ruler until that implement snapped in half. Thus early did I learn that we live in a man's world; even the women are on their side.

Most of the children stayed only for a month or two, and my worst times were when I saw them preparing to go home. My companions in the ward changed several times while I was there. One of Nurse Jones's favourite tricks was to tell me I would be going home "soon", or in a day or two. Anxiously I would watch for the "going home" signs. The doctor's examination, the collecting of personal belongings, and the non-issue of clean clothes, but none of these appeared, and eventually I refused to believe anything that Nurse Jones said. I would take no orders from her unless it was confirmed by another nurse, so that when the day actually came for me to go home I didn't believe it. I was ready quite early in the morning, but because of a railway strike Aunt Ada and Uncle George didn't get to Holt until late in the evening. After ten months my own clothes no longer fitted me and Miss Taylor had been obliged to run me up a dress of rough blue serge. Somehow I squeezed into the coat, now more like a jacket, but was unable to cope with the tyranny of a hat. Without a word I marched to the waiting fly and no persuasion by Aunt Ada or Uncle George could make me say "good-bye" or "thank you" or even look back at the building, though I knew that practically everyone in it was watching my exit.

We managed to get the last train to Norwich, and it was nearly midnight when we reached home. On the way Aunt Ada told me that Mr Mason was now married to his young lady, and that Uncle Ted lived with us in his place.

"You remember Mr Barber what work on the roads," she said; "well, that's him."

I had often seen Mr Barber on the roads. He was

considered "a proper caution" because of his fund of jokes and stories, and now this humorist was to be my companion. It made homecoming even more sweet.

I don't think I slept at all that night but lay in the small bed Aunt Ada had bought for me while I was away, looking at the stars and enjoying the soft warmth of the mattress, and the unclinical smell of the sheets. Enjoying too the things there wouldn't be any more. No more bells, red dresses and sputum bottles. No owls, or dark bear-inhabited woods — and no Nurse Jones.

It was pleasant to meet again the neighbours and the children I had known, it seemed, years ago. Time has no meaning for children, especially when you cannot read the clock. Five minutes can be an eternity, and my ten months' absence seemed a lifetime. After the delight of homecoming was over Aunt Ada began to notice a change in me. I was more difficult than ever, more discontented and harder to please. Naturally people were interested to hear about the sanatorium, but I found it impossible to talk about my life there. Their questions annoyed and irritated me, and I would always answer, "I don't remember." I didn't know what to do with myself, for I wasn't allowed yet to go to school. I found I could no longer read, and although I would sit for hours looking at the printed page it was just a baffling collection of signs. I could not hold a pencil to form letters or even draw, and I couldn't recite the alphabet after M or count more than twenty.

Aunt Ada was completely mystified, failing to understand how I could forget things I had once known so well. She would show me the H.P. Sauce bottle and say,

"Now what's that word?" I would stare at the word, but it might have been ancient Hebrew for all the sense I could make of it. "But you could read the whole bottle once," Aunt Ada would sigh with despair. She bought a slate and pencil and tried her best to teach me to read and write again, but I shut my mind to her efforts and refused even to look at her beautiful copper-plate letters. And of course she complained, to the neighbours, the doctor and the clergyman. These complaints in my presence always made me "put on my parts" more than ever. One day the clergyman called and at his knock I crawled under the table and pulled down the red chenille table-cloth so that it hid me. The Reverend Smelt had a small white pointed beard, and during the conversation I could be heard chanting, "He's a goat, a billy goat, a silly goat, a dilly goat" and so on, using every genuine and made-up word ending in "illy" I could think of. I had not consciously meant to be rude to the clergyman, but according to Aunt Ada he had been very shocked, and she "hadn't known where to put herself". It was about this time that the sounds of words began to fascinate me, and I would say them over and over to myself until they lost all sense and meaning. I swung on the gate saying things like "deaf — death — death — deaf" and I once startled a group of children by shouting "Yonder lies the horizon." I earned the nickname "Barmy Burrows" and only the bravest ones would play with me.

After Easter I was allowed to go to school in the mornings, but now I did not enjoy it. The only things I excelled in were reciting and knitting, and the children who were so far behind me before my illness were now way ahead. I would make no effort at all to learn, but after every lesson gave in a completely blank exercise book. The angelic Miss Emney used as much patience as she had, but it was easy to see I no longer amused her.

At home I fussed and picked at my food, and flew into a temper if the meat and vegetables even touched each other, they had all to be in separate compartments on the plate. I refused anything "mixed up" such as cakes and puddings, and although I ate custard and fruit by themselves, I pushed them away if they were served together.

Not only were Aunt Ada's days made troublesome, but her nights were disturbed by my screaming nightmares. I would sit up in bed, my nightdress saturated in perspiration, leaving a perfect sweat silhouette of myself on the sheets and pillow, like Peter Pan's shadow. Holding my head I shrieked and moaned about a horrible story teacher had told us. "It hurts my head," I yelled. Uncle George and Uncle Ted would stumble sleepily from their double bed in the back room, tripping over their nightshirts as they came up the two steps into the front room. Uncle Ted sat on the commode by Aunt Ada's bed and dried my drenched hair and body, and changed my nightdress, while Uncle George helped Aunt Ada change the sheets.

At last Aunt Ada came up to the school with me to find out from Miss Emney what this awful story was. From the clues I gave them it turned out to be the Crucifixion, and in particular the part concerning the crown of thorns. It may be that I was taken back to the pain I had suffered over the mastoid four years before, for I know that in my dreams it was on my head that the crown of thorns was rammed. I am quite sure that it affected my whole outlook on religion. To me Christ was a fearsome figure, both on the cross and in the pictures I saw where he sternly pointed out the right road. I have never lacked religious teaching; there were plenty of people willing to instruct orphans in this matter, for we were supposed to need it so much more than other children. Besides it cost nothing, and many people used us as the little steps by which they could get to heaven. But I was a very faulty rung in this ladder, for I *could* not accept some things, and church ritual was no more than rather dull play-acting.

God was quite a different matter. Through mishearing the phrase "a voice as of thunder" as "a voice on a tumbrel", God was always in my imagination a fat jolly farmer. Once when passing the public house I watched barrels being unloaded and heard them rolling along the cellar floor. Later on during a thunderstorm, of which Aunt Ada was terribly afraid, I tried to comfort her. "Don't you worry, that thunder is only God rolling beer barrels acrorst the sky." Far from being comforted Aunt Ada was outraged and smacked me for saying "wicked things", but it took her mind off the storm.

Some of the lighter and happier moments of my time at Brooke I have described in my radio sketches *Days from a Norfolk Childhood*. There I have tried to do justice to those people who had a hard time caring for me. They were poor, and not very well educated. They could not be expected to know how to deal with a difficult sickly child, who was so different from what I should have been. They loved me as much as they could, that it didn't satisfy me

52

was my inherent fault; I couldn't inspire more than they gave me. Aunt Ada kept me clean and well fed, and Uncle George showed me the justice and reason of things. But from Uncle Ted I think I had the greatest gift. One could not live with him long without catching something of his nonsense and appreciation of the ridiculous. He never criticized anyone directly, but he had a way of throwing off a sentence which immediately spotlighted a foible or pretension. He worked long hours and tramped miles as a road mender, but however late he came in he always had a joke or a "rum tale" to tell. Whenever I could not express myself properly, he knew exactly what it was I wanted to say.

Finding my whining unbearable one morning, Aunt Ada wrapped me up and sent me into the garden. The apple tree was full of blackbirds and I was sure they would peck out my eyes or carry off my nose. I begged to be let in again, but Aunt Ada locked the door, so I stood on the step covering my eyes and nose with my hands. Uncle Ted trudged round the corner of the house, his face grey with dust and weariness. "Come you along o' me, Elsie, we'll go to Mr Boast's for some baccy," he said, then when we were out of the garden, "thass only an old tale, you know. A lot o' squit. Them blackbirds are hundred times more afraid o' you than what you are o' them. Why if they worn't half the people in the country'd be without their snouts. Now tell me, hev you ever seen anyone without one?"

I had to admit that all the people I met were equipped with noses; though I added inconsequentially, Mr Tooke hadn't a finger.

"Well, there y'are then," said Uncle Ted, "that stands to reason," and stands to reason it did, for I lost my fear of birds.

He has been dead these many years and he had as he would say "neither chick nor child of my own. When I'm gorn no one'll mind Ted Barber." There for once he was wrong.

Perhaps if they had all persevered a little longer I might have become a different person, and eventually settled down. I think though that Aunt Ada was temperamentally unsuited to have charge of me. She was constantly changing her mind and her habit of discussing me in my presence gave me a feeling of inferiority.

Had she not talked about it so much I would probably have caught up on my school work sooner than I did. One minute she couldn't bear to have me with her a day longer, and the next she "wouldn't part with me for love nor money". Kisses and slaps were irrationally bestowed, which in itself gave me a sense of insecurity. My next foster-mother always kissed me good night whatever happened during the day, and I knew exactly where I stood with her.

It was the Ministry of Pensions who finally made up Aunt Ada's mind for her, when they belatedly discovered that the house was "full of men". This exaggerated circumstance they didn't think a suitable environment. So once more the tin box was packed and as usual we met Aunt Minnie, who came with us to the Pensions office, now moved to Thorpe Road. I don't know why I should remember this particular date, but it was 3 December 1924.

CHAPTER
THREE

Aunt Ada and I were shown into Miss Hayhurst's office at the Ministry and after a short conversation Aunt Ada just turned and went. She didn't say "good-bye" or even look at me, and I suddenly realized with a hopeless sense of finality that she was gone. I set up a loud wailing that rose and increased on the chance that somehow I could reach Aunt Ada and bring her back. Miss Hayhurst just went on writing as if I and my crying were non-existent. Another woman was shown in. Putting down her shopping-bag, she came straight across to me, ignoring Miss Hayhurst who had risen and was holding out her hand.

"Don't you take on now, my mawther," said the woman, kissing me. "You'll be all right along o' me. Do you know what I a got back home? Why, three old pussy cats, and look you here." From her pocket she brought out a little poke-bag of sweets, of the kind known as butter balls. I can still recall the salty sweet taste of them. The salt was from my tears which continued to flow, though quietly.

Then the woman turned her attention to Miss Hayhurst, and together they filled in the indispensable forms, while I studied my new foster-mother. She had that cut-out-of-rock kind of face, very common with Norfolk women, with deep furrows round her mouth and laughter crinkles running away from her eyes. She seemed older than Aunt Ada, but was in fact about the same age. There was not an ounce of superfluous flesh on her, and her skin was tanned by wind and sun. Even through her glasses you could see the bright blue restlessness of her eyes. She spoke with a broader Norfolk accent than I had yet heard, and like many people used to an open-air life, she more often than not forgot to turn down the volume of her voice indoors. I don't think she was capable of whispering, and her loud responses in church, and the well-articulated remarks she would fling off about other people present at a gathering, later used to cause me acute embarrassment.

To Miss Hayhurst's query she gave her full name, "Elizabeth Mahala Gooch, Miss. Did you ever hear of a dafter name?"

We had to catch a bus at the Recorder Road depot, but before going there she took me down St Stephen's Street to Brenner's Bazaar, all decorated for Christmas. There we spent threepence, and then caught the big yellow "United" bus out to Tacolneston.

We alighted at the top of a lane. "Now," said Miss Gooch, "this is Chainey Lane, and keep you behind me corse thass wholly muddy. Step you where I step." Like the page in the carol I marked her footsteps, a difficult proceeding, for her strides were very long, and I was carrying the tin box for the first time in my life. I don't think I had ever carried any heavy article before. We were met at the cottage gate by a procession of cats in ascending sizes. There was a tortoiseshell kitten, a black-

and-white half-grown cat, and a monster in ginger and white. Behind the cats flocked the ducks and chickens, giving us a raucous welcome.

"Hullo, my beauties," called Miss Gooch. "Do you want your supper, then? Well then, you shall hev it."

She took the key from under a flower-pot and unlocked the door. The first thing she did was to remove her hat, and jabbing the hat-pin through it she flung it on the table.

"Do you know, I'll feel that thing round my hid all of tomorrer," she said. She fed the fowls and cats and then we went into the living-room, which delighted me. The wall-paper had a pattern of red roses as large as cabbages. Whenever I hear the expression "a riot of colour" I think of this wallpaper, that almost shouted as it climbed and weaved and spattered up the walls. In some large mansion it probably wouldn't have been so noticeable, but in this little room about eight feet square it was omnipresent. I loved it, but Miss Gooch I found was a little ashamed of it. It had been there when she bought the cottage and as it was still in good condition her frugal mind and slender purse prevented her covering it with something quieter. When I could drag my eyes away from the walls I noticed a little cane chair.

"Can I sit on that dear little chair?" I asked.

"Yis, except when Nonny come; she call that har chair."

"Who's Nonny?"

"My little grandchild. Now then, Betty, git on with it."

"Who's Betty?"

"Oh, thass the kittle, and the saucepan's Susie. I talk a lot to my things, and the birds. I'm a funny old woman." Her face creased into a self-mocking smile. Although she didn't seem as old as Gran, I certainly thought she was funny. For one thing she talked to me, not as a grown-up to a child, but as one woman to another. She also expected me to know and do things that had never been asked of me before. I was old enough now to know that this was to be my home, and I suffered no longings as I did at Brooke for Granny Sparkes. I put Aunt Ada, Uncle George and Uncle Ted right out of my mind and scarcely ever thought of them; when I did it was as of people in books. This facility of putting the past behind me has been of great service to me. I have been able to come through partings and unsuccessful love affairs with my mind and spirit unscathed. The tentacles of nostalgia have never made a prisoner of me.

As we sat at tea I brought forward a problem that had worried me ever since we met.

"What shall I call you?" I asked.

"What did you call Mrs Everett?"

"Aunt Ada; but I'd rather call you Mummy."

"Thass all right. I er bin called a thing or two in my time. Mum's better than most of 'em."

So Mum she became to me until she died.

She was a highly individualistic person, and looking at myself now I think I absorbed a great deal of her independence. She was a supreme optimist, and always had ideas for making money which never quite came off; chiefly because she was too kind-hearted. She had a rock-like hardness which came from poverty, but a sense of humour which prevented this poverty from making her crabbed. "If you can't git the better of anything — or anybody — then you'd best be friends with it," she would

58

say. Life with her was much tougher than with Aunt Ada. There was no nonsense about dressing before the fire, for except at week-ends she didn't light it until dinner-time. She had no patience with my dread of the dark, and wouldn't hear of leaving me with a candle until I went to sleep. "Stuff and nonsense," she snorted that first night. "Who do you thinks a comin' arter us?" So certain was she of safety that I didn't really mind going to bed in the dark.

From the start she made me understand that I was not going to be a mere passenger. Setting the table, clearing away and washing up were always my responsibility, and on Saturdays the chicken houses had to be cleaned, the paths weeded and the errands run. Being by nature lazy and always considered delicate I found these jobs very heavy going. Mum would declare "Yar the laziest duzzy old mawther I ever set eyes on." But I really think some of it was due to physical exhaustion. My heart knocked against my ribs whenever I tried to run, and a roaring tempest came into my head whenever I bent down.

Whatever it was, "I fare gave Mum the creeps." She was the kind of woman who could not be idle. Only when she was very old, crippled with arthritis, and glimpsing death out of the corner of her eye did I ever see her sitting with her hands in her lap. She was for ever gardening, cleaning or mending. She had a green-and-gold-lined bicycle, the pride of her life, and on this she would tear round the neighbourhood doing odd hours of housework for other people. With fine impartiality she cleaned both the church and the Primitive Methodist chapel, while seldom worshipping in either; the reason being that she would have to wear a hat. She had no income, save what she earned and was allowed by her son. She was rigidly honest. I have known her go three miles back to a village to return an extra halfpenny she had received in her change. Everyone knew she had a grown-up and married son, but she would never take the courtesy title of Mrs, nor accept it from anyone else. She was not a native of Tacolneston, and her oddities and caustic tongue made her something of an outsider. This helped to make life very difficult for me when I started school, for I was mocked and ill-treated as much on her account as my own.

I have not been to Tacolneston since I left, and do not know what the male population is like. It cannot surely be composed of such dreadful men as the small boys of my day gave promise of being. Otherwise the place would be famous for something worse than a television transmitter.

There are I suppose good reasons, consanguinity and so on, for some communities to take on certain characteristics. In my adult life I have had many dealings with small boys, but I have never encountered any quite so beastly as the ones living in that village. If boys of today did a quarter of the mischief those did, the juvenile courts would be choked and the Borstals overflowing. They roamed about in small gangs and their victims were the old, the weak, the crippled and the peculiar.

On the other side of the lane from our cottage an old man lived alone in one room of a crumbling cottage. On dark nights the boys would climb on the roof and cover the chimney with a sack, so that the poor old man would be smoked out. As he tottered out of the door he would be sent sprawling by a wire stretched across the threshold.

They tried this trick once, but only once, on Mum. Her roof was high, and the chimney could only be reached by a ladder, which one of the boys brought from his father's shed. As Mum had very acute hearing she knew what was happening, so armed with a whippy piece of hazel she went outside. First she removed the ladder. She put it in the back kitchen and waited under the thatch overhang. It was a cold night and it soon began to rain. The boys on the roof had no alternative but to jump, and as each one did so he received some stinging whacks from Mum's stick. "You can tell yar father," she yelled after them, "he can come for his ladder any time he wants." He never did, and it came in very useful round the house.

There was a smallholder nicknamed "Bumfer" who suffered from these boys. He had a cleft palate, and his speech was consequently defective. He would find his eggs smashed, his young chickens stamped on and his cows tied together by their tails. The boys would stand outside his yard mimicking his speaking until in a rage he gave chase with an old shotgun. He would roar out of the yard like a character in a Wild West film, the gun crashing and smoking until he became enveloped in a cloud of dust and cordite. Although I was innocent of wronging him, passing his gate was a terror I faced four times a day.

Every afternoon I had to plod through the mud to a farm at Forncett End for the milk. At the end of the lane was a windmill, at that time still working. This great monster was anything but beautiful to me, and I have never been able to understand the present generation's sentimentality about windmills. Even at a distance, especially silhouetted against a clear East Anglian sky, I find them frightening and imbued with some kind of evil life. To get the milk I had to pass almost under the sails of the one at Forncett, and no matter how still the day, something about it was always moving. There was always a slight wind slithering through the sails and the machinery moaned and creaked so that the whole structure seemed populated by tormented souls. When the wind was high, and the sails working, I used to fear that I should be sucked into their orbit and set whirling round and round until I died. Or again, a sail might break off and cut me in two. But it was not only the windmill or the farm dogs, or even the approaching darkness, that made these evening journeys so hazardous to me. There were the boys; waiting to throw me over the hedge, or into the ditch, or to commit their fortunately immature sexual explorations. Non-consent meant a beating up, or worse still a threat to tell Mum of former lapses. I could not understand what it was all in aid of or why they liked doing it. I certainly didn't. The so-called "facts of life", which are anything but the facts, had never really worried me. I once asked Aunt Ada where babies came from and she said "the doctor's". I imagined stacks of babies like deflated balloons stored in a room in the doctor's house. If you wanted one he blew it up and brought it round. Later I noticed that some people had babies they didn't want, or had a boy when they'd hoped for a girl, so I knew this theory couldn't be right, but any connection between babies and what the boys did behind hedges never occurred to me then, nor for many years after.

The school was quite a distance away, so to begin with I only went in the mornings. Because of my backwardness I was put in the infants' room with Miss King. The other children looked upon this as a disgrace and shouted "dunce, dunce, double dunce" after me. I had grown very tall for my age and looked older than I was, which did not help my troubles; I dreaded going into the "big room", where the bigger boys, great farm lads of thirteen and fourteen, used to jeer at me and terrify me. Or so it seemed. It is quite possible they didn't give me a single thought — but they seemed so large, and their voices so loud it was a daily wonder to me when I arrived home alive and in one piece. Life has been made much easier, both for teachers and younger children, since the system of dividing schools into primary and senior became generally accepted. Compulsory education came hard to Norfolk, and these boys and the girls too had inherited from their parents, who were allowed to go to work as soon as they had satisfied the authorities they could read and write, a rebellion against sitting in school, being taught a "lot o' old squit", when they could be out earning money. Their attitude was resentful of all authority and they worked it off on weaker and smaller things.

One afternoon on the way home from school I stopped to stir up the slime in a roadside ditch. As I broke up the green scum with my stick I was far away in a daydream, from which I was rudely awakened when some bigger girls crept up behind me and with a push sent me head first into the ditch. While they ran off and I sat smelling horribly, draped with pond weed and shrieking like the damned, one of the teachers from school came along and helped me out. I shall never forget the look of understanding in her hurt, troubled eyes. The fright I had suffered from the ducking was nothing to the fear of Mum's wrath when she saw my clothes. The teacher came with me down the lane, just as Mum was coming up. Her acute ears had heard my yells and she was on the war-path and her bicycle. At the first sight of me she almost fell off it in uncontrolled laughter, and I suppose I must have looked an oddity, festooned as I was with water weeds and covered in mud.

"Well, you do look a poor little old mawther," she said. "Run you home now and get them things orf in the backus. I'll be back in a minute to light the copper."

She was not long behind me with a halfpenny bar of toffee for a comforter. There was nothing for it but to go to bed, as I had no other top clothes. While the copper was heating Mum sailed off on her bicycle to give a "piece of her mind" to the girls concerned. It must have been a good piece for I had no more trouble from that particular set.

The others, though, still tormented me. I have seen an owl mobbed in the daytime by a heterogeneous collection of birds, united only by the desire to oust the stranger. The same kind of thing happened to me; not only because I was an orphan — there were several others in the village — but because I was odd, and lived with a strange eccentric woman, in a "bad" village.

Sometimes when I complained to her she would defend me, but more often she would say, "I can't fight all your battles. There's two things you can do, either fight and beat the lot, or take no notice of them. Pretend they just aren't there." But they were there, and I couldn't fight any of them.

One day a new temporary teacher, Miss Brown, arrived at the school. Miss Brown was red-haired and large, and the first day she caned every child in the school. She must have been a very weary woman when the time came for dismissal. With the voice of a sergeant-major and a liberal use of the cane, or rather, several canes, she eventually restored order and paved the way for a permanent teacher, and a pupil teacher. I began to learn again.

I didn't stay long with Miss King in the infants', for I suddenly found I could read again. We were having a geography lesson, and reading a paragraph each from the book. It came to my turn and I kept my seat, nudging the next child to carry on.

"Stand up, Elsie," said Miss King.

"Please, Miss, I can't read," I muttered.

"Nonsense." With that one word Miss King made the whole idea ridiculous. "A big girl like you, of course you can read. Stand up and carry on."

I stood up and carried on. I read right through the paragraph, about grape harvesting in Italy. I stumbled only once, over the word "kerchief". I had never heard of it, and read it as "handkerchief".

I ran nearly all the way home, feeling like a prisoner newly freed.

"I can read," I shouted to Mum from the gate, but she was indoors laying the table. "I can read," I repeated, all the way up the path to the sitting-room door, and demonstrated the fact on a jar of "International Stores" jam.

"Well, blow me down!" said Mum. "You must a had a brick or suffen in yar hid a blockin' things up all the time.

That clout o' the ear I give you this mornin' must a shifted it."

Now that I could read, a more peaceful period set in. I was in a class with my own age group, and the cry "dunce, dunce, double dunce" could no longer be hurled at me. The children still teased, but following Mum's advice, I ignored them, and except for sporadic outbursts I was left alone. With the boys I discovered that if I attacked first and quickly, I could usually get well away before they got their wind back. I developed a strong right leg kick to the stomach. As I wore iron-shod boots this kick came to be feared and I only had to start running towards a boy for him to disappear.

I was lonely and had no friends, but I don't think I really wanted them. Children's conversation, mostly "Ooh-ers" and "Yes, you did — no, I dint's", was dull compared with Mum's picturesque and often acid gossip. The cats were my toys, though I am ashamed to say I didn't at first treat them very well. I had christened the black-and-white one Felix, and I used to pick him up and swing him by the tail. I liked the noise he made. When Mum caught me doing this she told me that a cat's tail was joined to its spine, and to pull it hurt the animal right up to its head. This just hadn't occurred to me, and filled me with remorse. I tried to make friends with Felix; but he was very wary and eventually went to live with someone else.

Often on Sundays Mum's son and his wife and daughter would come for the day. He was a silent man with his mother's craggy features. He spent most of his stay in the garden or chopping wood. His wife was full of jokes, and the little girl "Nonny", then five years old, was a pleasant bossable companion.

Her son was the light of Mum's life. Once just after they had gone she said to me, "That was a rare sinful thing I did — so they say. Yit — where is there a better man than Willie?"

I didn't understand her reference to sin, but there certainly wasn't a better man than Willie anywhere. By her very nature Mum couldn't have grown into an easy-to-live-with person, but unlike most people she knew this herself, and always, in spite of their repeated invitations, refused to make her home with her son's family. When she felt herself getting beyond work, she went, all unknown to them, and got herself admitted to the Great Hospital in Norwich, where she died at eighty-five. She had nursed her parents through their helpless old age; a prisoner for years of their querulous infirmities, her great spirit tied by duty to them as firmly as they were to their beds. Her constant prayer was that she "wouldn't be a tie to anyone such as they were to me. I only hope I'll keep my faculties to the end." But even this poor prayer was unanswered, for she became bed-ridden with arthritis, though mentally still alert and able to indulge in bitter verbal wars with her ward mates. It was Willie who brought home her soiled clothing, and he who washed and ironed it, refusing to allow his wife and daughter to help, saying, "She is *my* mother, and it's my job."

But when I lived with her she was a maelstrom of activity and expected me to be also, although all I ever wanted to do was to hide myself in a book. Often in the evenings I would read to her as she darned and sewed.

Once when she was adjusting the lamp wick I asked, "Where is Czechoslovakia?" "There isn't such a place," she retorted. "There is, that says on the glass 'Made in Czechoslovakia'."

"So it do," she agreed. "I don't know where it be. Let's look in the maps in the Bible." But of course it wasn't there and she was restless until she found some excuse to leave her darning and to find out more about this strange unheard-of land.

In a short while she was back triumphant. "I met the policeman and he knew. Thass a new country they made after the war out of bits and bobs that used to be Austria, only you say it Scheckoslovakia. Well, that's settled; I can't abide not knowin'. If you don't know — find out."

This was her motto, and I inherited it; and her restless questing to know things, just for the pleasure of knowing.

Cleaning the lamp glass was one of the jobs I didn't mind doing, and now it was a pleasure to look at the rampant lion stamped on it, with its four broad-spread toes on each foot, its curly tongue and double lace-patterned tail, and to know it came from Czechoslovakia, a country made out of "bits and bobs".

Sometimes on a wet day or in the evenings I would play ludo, throwing for her as well as myself. I never cheated in those schizophrenic games, and Mum seemed to win most of the time.

Life might have gone on quite pleasantly. I was winning most of my battles. Mum and I understood each other, and though neither of us was demonstrative, there was a stronger link between us than I had known with Aunt Ada. I knew where I was with Mum. If she said a thing she never went back it, and once she made a promise she kept it. Perhaps she expected too much of me; but she was nearly sixty and her own hard childhood was far away and forgotten. Although she was poor we always ate well and during the appropriate seasons we scoured the fields and hedges for their free gifts. Many mornings she pulled me out of bed at four-thirty to pick mushrooms, and these with blackberries and eggs were sold to a Mr Burrows who came round with a horse and cart. I remember him because he bore my name, and although I never dared ask him I used to imagine he was my uncle and secretly very rich.

Mum's strange passion in life, another thing to set her apart from her neighbours, a barrier to gossip, a country they couldn't enter, was for orchestral concerts. The names Ernest Lush, Thomas Beecham, Mendelssohn and Tetrazzini were household words to her, and verbal playthings for me. How satisfying to shout "You're a Rachmaninoff Tetrazzini" to someone who could only reply "and you're a duzzy grut fule".

Mum's great moan was that now she had me she wasn't free to bike off to St Andrew's Hall to hear those wonders. The buses were not accommodating and anyway she couldn't afford two tickets. I don't know if it was for this reason that she made what was for me a fatal mistake. She took a lodger. Not only a lodger, but a gamekeeper, a man with guns and two large black dogs. I have always hated gamekeepers as a race, and I haven't so far found one undeserving that hatred. Whatever their looks to begin with they end up looking and acting like weasels. I was terrified of firearms, and even toy pistols would make my heart miss a beat; and the dogs might just as well have been lions. Added to this, the man himself, Clarence Clarke, was to me a particularly unpleasant individual. He smelt. Not of dirt for he was for ever washing, but of greased buskins, cordite and plain animal man. Young ladies found him irresistible and perhaps that is why he disliked me so much. I was the only female he failed to captivate. I was impervious to his charm, his bullying and his strange sense of humour, which showed itself in silly practical jokes. He was a great red-faced, blond-curled man, who had to stoop through every doorway. Great was my joy when he sometimes forgot. He had a cupid-bow-shaped mouth, dimples in his cheeks and enough blarney for ten Irishmen. I don't know if he was a Norfolk man — I rather think not. Even Mum wilted under his dimpled smile, which made me feel sick.

Years later when I was grown up, Mum and I were talking of the past. "Do you know," she said, "I was proper sucked in by that man Clarke."

"I wasn't," I answered.

"No, you weren't," she agreed. "I did wrong there, I see it now." One of Mum's most endearing traits was her willingness to admit she was wrong and to castigate herself as a "proper old fule".

To make room for the lodger I had to turn out of my little lean-to room, and have a bed in the corner of Mum's room. I had at first been frightened of sleeping by myself, but Mum was so sure that no harm would come to me that I took courage and came to love my *own* room. To get into it at all you had to crawl on hands and knees through a doorway on the stairs. The door lifted out from slots, as

70

there was no room for one to hang. There were two windows. To see out of one you had to crouch on the floor like Alice in the hall of tears, and to reach the other you had to grow like Alice by means of a chair placed on a trunk. The wall, there was only one, the rest was roof, was adorned with texts and religious pictures. There were none anywhere else in the house, and I think Mum must have had a filing cabinet kind of mind. All calendars for instance were put in the lavatory, which made the long journey from the back door doubly useful.

My favourite picture in the bedroom was a massive frame, showing the high and low roads of life and their ultimate endings. All the way up the road were groups of people doing good works, and finally entering the angel-guarded gate of Heaven. Down the road were other groups, drinking, gambling and sinning in other then incomprehensible ways, but appearing to be having much more fun than their friends on the upper road. They ended of course in a fiery pit, with devils and forks and repentance too late. It was a lovely picture! Across the top and bottom of it were scrolls of words, unfortunately in a foreign language. I believe it was German. I insisted on having the picture in the other room if I had to move out. I couldn't for the life of me think why Mr Clarke shouldn't sleep there and leave me where I was. When I suggested it Mum roared unexpectedly with laughter but said it couldn't be done.

"Why not?" I demanded.

"Mrs Mayes, where he a bin stayin' say he snore like old Bumfer's bull."

He did too, rattling the door of his room and shaking the whole house; another terror added to my nights.

I have never seen a man eat so much, with such a noise and at such speed. One of the things which annoyed him was the way I stared at him during meals, but I found it difficult not to, he made food disappear so fast.

I resented the time Mum spent talking to him; it had formerly been given to me, and I became once more bad tempered and insolent. He soon found out that I was afraid of guns and whenever he met me he thought it great fun to point his at me and pretend to fire it. My greatest fear was when he brought his guns into the sitting-room to clean them. His dogs were not allowed in the house, but were tied up to the apple tree outside the back door. At nights, particularly when it was moonlight, they would howl mournfully. The poor things were probably cold, but to me their howlings presaged death, and I would be afraid to sleep in case I didn't wake up in the morning.

Clarke's job demanded a high skill in shooting, but he was exceptionally good and loved to show off; standing at the back door potting at sparrows and robins. He was very vain about his clothes too, insisting that his shirts were ironed all over. In those days when shirts were more voluminous than now, busy housewives would only iron the fronts and cuffs, smoothing the rest out in the folding. Men, even in the hottest summer, rarely showed themselves in their shirts. Clarke scorned the high-buttoned waistcoat, part of a gamekeeper's uniform, and wore new-fangled things known as pullovers, knitted for him by his lady loves. Most of his possessions were marked with his name, and he was very proud of his fountain-pen, on which it was stamped in gold letters. To mark things with one's name implied a dishonesty in other people, and a

72

daftness in oneself if one couldn't recognize one's own possessions. This fountain pen was a present from his fiancée. I don't think this particular lady married him, but at that time they wrote to each other every day, and once she enclosed a spray of rosebuds. Mum called it "proper soft", but the maudlin keeper put them in water and fed them with aspirin tablets, and they lasted quite a long time. All these details I was able to pass on with many sniggers and giggles to my school-fellows, and once to my shame I purloined one of her letters which was passed round the class. Its nuances were lost on me because it was a long time before I could read handwriting, but it gained me a moment's popularity.

Looking back now and remembering the strong, deadly hatred I had for this man I have probably done him an injustice. There may have been no harm in him, just the vanity and cruelty present in all young men; he was possibly little more than a boy. A lot of his work was done at night, so that he would often be around the house during the day, and for this reason I stayed away as long as I could, only appearing for meals. Whenever Mum wanted me she called "El-see! El-see!" from the back doorstep. By some trick of acoustics this call could be heard all over the village. It would often amuse Clarke to imitate Mum in this way, and I would rush home to find him grinning at the gate with a "had you that time". But I had my ways of annoying him too. I sometimes met the postman and took the letters to save him walking up the long garden-path. The one from Clarke's fiancée I would keep, enjoying the moody silence in which he ate his breakfast. Just before I went off to school I would throw the letter at him and tear off down the path. I made up yarns about pheasants' nests and foxes that sent him tramping unnecessary miles. He had a "carbide" lamp for his bicycle which he took off during the day and placed carefully on the window-sill. By twiddling the knob at the top I could make the lamp give out a horrible smell and in some way so upset it that it took him a long time to put it right. This was a war in which I was inevitably the loser. All my annoyances of him were reported to Mum, and when I complained of him she would say, "Don't be so sorft, thass on'y his fun." That sensible, down-to-earth Mum could find him funny was entirely beyond my comprehension. But she did, and would bellow with laughter when he sent her on fruitless dashes; as the time she went tearing off to Forncett to bring back her runner ducks, which he had already shut up in the shed. Or paying her the week's rent entirely in pennies. He went a little far, though, when he brought in a rabbit, already skinned. After it had been eaten, he said, "You know what that was, don't you?"

"Why, yes, a rabbit," answered Mum.

"It wasn't, you know — it was Mrs Lord's old tom cat."

Now cats were fellow-creatures to Mum, and she was the only person I have met who could really control them. They would do exactly as she told them, in the way that dogs will, and the thought that she might have eaten one made her ill for several days. I knew it wasn't a cat, for I had seen him take the rabbit out of his pocket that morning and Mrs Lord's cat was still sitting on the gate-post. Deep down Mum didn't believe it either, but the doubt was there. When we were alone she would say, "That worn't a cat, were it, Elsie?"

"Of course it wasn't, it tasted just like all the other rabbits we've had. A cat would be bound to taste different."

"Why would it be bound to?"

"Well, it stands to reason; a cat eats mice and fish and things, but a rabbit only eats grass," and for a while she would be comforted; but she would eat no rabbits after that.

All these jokes must have taken a great deal of thinking out and trouble to execute. For instance, it must have taken him weeks to collect enough pennies to pay the rent. After the rabbit incident Mum never found him quite so funny, and even discouraged him from teasing me. But it was too late. During my daytime absences I had joined up with a band of really bad children. There were four of them, two girls and two boys. Three of these were war orphans like myself, and one was boarded out by the Poor Law authorities. Their foster mother was a widow, and a sort of friend of Mum's, which is how I came to be with Mum at all. Mrs C. had a council house and was willing to fill it with any number of children. She would have taken me, but for the Ministry's stipulation that because of my past ill-health I should be the only child. She had spent most of her life as a foster-mother, generally for the Poor Law, and had only taken the three "pensions" children because of the higher allowance. She always wore a fur coat of some sort and was cross-eyed to a distressing degree. I could never bear to look at her and was thankful I didn't have to live with her. Whenever she called she would commiserate with Mum about the Ministry's ban, because, according to her, keeping children was only profitable when done in numbers.

"But," she would declare, "once I get rid of these three I'll never take another pensions child, not if they pay me double. They're the wickedest little thieves and liars I've ever come across in all my born days. Wicked, wicked they are." Thieving and lying was just what I caught from them. They were as wild as unbroken colts. Their reply to threats and punishment was "Don't care", and they didn't care either. They would boldly display the pennies they had stolen, together with the stripes left on them by Mrs C. for their last offence; she was, as Mum said, "a rare handy woman with the rod". Their leader was Doris, at that time about twelve years old. She was extraordinarily pretty, and could face out grown-ups with an assumed innocence that was scarcely believable. She also had a beautiful singing voice, and this, with her good looks, saved her from the consequences of many of her sins.

Most children between the ages of eight and twelve develop a passion for sweets. I have noticed this so often in children of this age that I think it must be something to do with the process of growing. Younger children live quite happily without them and older ones gradually get a taste for savouries or cigarettes. But in mid-childhood sweets are a passion as strong as alcoholism; they are, in fact, the currency of those years. Mum promised me a penny a week, providing I had behaved. More often than not I hadn't, so I rarely got the penny. Sometimes I earned pennies and halfpennies by running errands for other people. It infuriated Mum if I spent this money without asking her first, and as she usually refused permission to spend, or as she said, waste it on sweets, I stopped telling her when and for whom I ran errands. Sometimes she found out in roundabout ways and although I would try, like Doris, to look her straight in the eye and lie like a trooper, she never believed me and my much abused behind would feel the weight of her hand. I hated being smacked; not so much because of the hurt suffered, but for the violence roused. I was convinced that Mum didn't like me, and with all my being I longed to be liked — by anyone. But no matter what she did my passion for sweets was unassuaged and my determination to get them equally strong. Doris and company stole them direct from the shop, or took the money from Mrs C.'s purse. She, poor woman, was constantly racking her brains to find new hiding-places, but she never succeeded for long. Even when she stitched it up in the hem of her petticoat, her habit of sleeping after dinner was her undoing. By wheedling and promises and performing unspeakable "dares" I managed for a time to share their spoils, but there came a time when they insisted on a contribution from me. I was threatened with a "bashing" and Doris said she would tell Mum of the things I had done for "dares". Her blackmailing became unbearable. She would hang about our lane and if she met Mum and me she would say "Miss Gooch —", but this was just a warning to me. The next time she would say, usually when Mum was talking to someone else, "Miss Gooch, do you know what Elsie done?" So it would go on, every time we met Doris would say a little bit more, and a little bit louder. At last one Saturday morning, with a pounding heart I snatched a penny from a pile on the mantelpiece. From then on it became easier, a penny and a halfpenny here and there, and it seemed I was getting away with it.

Of course I overdid things. I had heard Mum tell Clarke that it would soon be her birthday and asked him, in fun, what he was giving her.

"A wheelbarrow," he answered. He said it quite seriously, and I really believed he would give her one. I later learned that this was some kind of joke between them. In that case I was determined to give her something too. For days there was no convenient money lying about, and in desperation I opened the tea caddy at the end of the mantelpiece and found a ten shilling note. I had no idea of the value of money, and it seemed no worse to take a ten-shilling note than a halfpenny. The absurdity of buying someone a present with their own stolen money was also lost upon me. Nor did I realize that ten shillings, probably half her weekly income, was so large a sum as to be instantly missed by Mum. I took the money in the dinner hour, and without the slightest feeling of guilt, but rather in a high state of elation, I went off to afternoon school. I intended when school was over to go on to the next village, which had a fairly large shop, to buy the present. The temptation to buy sweets was, however, too great to resist, and I went into Mrs Cork's shop, by the school, and bought the tremendous quantity of a quarter of a pound.

"Where did you get all this money?" asked Mrs Cork.

"I had a present," I stammered. She said nothing, but gave me the sweets and the change. No trouble that came afterwards could take away the bliss of handing round these sweets and rattling the change in my hand. A form

78

of showing off among the children was to ostentatiously hand anything of value to the teacher for safe keeping, and this was another gesture I could not resist. Like Mrs Cork, she asked where it had come from and I gave the same answer, confidently now, elaborating about an uncle who had returned from sea with "sacks and sacks of money". Miss Squire was openly doubtful, for had I not once put a threepenny piece with a hole in it in the Flanders Day collection box? A deed so wicked and unforgettable that I had probably already lost any hope I ever had of getting to heaven. But what was far-off heaven compared with the glory of wearing the superior poppy my false coin had bought? Although Miss Squire could not really believe even I was so bad as to steal ten shillings, she wasn't taking any chances, and to my horror when school was over she wrote a note, and sealed it, with the change, in an envelope to Mum. Calling two or three bigger girls who went my way home, she gave the note to one of them with orders to deliver it and me to Miss Gooch.

Now I was to know exactly what King Charles or anyone else felt like on the way to execution. My *via dolorosa* was over two miles long, and I was too numbed with fear to speak or look at the jeering children who lined the way — the same ones with whom I had shared the sweets such a short time before. Urgent heralds had gone ahead shouting to their parents, "Elsie Burrows hev stole ten shillin'. Elsie Burrows is goin' to the reformatory." The mothers in amazement came to their doors, or drew aside their lace curtains to see me pass. Kindly Mrs Doe, who kept the little shop at the top of the lane, looked out and murmured sadly, "Oh Elsie, Elsie, what will become of you?" "She's goin' to a reformatory," called back one of the girls — all knowledge and spite. I had refused to hold their hands, so two of them grasped the tops of my arms, and one held the belt of my coat.

No one had been brave enough to run ahead and tell Mum, so the deputation took her by surprise as she was digging in the garden. Wiping her hands on her apron she took the note, and as I watched the horror rise in her face, my guilt seemed to explode inside me and I turned on the girls and punched, kicked and scratched at everyone I could reach.

"That'll do, Elsie," shouted Mum, and to the girls she said quietly, "Thank you for bringing me the note. You can go home now."

Rather disappointed, they turned away, all but one, who said, "She'll go to a reformatory, won't she, Miss Gooch?"

"No," said Mum very clearly, "she will *not* go to *no* reformatory. Good-bye." They went in silence down the path, closing the gate very carefully and quietly. Mum turned on me a look so full of sorrow that I suffered almost physical pain.

"Go indoors," was all she said.

Now of course I realized that I had done a dreadful thing; something which had deeply hurt Mum as well as harmed myself. Shaken by deep strange sobs, so unlike my usual high pitched yell, I took off my boots, washed my hands and with great care laid the table for tea. Still sobbing, I meticulously cleaned my boots, taking the dirt even off the soles, so that the studs, iron heels and toecaps shone up at me like stars. Mum still didn't come in, so I laid and lit the fire, which I had never done before. Always I had to be nagged to do a job, but now I wandered round seeking work as a penance; but there was nothing else to be done, so I just had to sit and wait.

At last Mum came in; her eyes took in the table, and the fire, and my boots standing by the hearth.

"I reckon that's me what ought to be cryin', not you." She did not speak in her usual rage, but slowly, quietly as if she had suddenly grown several years older. "Do you know that I looked everywhere for that money. I thought I must have lost it somehow, that didn't enter my head that you could do such a thing. I suppose that's where all the other bits and pieces have gone. I thought I couldn't have made all them mistakes. Well, I shall hatta tell the Pensions."

"I'm sorry," I whispered.

"Sorry! I don't doubt but what you are. Sorry you've been found out, I reckon."

For a while there was silence while she gazed into the fire, then she said intensely, almost passionately, "Hevn't I done the best I could for you? Fed you, cared for you, given you what I could? Hevn't I loved you like my own?"

"Yes."

"And this is how you pay me back. Stealing what little bits of money I can come by. I'm afraid of what will happen to you when you're grown up. You'll be spendin' all your life in prison." With a sigh she stood up, "You can take away your place. You won't be hevin' any tea tonight. Wash yarself and get to bed. And you'll hev bread and margarine every meal for a week."

I had expected the thrashing of my life, but she caught me where it hurt most, in the belly. She went to my coat pocket and took out the rest of the sweets and flung them on the fire. She kept to her word too, and at every meal for a week I had nothing but bread and margarine, and every night after tea I went straight to bed. I have never spent a longer week, even though I managed to supplement the diet now and then with Clarke's dog biscuits, which with great daring I snatched from under the very noses of the dogs. Mum never thrashed me again, but discovered instead a new way to punish me. Whenever I did anything wrong she would refuse to speak to me and would sometimes go for days completely ignoring me. It was certainly a great strain on me, an eight-year-old, much given to chatter, and it must have been on her too, ordinarily so full of life and humour as she was. She must have been convinced that she was doing her duty, and that her duty was for my good.

Things were never the same after this, even though Clarke left and a milder gamekeeper came in his place, one who kept his dogs somewhere else, and never brought his guns into the living-room. Mum could never trust me any more, and because she was more watchful she discovered more faults in me.

Did I help myself to a spoonful of sugar, then Mum's head would appear at the pantry window. She was very fond of "Bluebird" toffees and would now and then treat herself to twopennyworth. She knew just how many there should be for the money, and if I helped myself to one on the way home it was no good pretending it had dropped out of the bag. I got away with nothing. There were always rows about the milk, which had to be fetched from a farm at Forncett End over a mile away. Mum would declare that I drank some on the way home. As a matter of fact I didn't care much for milk, and detested it out of anything enamel, like the can. The trouble was that I was terrified of the dark and in my hurry to get home the milk would splash under the lid and run down the side, a clear proof to Mum that I had been drinking it. Finally, I had sense enough to wipe the can thoroughly with grass at the top of the lane.

When not at school I would wander miles and miles round the countryside alone, for now all children had been forbidden to play with me. The policeman had even been to the school and warned the children against me, I don't know on whose authority, but the police were allowed more latitude then than they are now. Although it was Mum who had been wronged, Miss Squire still caned me in school for lying and stealing. But one or two people were kind. Mrs Doe at the shop would sometimes say, "Hev you any use for an empty box, Elsie," and she would give me a box, or a tin with a few sweets stuck to the bottom. I found a refuge too with a Council house family whose name I think was Marshall. Oddly enough, although I spent many hours in that house I can't remember what I did there. I think it was they who had the beautiful carved and painted toy, a fat man, containing a smaller one and so on right down to a baby about an inch high. I was told it came from Russia, and always thought kindly of a land that could produce such a lovely thing. Although it is possible to buy similar toys in England I have never met one so well made and pleasant to handle as this one; and for years I dreamed of possessing it. There were two old men who lived in the house who constantly played cribbage, and one, stone deaf, who played the violin. He kept his instrument in a white calico bag, and except when he was playing looked very forlorn and sad.

Officially I attended the Primitive Methodist Chapel Sunday School, at Forncett St Peter, both morning and afternoon. At each session we received a printed text about the size of a visiting-card. Twelve of these were exchanged for a large picture card, and for twelve coloured ones a Bible was presented. To get a Bible meant regular attendance over a long period, and Mum could never understand why I didn't get mine. One day she asked suspiciously, "You do go to Sunday School when you're sent, I suppose?"

"Of course I do," I replied, looking as aggrieved as possible, and so I did. My name was on the register of all the Sunday schools within a two-mile radius, in the fond hope that I would be eligible for all their Christmas treats and summer outings. This grand idea was hit on the head though when Mum found out, as she was bound to do in the way of gossip, and I was banned from *all* jollification in spite of the pleading of the Forncett St Peter superintendent.

I was always in trouble for loitering on the way home, particularly in the lunch hour. It was a long way and there was much to see. How high the beck was and what was in it for instance; and striking one's iron heels on the flints to see the sparks fly; it took time, there wasn't much traffic, and it was possible to kick a stone from side to side all the way along the turnpike. On two occasions, however, I was home in record time.

In those days the county exercise books bore a motto on the front "Whatever is worth doing is worth doing well", and on the back various safety rules, one being "Do not hang on the backs of moving carts and wagons." This lunch time I was wandering home, walking for some good reason of my own, backwards, when a horse and cart approached with several boys swinging on the back. One of the smallest let himself off and a rare following motor-car knocked him over. He was flung in a parabola to the side of the road where he lay motionless. I was quite sure he had been killed, and turned and tore home like the wind.

"Suffin's given you a frit," said Mum; "thass a pity that don't every day."

"Sidney Buck was knocked over by a motor-car," I gasped.

"Oh dear, dear. Is he hurt?"

"He didn't get up any more." I was trembling so much I couldn't eat my dinner, so Mum went up to the main road to see if she could get any comforting news, and no doubt to satisfy her own curiosity.

"Thass not too bad," she called as she came up the path. "His hid was cut and he was knocked unconscious. The people in the car 'a taken him to hospital."

For several days until the rain washed it out we would gaze morbidly at the patch of blood at the side of the road where Sidney fell. He reappeared at school less than a week later, a hero, with only a small scar to account for all the trouble he had caused. There was an inquiry at the school as to what had actually happened and I was the only one who said that he was hanging on to the cart. For this the whole Buck family, an enormous one, set upon me after school. It didn't make much difference whether I told the truth or a lie, I still got into trouble.

The second winter I spent at Tacolneston was appallingly cold. Snow lay inches deep for weeks on end and all the ponds and ditches were frozen solid. It was so cold that we had to sit in school with our coats and scarves on. Cold has a devastating effect on me, making me feel physically sick and almost mentally deranged and this winter was one of sheer misery. Every night I would pray earnestly for rain, knowing that rain and frost could not come together. Mum still didn't light the fire until midday, and I had to break the ice in the wash basin and scrub my face with a frozen flannel.

"Git a move on, gal, that'll keep yar warm," Mum would yell, but the colder it was the less easy I found it to move. None of us had gloves and hardly a child was without gaping chilblains on the hands. It was no rarity to see a child, and I was often one of them, stand crying for no reason but the sheer pain and difficulty of living. Better feeding, clothing and heating have taken away a great many childhood stresses of those "good old days" for which the erstwhile rich are always moaning. I never found snowballing much fun, especially when the snow was packed around sharp stones, but I did once attempt to join in the skating on the pond. I didn't dare go far into the middle, so I pottered around the edge. The boys made holes every evening and drew up water to throw over the ice. This froze again and smoothed out the rough places.

While skirting round the edge my right foot went through one of these holes up to the knee, and while struggling to the bank my left foot found another one. Now I would be in trouble indeed, for getting my feet wet was a major crime. I sat on the bank and took off my boots and rejoiced to see my socks steaming in the frosty air. When they stopped steaming I was sure they were dry and laced up my boots again and went fearlessly home, to be betrayed by tell-tale footmarks on the linoleum. Another evening tea-less to bed taught me the scientific fact that a warm moist object meeting cold air will steam but not necessarily dry.

I learnt by myself a further piece of elementary science, for I discovered that if you rolled a small snowball along it gradually became a big one. It was while trundling one of these that the other event occurred which sent me scurrying home in record time. There was a furious clanging of bells, and charging round the corner, pulled by four grey horses, came the fire engine. It must have been one of the last horse-drawn outfits left. It went at a furious speed with the driver fireman cracking his whip and the others clinging to the vehicle shouting, "Way there, way there." The noise, the furious foaming horses and the speed were all enough to terrify me, but my worst fright was caused by the reflection of the dying sun in their brass helmets. As they swung round the corner they appeared to have blood pouring from their heads. The fire was at the hall, and had been put out long before the engine arrived from its base at, I believe, Long Stratton.

I eventually became tolerated at Tacolneston, but never liked, partly because I was not very likeable and partly because Mum herself wasn't popular. At a Christmas party for the school where all the grown-ups were present there was a reciting competition, the prize for which was sixpence. There was no question of my ability in this direction, no one had a better memory or a clearer diction, but at the conclusion of my "piece" there was dead silence, and I knew instinctively that the teacher *dared* not give me the prize. Mum, who was washing up, put down her cloth, and very deliberately rolled up her apron. She came over to me and handed me my mug with one hand, and with the other took away the packet of sweets we had all been given. These she put down on the table and like banished exiles we left the hall.

In spite of all this nothing stopped me from trying to make friends, and I can remember one or two of them: Peggy Thompson, and a fat girl we called Maud Porker, but I don't think it can really have been her name. Then there was little Beattie Doe, but unfortunately one day I made her laugh so much that she incontinently wet her knickers, and was thereafter ordered to shun my company. I broke with all Mrs C.'s children when they were sent to Bunwell school, though Doris was to turn up to discomfort me twice more in my life.

It was towards the end of my time with Mum that I discovered that I could make children, and sometimes grown-ups, laugh. I collected a whole repertoire of questionable stories, mostly concerning parrots and clergymen, which used to send the other children into fits. I don't know where these stories originated, but only the other day I heard one on the radio. It concerned a bald-headed parrot and a bald-headed clergyman, and had the tag line "another poor devil been ordering coal". To judge by the studio audience's reaction it went as well then as it did in 1927. One of my favourites is still about a boy called Abram who had to cross a turnip field on his way to church. Feeling hungry he picked a turnip and hid it under his jumper. During the service the clergyman read "Abram, Abram, what hast thou in thy bosom?" Whereat Abram rose and called out, "A wholly grut old tarnip; do you want a lump?" Not great wit — but funny. The young pupil teacher who took my class sometimes punished the girls by making them stand in a corner with their pinafores over their heads. This was supposed to denote extreme disgrace. She only tried it once on me. On that occasion I chewed a hole in the pinafore and stuck my tongue through it. This kept the class in ecstasies of mirth and the teacher in a state of exacerbation, for however quickly she turned round she couldn't catch me at it.

It was the teacher who gave me one of the few pleasant surprises of this period. Very painstakingly she drew a ladder on a large sheet of paper and put the name of each child in the class on a rung. After the exams, which were done in special foolscap-size books, she put little coloured flags over the first three names. My name had a red flag, which meant I was at the top, and I kept the red flag all the time I was there.

Not long after the incident at the party, Mum came in after breakfast, and as she carefully wiped her boots on the mat she said, "Elsie, you're going away tomorrow."

My immediate reaction took her by surprise. "I don't want to go away," I shrieked.

"Why, my mawther, that's the best thing that could

happen. You're going to a place called Gimingham Hall Farm."

"I want to stay with you. I love you."

"But don't you see. You can start agin there. People'll treat you fair. There's nobody'll know about that ten shillin'."

At last, after so many months, I burst out, "I only wanted to buy you a present. For your birthday."

"Well, that was a rum way to go about it. But we shan't say any more, thass finished with. I've told you today so that you can say good-bye to your friends at school."

Wallowing in self-pity, I muttered, "There aren't any friends at school."

"Well, now you'll be able to make new ones at this other place. And now you're doing so well at school you'll git on all right; so long as you don't go trying to buy them presents with their own money."

I knew now that she wanted to be rid of me, that there was no longer any bond of fellowship or love between us. I had tried her patience too far, and I stopped crying.

There was a small tragedy about all this. War Pensions children were allowed threepence a week pocket-money, but I don't think this could have been made clear to their guardians, for only at one period of my childhood did I receive this. Had I done so, at Mum's and later foster-mothers', things would have been very different. With threepence a week I would have had a high standing among my fellows, who judged one only by worldly goods. I should also have been able to buy presents. It is only just being realized by people who deal with deprived children that the urge to give is often much stronger than

90

the wish to receive. Giving presents has always afforded me great pleasure, and I have a real knack of selecting the right gift for the right person; but for most of my life I have not been able to use this gift.

Once again I and the tin box arrived at the Ministry's office and I began another, and very strange, chapter of my life.

CHAPTER
FOUR

This chapter should be full of Dostoevskian gloom and introspection; if I was a psychologist I might lay all my troubles at the door of Gimingham Hall. Perhaps if I had written this book as an angry young woman of twenty-five I would have done so. Now nearly half a lifetime later I can see things clearer. It doesn't do to be too near-sighted about one's life.

Even my approach to the hall was strange. I was to be taken by Miss Duff, who lived not far away at Trimingham. But Miss Duff, a Justice of the Peace, and practically everything else, was at a meeting at Samson and Hercules House, in Norwich, so I was taken to the kitchen of that place, given a book to read called *Robinetta*, and left to watch the cook ice an enormous cake. I was terribly hungry, and the sight of the cake made me more so, but no one suggested any food and I was too shy to ask.

At last, when I was almost through *Robinetta*, and the cake had reached the silver ball stage, Miss Duff arrived. She wore pince-nez secured by a thin gold chain; they had an alarming habit of suddenly dropping off and getting lost among her neckwear. The naked blue eyes that were suddenly revealed somehow looked indecent. Her white hair was never quite so tidy as it might have been, but as she was always on her way from one meeting to another, from one good deed to the next, this is not surprising. Though she was in every respect a lady, she had the bright, breezy cheerfulness of the old-time music hall comedian. She praised and thanked God at every conceivable time and in every possible place. When I was a little older she caused me acute embarrassment on a staircase in St Andrew's Hall. We were discussing some problem of mine at that moment. "Well," she said, "let's ask the dear Lord Jesus about it," and there and then she sank to her knees, and in anything but a quiet voice addressed her Saviour, while I stood by frozen with fear that someone would come up or down the stairs, and determined if that happened to walk smartly away as if the lady was no connection of mine.

She did not resort to prayer, however, to resolve the problem encountered on our first meeting. I believe she had forgotten all about her undertaking to deliver me to my new home, for she had come to Norwich in her smallest car. This was a Morris two-seater, with a dickey seat. She didn't drive herself, and there was certainly no room for me between her and the chauffeur, who was, of course, called James. It was too cold for me in the open dickey seat; the problem was a tough one.

"Colonel, colonel!" called Miss Duff to a gentleman who had presumably been at her meeting. "Here is a mathematical problem. How do we get this little girl, her baggage, James and myself into this carriage?"

The colonel came over and mentally measured up the space under the dickey seat and compared it with my box and me, then gravely gave his verdict.

"You must first put in the box, and then get the child to curl up in the remaining space."

"Excellent. Splendid, splendid!" cried Miss Duff.

James pushed the box in as far as it would go, discovering an overcoat of Miss Duff's in the process.

"The coat you lost, Madam." He was a man of few words apparently; he needed to be.

"Oh splendid, splendid!" Her delight rang over Tombland; she pointed to the coat she was wearing.

"I had to buy this one today, Colonel, for six guineas. I'm so fat you know, it makes clothes terribly expensive; but the Lord made me so and I must put up with it. Now this coat will do for someone else. No one needs two coats, do they, Colonel?"

"Probably not, dear lady, probably not."

"Meantime," went on Miss Duff, "it will do to keep Elsie warm on the long journey." She swamped me in the enormous coat, and I was stuffed into the back of the car.

No doubt to keep me awake, she asked me if I knew any poems; if so, she said she would like to hear them. I hope she meant it, for she got *Curfew shall not Ring Tonight*, *Little Jim*, *The Relief of Lucknow*, *The Psalm of Life* and *Hiawatha's Wedding*.

After each rendition she said, "Very nice, very nice, don't you think, James?" and James answered, "Very nice indeed, Madam," in a voice that sounded anything but "very nice".

I liked nothing better than the sound of my own voice reciting these long narrative poems. The more tragic they were the more I enjoyed myself, but I shudder now to think of the boredom I must have caused the listeners and

94

what a blight I must have been at parties. I think though that it is a pity that reciting, as against verse speaking, is no longer encouraged in schools. The poetry may not all have been good, and a lot of it was plain mawkish and bad, but it trained the memory, gave confidence in speaking, and used up a lot of surplus energy. *And shall Trelawney Die?*, properly rendered, took it out of one!

I could not tell what kind of house Gimingham Hall was, for when we arrived there was only one room lighted. I stumbled out of the car, tripped over Miss Duff's coat, and finally landed in a room full of tables and backless forms.

The tables were covered with white oil-cloth and laid ready for breakfast. Miss Huntley, with Miss Garner in her lee, came smiling forward to meet us, and I felt very foolish when I tried to shake hands and couldn't find the way down the overcoat sleeves.

"So sorry to have kept you up," boomed Miss Duff in a hollow tone she took to be a whisper. While she explained all about the misunderstanding I unburied myself from her coat.

As she was about to get into the car she said, "Elsie recites beautifully! She has entertained us all the way from Norwich. Hasn't she, James?"

"Yes, Madam," said poor James, in the flat expressionless voice cultivated by chauffeurs. He was standing in the full glare of the headlights, and his eyes shone red like reflectors. I have since only once seen this phenomenon in a human being, which I suppose is why I have always remembered James. He was to inspire my first attempt at play-writing, a drama in twenty-one scenes, involving well over a hundred actors, called *The Red-eyed Ghost of John of Gaunt*.

Miss Duff waved and left me with no explanation as to where I was, and who the ladies were who seemed so pleased to see me.

This was something I began to notice as I went through life; people were always pleased to see me come — and go.

I was soon shown to a candle-lit bedroom. Three beds were occupied by lumps, presumably people; had they been elephants I was too tired to care. When I was in bed one of these forms rose up and came over to my bedside. She was swathed in an immense striped nightdress, giving her the appearance of a mattress, and long black hair covered her shoulders.

"Do you require the article?" whispered the mattress.

"Pardon?"

"Do you require the article?"

I said "No, thank you", without having the slightest idea what "the article" was. Later I learned that it was the polite name for a chamber-pot. I had to revise my whole vocabulary for the natural functions. I learned that ladies always did "No. 1" and "No. 2" and that they asked "permission to retire". They *never* went to "the closet".

Apart from the sanatorium, Gimingham Hall was the largest house I had ever lived in. It was reputed to have been built on the site of a castle once owned by John of Gaunt (hence my drama), and it was said that a tunnel ran from there to the ruins of Bacton Priory. As Bacton was well over five miles away this was quite impossible, but I believed it then, and for many years did the equivalent of "dining out" on the stories I made up about this tunnel and my adventures therein; although in actual fact I was terrified of going more than two steps down the cellar stairs. It was not an over-large house, but it was full of odd little rooms and corners. With the perversity of childhood I was reasonably happy there, where by all the laws of psychology and what-not I should have been most miserable. When I was grown up I tried to discover from the Ministry of Pensions why I was sent there, but they were non-committal, and the officer I questioned was obviously afraid I might make a fuss.

I am inclined to think that my awkward questions may have led to the premature destruction of my file.

I believe it was a genuine mistake. At Seething Hall, Miss Huntley had run a home for difficult children with some success, and who was more difficult than I? When she moved to Gimingham the landlord had refused to allow boys on the premises, so they had to go, and gradually I suppose the character of the place changed, for the gaps were filled by elderly and middle-aged gentle-women, all a bit "gone" in the head. They were, I expect, more profitable and less trouble than children, and though none of them was raving mad they were the sort of relations one would rather not see, especially if one had a title or high position. Although I did not of course realize it then, the place in my time was definitely a private mental home, and registered as such with the Board of Control. Whenever the Board's inspectors came down I was always sent for a walk with Miss Garner, and Miss Huntley was always referring to me as the only "normal girl" there. There were about twenty-five inmates, most of them between forty and sixty. There were a few teenage girls, and Cissie who was eleven and myself, then nine and a half. Miss Huntley was always referred to as "Ma'am" as if it was her name. Miss Garner was her partner, and shared her life in the drawing-room, but Miss Denny, who was a kind of help, lived with us.

Old Mr and Mrs Huntley had rooms of their own and were never seen in our part of the house. Mr Huntley drove the pony and trap and I often went out with him. He kept a large school bell on the floor of the trap and rang it whenever he approached a corner. He seldom spoke, and when he did it was in such broad Scots I couldn't understand him. Mrs Huntley did the cooking, but in all the time I was there I never remember speaking to her. Sometimes in the dusk I would watch her from the bedroom window gliding along the paths of the vegetable garden, wrapped tightly in a plaid, with no arms showing at all. Occasionally she would sing, not wild Gaelic laments, as I thought she ought; for I had read all about Flora MacDonald and Bonnie Prince Charlie, but frivolous modern tunes, such as *It's nice to get up in the morning, but it's nicer to lay in bed*; and the words I thought she sang to *Mary Brown* I put down to my mishearing of her Scots accent.

There were no servants of any kind on the premises, all the work — in the stables, garden or house — was done by the "girls". Some had jobs to which they clung as if they were hereditary privileges. Miss Bell always worked in the laundry, and would never do anything else, even when there was no washing to do. Miss Watson cleaned the silver, and Ella Barton looked after the pony and stables, and supervised the gardening. Beautiful, consumptive Margaret, who was subject to alarming haemorrhages, trimmed and lit the twenty-two oil lamps, and sewed. Audrey, who was lame, crocheted borders for the church altar cloths. These people never changed their duties, but the others changed about from time to time. Sometimes Polly would be parlourmaid, and sometimes Edna, and once I remember they both claimed the same week. Every time the doorbell rang they both rushed to the door and an unseemly scuffle ensued while they fought for the handle. The door would eventually be flung open and the surprised visitor confronted by two parlourmaids chanting in unison, "Good afternoon, sir; Miss Garner is at home, but Miss Huntley is not." They would then both snatch the minute brass tray to receive his card, for calling was still done according to the rules. Cissie and I, who had witnessed these incidents from the shade of the great copper beech on the lawn, were convulsed with laughter; but such an unseemly state of affairs could not continue, so Ma'am took them both off the job and tried out Elizabeth.

But as she welcomed her first visitor, and I heard her, with the words "Good morning, Sir or Madam, as the case may be", she didn't last long, and was banished again to the raspberry canes.

I could never understand what was wrong with Cissie, she seemed to me no worse than other children I had been at school with; apart from being very slow on the uptake she seemed all right. We had a lot of fights and quarrels, chiefly because she couldn't keep pace with me mentally. I was impatient and thought she did it on purpose, and she naturally resented being bettered at anything by a younger child. Miss Huntley thought I would be good for Cissie and bring her on, but actually I think it had the opposite effect; seeing that she couldn't keep up with me she didn't try. In one thing, however, I benefited from her, for she spoke very well and had beautiful manners. We would often profess to "loathe, detest and abominate" each other, but I don't think there was any real bad feeling between us.

When I looked back at Gimingham Hall from my 'teens it appeared in a terrible light. I thought it was dreadful that all the work of the house and grounds should be done by senile and defective women, whose relatives paid for them to be there. But now that I know the subject a bit better I can see that it was the only thing they could do. Occupational therapy was a term little used then, but it was practised by Miss Huntley, even if it was mixed too much with a harsh and stark religion.

Herein, if she failed, was where the failure lay. She appreciated that Miss Watson was only happy when she was cleaning the silver, and allowed her to do it every day. In fact, she would often pick up at jumble sales some discarded and useless piece of plate merely for Miss Wason to clean. When this work was done Miss Watson would just sit with folded hands, and talk about the forthcoming letters and visits from her sister. There were no letters ever for her, and no visitor, so it may be that the sister was purely imaginary; but whenever she was annoyed she would always threaten us with the dire penalties we would suffer when her sister came. Miss Huntley could not admit that a mind so frail as this was incapable of appreciating either the promises of heaven or the threats of hell, and of getting by heart the collect for the day, a duty imposed on each of us every Sunday; and every Sunday poor Miss Watson was in disgrace, and deprived of the cake at tea-time.

Cissie and I decided that on Easter Day, at least, Miss Watson should have her cake, and as the collect for that day is very short, or so we thought, we taught it to her line by line during Passion week. "Christ our passover is sacrificed for us: therefore let us keep the feast: Not with the old leaven, nor the leaven of malice and wickedness: but with the unleavened bread of sincerity and truth." On Easter morning she was word perfect, but we found to our horror that what we had taught her was not the collect proper, but the words of an anthem for Easter Day. We had been careless in our reading of the Prayer Book. Miss Huntley was convinced that because of its reference to bread Miss Watson had learnt the verse to be "impertinent", a favourite adjective of hers; and as Cissie and I had not learned the correct collect either she looked upon it as a plot. There were three of us without cake for tea.

Ella and Frances had epileptic fits, which frightened me at first; but there is nothing so awful that, if repeated often enough, one cannot get used to. I became quite an expert on epileptic fits, and a great help to Miss Denny who had to deal with them. I noticed that Ella always had hers in the orchard, and Frances behind the laundry door. That a day or so before a fit was due Ella's left hand would tremble, but the whites of Frances's eyes would turn green, and the pupils appear to spin round, like the dog's in the "tinder box" story. Whenever I noticed these signs I

101

warned Miss Denny, who always had too much to do, and she kept watch. I was never once wrong. Later, after I left, Ella was found dead, having suffocated during a fit.

Apart from Ella's and Frances's fits no one was alarmingly mad; they were merely a little odd. Miss Bell for instance had suicidal tendencies, but she never went further than making a collection of suitable knives for the job. These she hid in her blouse and went round the house rattling so much that she was soon relieved of her weapons. Then she would dissolve into tears and moan for a nunnery, and fashion herself a crucifix with two sticks. This was hung round her neck with a piece of string until Ma'am saw it; then there would be fireworks indeed; for a crucifix meant idolatry to a Presbyterian Scot, even if it was only made of firewood and clutched by a feeble-minded old woman. Here again Miss Huntley's blind spot was in evidence, and although I was a little frightened when I met Miss Bell on the dark back stairs, and caught the gleam of steel through the *broderie anglaise* of her blouse, it was nothing to the terror I experienced at Ma'am's high passionate rage over the crucifix. She was the Grand Master of religious invective. When Miss Bell was "all right" her favourite pastime was doing very easy jig-saw puzzles.

There were one or two kleptomaniacs and periodically their drawers and boxes were searched by Miss Garner and Miss Denny. Quite a haul of missing articles came to light, and I could never understand why nothing was ever said to these people. If Cissie and I whipped a bun from the larder, or an apple from the orchard, we were severely punished, and we felt very bitter about it. No one bothered to explain that the sort of stealing carried out by these women was a disease. The thing that marks a kleptomaniac is her — for some reason they are nearly always feminine — jackdaw-like habits. She will take things for which she has no use whatever. One of these women hoarded sixteen thimbles, seven Bibles, two tins of grease for horses' hooves, and eleven bath bricks.

Miss Huntley had all the economical traits of her race, but in spite of this we fed quite well, even though the diet was on the stodgy Scotch side. There was plenty of it, and we were seldom refused a snack between meals if we asked for it. One had to be really hungry, though, to do this, for it meant an approach to Mrs Huntley in the kitchen, who was, I thought, more odd than all the other odd women. We had our penny a week for sweets with absolute regularity.

Apart from running this extraordinary establishment Miss Huntley still had enough energy left over to devote to church matters. Every summer she arranged at least two garden parties in the grounds and did a concert in the village hall in the winter. On these social occasions I was always amazed at the change in her. She was the type of Scot always described as "raw-boned". Her height was accentuated by the Chelsea bun of hair on the top of her head, from which stray frivolous curls were always escaping. She always wore long skirts, but these did not hide the gouty ankles hanging over the narrow pointed shoes. Indoors or out she had draped round her neck a feather boa; and in the winter she sported a plaid dolman as well. Her nose stuck out like a beak in a lined purple-streaked face, and her lower lip was loose like a ventriloquist's dummy. She reminded me of a picture I had once seen of a Maori chief. On fête and concert days she wore black velvet and many rows of jet beads, clashing together over her midriff. Her "best" feather boa, made from black ostrich feathers, was secured at one end only by a large cameo brooch. On these days she would become skittish, and somehow, though at her age and with those legs it should have been impossible, give the impression of skipping about. A breeze would catch the feather boa, sending it streaming out behind her, and she would stand making girlish squeaks and ineffectual grabs at it, until a MAN, or better still MEN, came to her rescue. At these times I would be heartily ashamed of her. But her garden fêtes and concerts were always highly successful, and by these means she provided new lamps for the church and extended the village hall; as well as making a subscription to St Dunstan's. We worked for these events the whole year round, sewing, knitting and fashioning objects in papier-mâché. My favourite pastime was making paper beads for curtains, for which Miss Huntley bought me a little machine, intended really for rolling bandages. The beads were made from discarded wallpaper pattern books, which in themselves were a delight to handle. Bead curtains were such fun to make I almost regret they have gone out of fashion. Apart from beads, and the mashing part of papier-mâché, my contribution towards the handiwork wasn't much; but some of the girls did exquisite embroidery and crochet work. Margaret I remember made the lace for an altar frontal, which I should think is still in use at the church.

Miss Watson could sometimes be prevailed upon to do

tatting, or French knitting, but not often. Miss Bell was handy at leather-work and Cissie painted pretty calendars. Even poor Frances, who had a paralysed hand, could manage large knitting-needles, and made dish-cloths. While all this industry went on, Ma'am might read to us, or if there was anything suitable on, we could hear the wireless. This was the very latest thing in loudspeakers, and I think in many ways more convenient than present-day sets. The speaker part, a large aluminium plate on a stand, was separate from the cabinet and could be carried from room to room without disturbing the rest of the works. It had been given to Miss Huntley as a present so that we could hear the church service, always I think from St Martin's-in-the-Fields, instead of making the long trek down to evensong in the winter. We all worshipped "Dick" Sheppard with as much gush as "pop" stars are worshipped today. Just to hear his appeal for funds to be sent to "The Vicar — the Vicarage, Trafalgar Square" sent shivers of delight down one's spine. "Children's Hour" on the other hand was not a success with me. A lot of the time was taken up with reading birthday greetings, and the first time I heard the "Uncles" and "Aunts" growling "Hullo-o, Twi-ins!" I ran from the room in terror.

The only person who made no contribution, either to housework or handicraft, was Miss Pankhurst She was like a Gillray cartoon, almost as broad as she was long. She had to be turned sideways to get through some doorways. There was a rumour that before a serious illness she had been very clever and musical, but I doubt that now, for she had several characteristics of the "mongolian" type of deficient. The tiny lobeless ears, and the dead hair, standing straight out from the scalp for about a quarter of an inch before falling downwards; rather like a scratch wig. She did not talk, but only made bumbling noises. Most of the time she sat making faces and cracking her finger joints. This last habit Miss Huntley found extremely irritating, especially during prayers; and no amount of roaring and lecturing could bring the light of God to that dark mind. Miss Denny would have to lead her away so that prayers could proceed. "If it were not for the promise of God," said Miss Huntley on one occasion, with the slightest suggestion of a sigh, "and the sacrifice of Jesus Christ, I would be forced to believe she had no soul. As it is, we must believe it is asleep, and pray for its awakening."

The thing I found most annoying about Miss Pankhurst was the way she would lick the end of her nose with her tongue. To be able to perform this, I have been told, it is essential to be mentally deficient; as is a complicated finger trick, which Miss Pankhurst could also do. It is something to do with the co-ordination of the muscles of the brain. Except once at bath time, Miss Pankhurst didn't give much trouble. After the combined efforts of Ella Barton, Miss Denny and Miss Huntley had failed to get her over the side of the bath, I, not being able to stand those pig-killing screams, and remembering my first day at the sanatorium, timidly suggested she might get into a smaller bath.

Miss Huntley, hot and flustered, sank on to the covered w.c. seat and fanned herself with the end of her boa. I was not in the bathroom, but speaking through a crack in the door.

"Who asked your opinion?" she panted. "Go away."

"I don't like the noise" — as usual when attacked I grew bolder — "she's afraid of the bath. You're wicked to make her get in."

"Don't be impertinent." Miss Huntley was recovering her powers of speech. "Go downstairs this minute."

I ran downstairs and out to Miss Garner, who was weeding the borders by the front lawn; there I burst into tears. "I can't stand the noise," I sobbed, "I shall run away."

Gentle Miss Garner, so quiet, so much a lady, I cannot now understand how she became yoked to the tempestuous dragon that was Miss Huntley. There must have been a great bond between them, for they spent not only their working life but their retirement together. I can always see her in my memory that evening, on her knees by the border, her delicate hands protected by gardening gloves, rough leather things which seemed to do them violence; her brown hair covered by a large straw hat, and tawny montbretias reflected in her glasses. She sat back on her heels and gazed at me with all the pity in the world.

"It will be all right," she said. "It is only noise."

"It gives me a pain."

"You mustn't let it. It is only noise. You'll hear worse and louder before you die."

"There isn't any worse noise than someone afraid." All the noise of Hitler's bombardment has not shaken me in this opinion.

Miss Garner bent over the border again. "Have you been rude to Ma'am?" she asked.

"I said she was wicked."

A shudder, which may have been of horror, or a suppressed giggle, ran through Miss Garner.

"Then you must go and apologize," she said. I went into the house and collided at the door with Ella Barton, carrying in an old hip-bath from the stable.

Miss Pankhurst had no objection to the hip-bath, which was perhaps why, when I went to apologize, Ma'am gave me a Fox's Glacier Mint from the bag she always carried.

Miss Pankhurst brought with her some children's books which she pored over for hours, following each word with her finger and going "Burr, burr" all the time. For several years the Ministry of Pensions sent me *Uncle Oojah's Annual* each Christmas, and I presented the oldest of these to Miss Pankhurst. At first she was shy and would not take it, and then I wrote her name Lilian Pankhurst on the fly-leaf and she was delighted. After that she followed me wherever she could, and I got used to her great shambling performing-bear-like figure in my wake. She even managed to say my name, and sometimes managed "Pret-ty El-sie", which always made me laugh, for only an idiot would think me pretty. She hated soup, and would slap the plate with her spoon, spattering herself and everyone within reach. I would say, "No, Miss Pankhurst! Naughty!" and she would stop immediately. I don't know what finally happened to her; I believe she missed me when I left, and was gone when I paid them a short visit some years later, Miss Huntley saying she had become "too dirty in her habits" for her to keep.

According to the regulations of the Board of Control, fire practice had to take place at regular intervals. The ladders were wheeled up and hooked into slots on one of the bedroom window-sills. First of all Miss Huntley went down. Whenever I hear about people going "over the top" I always think of Miss Huntley disappearing from the window, for it must have taken a great effort to heave her enormous frame and gouty legs over the window-sill. Miss Garner, who had no head for heights, went next, with lips tightly compressed and eyes closed. Miss Bell descended grumbling and pining for the "little sisters of the poor", and Miss Watson twittering about her sister's revenge. The first time we did this drill after Miss Pankhurst came, a great difficulty arose, for Miss Huntley had to sign a document saying that the drill had been done and *everyone* had performed it. She was too conscientious to sign it unless everyone had taken part; but to get Miss Pankhurst over the sill and down the ladder seemed impossible.

"Please, Ma'am, I know," I volunteered. "If you tied a rope round her middle and Ella held on to it upstairs, I could guide her feet from behind." Ella was well known for her horse-like strength, so it was decided to try, Miss Bell meanwhile being ordered indoors for her suggestion that Miss Pankhurst be allowed to fall out of the window and "break her silly neck".

Miss Pankhurst snorted and giggled while the rope was being tied round her middle — she had no waist — for she was terribly ticklish. We managed to get her the right way round, and on to the first rung of the ladder, and there for a while she stuck, while I below grasped her ankle saying, "Come on, Miss Pankhurst, move this tootsy-footsy. Elsie won't let you fall", trusting that the rope would hold, and Ella wouldn't choose this moment to have a fit, so that I could keep my promise. At last she moved her foot on to the next rung, and Miss Denny above moved her hand. "Now the next tootsy-footsy"; thus while Ella paid out the rope I baby-talked her down. It took forty-five minutes, long enough for the house to be burnt to ashes, but Miss Huntley could sign the form with a clear conscience.

Miss Pankhurst was not often seen by the village people, as she could not be taken to church, and on fête days she was kept indoors. Those who did see her would murmur "Poor soul, poor soul. It would be a happy release if she were took." But I don't know, she would sometimes sit and shake with silent laughter for minutes at a time, and making a long nose with her hand, as if she had discovered that the whole secret of life was no more than a dirty joke. Within her limitations I think she was perfectly happy, except when having her hair washed, or when she discovered that she had wet her knickers. Then *Tiger Tim* and *Uncle Oojah* would be splashed and blotted with the largest tears I have ever seen cried.

The discovery that all these women were in some way abnormal did not come as a sudden shock, I gradually absorbed it. Norfolk, after all, has always been the cradle of eccentrics, and now it is their last refuge. Aunt Ada was one in her way, and so was Mum; and I, as I remember hearing Granfa say, "was born crorse-cut". The differences between eccentricity and mental deficiency are not always immediately apparent. In many ways we two, Cissie and I, were made much of, petted and coddled like babies. We were always referred to as "the children",

110

while anyone under thirty was a girl, and over that a lady. This treatment was in direct contrast to the stern rigidity of life with Mum, and I wallowed in it. On cold mornings we were allowed to dress before the fire, and were given warm water to wash in. We were swaddled in scarves, muffs and gaiters to guard against the solid wall of wind coming in from the sea. Mrs Huntley wrapped large baked potatoes in napkins, which placed inside the muffs kept our hands warm all day.

The winter of 1927-8 was the wildest I have ever known. It was then that Coxswain Blogg fought his three-day battle for the lives of fourteen men clinging to half of the *Royal Sovereign.* Every morning, both at home and at school during that week, we opened proceedings with "Eternal Father strong to save". Each noon and evening we called at the Post Office for news, and all the way home people battled to their gates with the same question — "Are they off?" At home we would scarcely be inside the door before Ma'am called from the drawing-room, "Are they off? Elsie? Cissie? Are they off?" For two days we had to say "No", with added encouragements, such as "Cogswain Blogg has fired a line. He's still standing by. They've poured oil on the sea." At last someone brought a note to the school to say that the men were rescued, and we all gave three cheers for Coxswain Blogg. That afternoon I think Cissie and I must have qualified as four-minute milers, for with the wind behind us we streaked home, calling out to everyone we met, "They're off, they're off, they're safe." It was an epic sea-story and we all felt part of it, and proud to be of one race with the great Henry Blogg.

The walk to school was long, but about as varied as any walk could be. It began with the farmyard, through which we walked warily. Cissie was frightened of the massive Shire horses pulling the red and blue tumbrels and wagons. I was frightened of everything else — be it on four legs or two. The wagons not only carried ordinary farm produce but sometimes great fascinating slabs of cattle cake, like very thick corrugated cardboard and tubs of molasses — the same, Cissie was quite sure, that appeared on our tea-table as black treacle, and which we always called "cows' cough mixture". The farmyard led into a lane nearly a mile long, with high banks on either side. Here in their seasons we picked primroses, purple orchids and harebells. The lane ran into the North Walsham-Mundesley road, and we turned east, down into the valley that lay behind the cliffs two miles away. It was this section that was so hard to travel when the winds were high, for there was no shelter until we came to the trees by the church: a group of enormous beeches wearing pierced hearts and carved initials, like medals from old wars of love. They seemed to catch the wind in their topmost branches, and play aerial football with it before tossing it contemptuously towards North Walsham. Beyond the church the river ran beside the road as far as the mill, whose wheel it turned before disappearing under the road. Then the village proper began, little odd clutches of houses and a small shop, and at last the school. This was built in the triangle where the road rose and divided, one half going to Cromer and the other to Mundesley.

The morning and dinner-time journeys were hurried affairs, but in the afternoon we could loiter. There was time to stir around in puddles with a stick; the ones that had petrol or oil spilt in them made a kind of kaleidoscope. In the spring the frogs left the river in millions, the road would be black with them. This migration could be heard, even though the frogs were less than half an inch long. Here and there, like army commanders, were full-grown frogs, chirping and croaking as they hopped over the road. Many never reached the other side, and their flattened drying bodies disfigured the road for many days.

Because we lived at "the Hall", and because Miss Huntley and Miss Garner were definitely "ladies", we were treated with the greatest respect and courtesy by the villagers and children, so we never suffered as I had done at Tacolneston from name-calling and bullying. Had either of us had leanings that way, we could have ruled with impunity, but fortunately we were both essentially kind-hearted children. No one ever referred to the peculiarities of the residents of the Hall — not even after the affair of Mr Huntley. He went out with the pony and trap one morning and did not return, until he was brought back very late by a policeman in a motor-car, followed by another with the pony and trap.

Cissie and I were quickly hustled back to our beds when we looked out of the window, but we just had time to see that his trousers were tied up with string.

All the next morning, Mr Huntley, usually so quiet, ranted and raged, and used bad language in his sitting-room. I heard Margaret whispering to Miss Denny, "There was a bottle beside him — empty."

"Tut-tut-tut," said Miss Denny, her favourite expression.

"A bottle of what?" I asked.

"Medicine," said Margaret; "he took too much by mistake."

But Cissie and I dared to think it was beer, the only alcoholic drink we had heard of. Mr Huntley was determined to be off again, and Ma'am could not stop him, so she took the precaution of putting his name and address in an envelope under the mat in the trap. Early that evening a young man led the pony and trap home. Mr Huntley had been found insensible by the roadside. He never came home again, but died shortly afterwards in Hellesdon Hospital. The young man said he had met the pony walking calmly homewards carrying her driving reins between her teeth. If this was true she must have been an unusually intelligent animal; at the time we believed it, and the wonder at Lady Jane Grey's cleverness lifted the shadow of Mr Huntley's death.

The ladies of the staff put on deep mourning, and the others had black and white check ribbons for their hats and mourning bands on their arms, but it was not considered "suitable" for the children, and Cissie and I were furious, feeling that we were being done out of something.

Now Mr Fairey from the village drove the pony and trap. We thought he was wonderful, because he had an artificial leg, having lost one in the war, but this misfortune did not seem to handicap him in any way. He even talked and made jokes about it. saying that he would never drown, as the leg, being made of cork, would prevent his sinking. I had always been taught never to "pass remarks" about anyone's appearance or disability and Mr Fairey's frankness was something quite new to me

The dreary dour Sundays were the worst things I had to contend with at Gimingham Hall; those and Miss Huntley's frightening rages. If the smallest thing upset her she would roar like a maddened bull and turn purple in the face. She often complained of her heart, so I suppose she suffered from that form of cardiac trouble which causes bad temper. In these moods she did not hesitate to use her hands, or any implement which happened to be handy. She once boxed my ears with a Bible, and on another occasion pushed me from top to bottom of the front staircase. I don't suppose it was intentional, but it was fortunate for her as well as for me that I suffered no more than eighteen separate bruises. Cissie and I counted them in the bath that evening, and she secretly brought a mirror from the bedroom so that I could see the worst one, on my bottom; or, as the ladies would have it, my "lower back". It takes a very hard knock to bring up a bruise on me and I was sore for several days afterwards. A favourite trick of Miss Huntley's was to rap offenders on the back of the head with her knuckles. She would do this without any warning or apparent cause, and I unconsciously developed the habit of ducking every time she came near me.

Prayers were held every morning and evening. The morning ones were perforce short, but the evening ones could last an hour or more. The tables of the dining-room were pushed back against the walls, and the forms arranged in rows; then one of us, usually Cissie, who was more sycophantic than I, knocked on the drawing-room door and said, "Please, Ma'am, we are ready for prayers." Through the open door Miss Huntley yelled "Silence!"

and when this was complete she entered. With people like Miss Bell and Miss Watson, silence was not attained easily, and the rest of us would sometimes have to wait, scarcely breathing, for nearly a quarter of an hour. Eventually, like a squire's page, Cissie came in with the footstool, with which she stood behind Ma'am's chair. Rustling and jingling, Miss Huntley followed and behind her came Miss Garner with a hymn book, the Bible, the *Daily Light* and the mark book. At their entry we all stood, and only when Ma'am was seated, and the footstool placed in position by Cissie, were we allowed to sit down again.

A review of the day then followed and everyone's sins were brought to light. Perhaps Miss Bell had "again been foolish", or Maria "relapsed into dirtiness", and more often than not I had "been impertinent". Black marks were entered in the book by Miss Garner, and we were then read a portion of the scriptures and a piece from the *Daily Light*. We took it in turns each day to choose the hymn, which we sang to Miss Loftus's accompaniment on the harmonium. Miss Loftus had her own ideas about which tune should be sung to which hymn, so the singing was not always successful

Then we knelt down, Miss Huntley on her velvet-padded footstool and we on the corrugated coconut matting, and she prayed. How she could pray! On and on without a break, presenting to God each one of us in the "vileness of our sins" and imploring Him in spite of these to show us mercy, "especially to the wretched little one, Elsie, who has further to go along the road to reach thine Eternal Throne. Oh, let her future not match her present;

take her not to Thee this night, but spare her for another day to blot out the sins of her past." Although these prayers gave me a great fear of dying in my sleep, which was never quite to leave me, I was not half so weighed down by my sins as Miss Huntley seemed to be.

One night we were expecting visitors, who mistimed their arrival in the middle of Ma'am's prayer. Polly, who was on parlour duty, was in a dilemma; should she creep out, or commit the unforgivable parlourmaid's sin of letting the doorbell ring more than once? "Excuse me, Ma'am," she burst out at last, "the car has arrived." Checked in full gallop, Miss Huntley turned a dreadful look upon the unfortunate girl. "Polly!" she exclaimed in a voice in which horror and sorrow were equally mingled, and went on praying. The visitors had to wait on the doorstep for fifteen minutes

But all this was nothing to Sundays. Silence was the rule from rising until church time. We all, except Miss Pankhurst and Ella, attended morning service and sat in our own reserved seats. The service was not inspiring, and the same words repeated Sunday after Sunday bored me to distraction. I used the time to learn the collect, which had to be repeated to Ma'am after the service. In the afternoon we all went into the drawing-room and wrote the answers to a set of questions in a paper called *The Christian*. The chapter and verse of the appropriate book of the Bible were given as clues, and one had only to look up these for the answers. Many of these I knew without having to look them up, and once the paper was finished there was nothing else to do. Silence was again the rule; not only were we not allowed to speak, but wriggling or creaking chairs was also forbidden. It was unwise to have such a thing as a cough, and even breathing heavily was taboo. While we were tortured round the table Miss Huntley lay on the sofa to rest, and often snored in a truly alarming manner. Toys and story books were of course out of the question, and one Sunday I amused myself by making a dramatized version of *The Little Duke* which I knew by heart. So absorbed did I become in this, that I did not hear Miss Huntley rise from her couch. I was soon brought back from mediaeval France by the rattle of her knuckles, which set my ears singing like a Sibelius symphony.

Yet this woman was extremely, even possessively, fond of me. She never went out without bringing back some small gift, and was continually arranging surprises. A trip to North Walsham in the trap, a visit to Miss Duff at Trimingham or a journey by hired car to Cromer. It is true these outings, always with Miss Garner, usually coincided with the visit of the Board of Control's inspector, but the significance of this was lost on me and the treats were very welcome. Sometimes there were little extras for tea when we came home from school, such as bananas or toffee apples, and of these poor Miss Watson was always terribly jealous.

Apart from going to school we had very little contact with the village people, though sometimes one or two bigger girls came up to help with the plays we did at Christmas. I remember Joan Gaze, the school teacher's daughter, and another girl demonstrating, with the aid of the scarlet-horned gramophone, the Charleston. We thought Miss Huntley would be shocked by what most conventional people thought a very vulgar dance, but instead she laughed until the tears rolled down her cheeks. I can't think why she found it so amusing, but I see now that to anyone nurtured on Scottish reels there would have been nothing vulgar about the Charleston.

One of the things which had confused me when I first went to Gimingham was a change in my birth date. I had always celebrated it, though "celebrate" is too strong a word, on 5 July, but Miss Huntley insisted it should be 17 May. I didn't mind a bit because I shared it with Miss Garner, and became two months older at one swoop. Mum still sent me a small gift on 5 July, so my birthday was spread about. Miss Huntley had probably read "5.7.16" as "5.17.16". When I left her I had to change it back again, but by then it was convenient to be two months younger.

One day Kathleen and Elizabeth, who could be "trusted", came to the school to fetch me home. They said there was someone to see me. I was excited, hoping that at last that earl had arrived to claim his long-lost daughter. I don't know why I always fancied an earl for a father, rather than a duke or a prince, but it was always an earl from whom I had been stolen. Kathleen, who hardly ever spoke in ordinary conversation, although she recited very well at concerts, said the visitor was a lady, so I switched the dream to one of my sisters. It was only a dream, so I wasn't very disappointed, when I went into the drawing-room, to find Miss Cozens-Hardy. She was a Ministry of Pensions visiting officer and I had seen her before. At first I had found her a little frightening because an illness had drawn up one side of her face, leaving her mouth crooked, and her speech, though intelligible, was strange in tone. Behind her plainness and affliction there was a soul of true feeling and beauty, and her friendliness shone through even to me, shy and fearful as I was. Now I was delighted to see her, for she was the first person I had met from my former life for two years. She looked aghast when she saw me and scribbled furiously into her notebook.

"What have you got on — underneath?" she asked. I understood what had bothered her. Miss Huntley never recognized that children grew, and the dress I had on was scarcely decent. I was very tall for my age and with my short socks must have looked all leg.

"A chemise, and stays and —" I hesitated.

"Knickers?" asked Miss Cozens-Hardy.

I nodded. These things were always referred to as "unmentionables".

"What kind — show me?"

I lifted up my dress and she felt the texture of the knickers. They were hand-knitted, by the girls, from unbleached Highland wool, of which Miss Huntley appeared to have an inexhaustible supply.

"Don't you find them uncomfortable?" asked Miss Cozens-Hardy.

"Yes," I said, though I never expected anything but discomfort from clothes.

After a pause she asked, "Are you happy here?" This was a question Ministry officials always asked, and I usually answered "Yes", because I knew that was what they wanted to hear. If I said "No" it would only call forth other questions as to why, and lead to a lecture on how fortunate I was that anyone should deign to give me a thought. This time I felt a certain unease in Miss Cozens-Hardy's manner so I temporized by saying, "Not always."

"But you are sometimes?"

"Oh yes, at school, and — and when people leave me alone"

"What do you mean by that?"

It was difficult to explain. I could not put into words that I was not, nor ever could be a little lady with a religious vocation. This was the mould into which Miss Huntley was always trying to pour me, but I was not malleable material.

Miss Cozens-Hardy waited patiently until I finally burst out, "I want to do as I like."

She smiled faintly. "I am getting an old woman, and I still can't do as I like, but I think I know what you mean. Go now, child, be a good girl, we will see what can be done."

Many years later, after she was dead, I was told how shocked and appalled she was to find me in the company of senile old ladies, and that she fought a stormy battle on my behalf with the local War Pensions Committee.

A month or two later a doctor came to the school and spent the whole afternoon examining me. He asked most odd questions and gave me puzzles to do; measured my head in all directions and inspected my exercise books. In the end he flung his papers on the desk and muttered, "I can't think what the Ministry are playing at. Dragging me out to this wilderness to examine the most intelligent child of her age I've ever met." He rummaged among the papers as if seeking a clue, "Are you sure this is the right child?" he asked Miss Green, the head teacher.

"Oh yes," she replied, smiling a little triumphantly, "this is quite definitely the right child." She could of course have told the Ministry all they wanted to know had they asked her, without all this palaver with a mental specialist.

Soon Margaret began making me a new dress, and Miss Huntley didn't cast me in the play for the next concert, so I knew my days at Gimingham were numbered, and I was looking forward to a change. No one, and nothing, except perhaps the life-sized baby doll Miss Huntley had given me, had engaged my emotions, for there was no one I could love. The doll was mine to take away, and my imaginary father, the earl, was in my head, so there were no roots to tear up. I was now almost eleven, and a very different child from the one who had arrived in the dark after that reciting marathon two years before. Some rough edges had been smoothed, and I spoke with hardly a trace of my Norfolk accent. I was not always to find this an advantage among the children I met later. "Lady Muck" and "Madam La-di-da" were the names that standard English earned for me.

It was odd that Miss Huntley, so strict in most matters, should have made no attempt to control my reading. She once noticed a book by D. H. Lawrence in my hand and took it away as being "too old" for me. I always *thought* it was *Lady Chatterley*, for I have certainly read it and can't remember any other books by this author, but I don't think the cut version was published at this time, and imagination boggles when I speculate how the original book could have entered that strange house. All over the place there were bookshelves crammed with a hotch-potch of literature. No one else in the house seemed to read at all, so I had command of the lot, and I read anything. My preference, I regret to say, was for those "drunken-father-death-bed-conversion" tales, and there were plenty of these. *A Peep Behind the Scenes*, *Christie's Old Organ*, the *Little Match-girl* and so on. I went through the whole of Dickens, several bound volumes of *The Spectator* and *Punch*, the *Life of Ruskin* and a perfectly ripping story called *Burton of the Flying Corps*. Apart from the last-named my undigested reading made me look at the world with mid-Victorian eyes. Much as present-day Russians are supposed to do, I thought there were still little boys in London who swept crossings to support their ailing mammas, and that if ever I ran away I could always earn my bread by cleaning doorsteps. I also believed that you had a baby if you allowed a man to kiss you, for this was always the sequence of events in the books. I had a vast knowledge of the Bible, and once learnt all the "begets" from the first chapter of St Matthew, just to show off. By the same token I learnt the first three chapters of what must have been the original edition of *French Without Tears*. When Cissie annoyed me I would chant "Un, dux, troys, quartrie" at her until she nearly went mad. Later I had great difficulty in remembering French numerals, and could only do so if I first said my English version to myself.

It was no doubt this unrestricted reading, and my ability to escape into my imagination, which saved me from being tainted by the lunacy around me. A less intelligent and self-sufficient child would have suffered irreparable harm. If I was untouched by madness, I was equally so by religion. I couldn't understand people who claimed to be "saved", and who were so absolutely sure about the will of God. I was often told that it was God's will that I should be an orphan, and when I retorted that if it was I had nothing to thank Him for, I was considered very wicked indeed. I once went with Miss Garner to visit an old lady who had lost four sons in the war and had been recently widowed. I expected to see a woman bowed down by sorrow; instead, we were met by a perky little sparrow who assured us that "the Lord was merciful", and that "He had a plan for every man".

In the trap going home I said, "I think it was a waste of time the Lord giving her four sons if He'd planned to take them away again."

Mr Fairey quickly turned away his face, but Miss Garner was very shocked and warned me not to mention such a thought to Miss Huntley. I didn't, remembering the retribution that had befallen me when I asked, "Why couldn't Protestants *pretend* to be Catholics instead of getting themselves burnt at the stake?" This was bad enough, but I had argued that if God could see into people's hearts then He could see what they really were. I stuck terrier-like to my point, and advanced the heresy that "it was nothing to do with God at all, only people", and "if you make people sin against you, then you can't be doing right". Even as I said these things I didn't quite know what I meant. They were things I felt, much as thirteen-year-old Cissie assured me she could feel the "everlasting arms of Jesus". After the argument the prayers were very long and earnest for me, and as everyone was so certain I was wrong, I was a little worried about my spiritual state. But not for long; I laid that problem, with others, aside, content that one day I should understand.

Meantime there were day-dreams in which to perform heroic deeds. Sometimes, when being particularly courageous, I would meet my untimely death, and the funeral service would be so impressive, and the oration, spoken always by the Prince of Wales, so heart-rending, that I couldn't control my tears and would weep at my own obsequies. Words as such still fascinated me, and I was once overheard addressing an oak tree "it is impossible to exaggerate your importance to agriculture —" and at that time I had never heard of George III, who had a similar habit.

Suddenly without warning Miss Huntley produced my tin box, and it was packed with gifts from nearly everyone. Miss Bell slipped in her favourite jig-saw puzzle, the one with pieces shaped like animals The next day they all crowded round to say good-bye, and Miss Watson, who had been so jealous of me, wept. In two years I had learnt to speak good English, and to recognize an epileptic fit, both useful accomplishments. But I had lost something too, a certain trust and innocence. I had seen grown-ups cry, known them to steal and wet their beds. Now I knew they were only older children, and I was never again to respect or fear them merely for being grown up.

CHAPTER
FIVE

I was so used to moving now that the only sensation I felt on leaving Gimingham was one of curiosity about the future. With the tin box at my feet, and the baby doll in my arms, I awaited my new foster-mother. She, when she arrived, not for some reason at the Ministry office, but on the steps of the now familiar Samson and Hercules House, gave me a look reminiscent of the one I had received some years before from Aunt Ada. All the time I had been waiting on the steps I had been conscious of the bumbling lecture of my escort, Miss Hayhurst's successor at the Ministry. "A very nice foster home — must behave — should be grateful", and so on. Is there a more difficult emotion to sustain than gratitude? I have no memory at all of this officer, except of her millstone-turning voice. The burden of her lay was so familiar that I could listen and think of something else at the same time.

The exciting thing about this next foster-mother was that she had a baby, and a baby was quite new to me. It would be different, I was sure, for with a baby to look after who could be lonely or miserable? I still had faith that different circumstances would make me different; it was to take me years to face the reality that only I, myself, could change the essential barbarian me. I interrupted the officer's monologue to ask if it was a boy baby or a girl.

126

"A little girl, and you must be very kind to her" — kind, already I loved this unknown baby. "And you must remember," went on the well-meaning woman, "that she is Mrs Grant's own child, and you are not. You mustn't expect the same treatment." No, I never expected the same treatment, which was just as well, for I never got it.

Mrs Grant was no less kind and long-suffering than any of the other people who had been unfortunate enough to have me in their care; I cannot blame any of them. I was a lanky, plain girl dressed in a strange assortment of clothes, all too small. I must have looked rather odd on the Samson and Hercules steps, in boy's boots and short striped socks, with an enormous length of bare leg and thigh, a coat that had been indifferently dyed from white to ginger, a hat that was almost a bonnet, Granfa's muff, and that great baby doll.

She lived in a semi-detached house in Sprowston, which was shared with a married couple who were somehow related to her. I very rarely saw them, but often heard myself discussed in the next room. By this means I learnt that Mrs Grant thought that I hadn't "a rag fit to wear".

The baby was not quite what I had expected. Moyra was already two, very talkative, and extremely self-possessed, but we soon set up a mutual admiration society. My only happy moments at this place were when I was dressing Moyra, or taking her out for a walk.

My stay in Sprowston was very brief, less than six months, but the time was fairly eventful. My mania for sweets, which for some reason had been inactive at Gimingham, flared up again. It is true Mrs Grant gave me a penny a week, but with this I had to buy a penny stamp, which was put on a form, obtained at the Post Office. For twelve stamps it was possible to start a savings account. Savings and I have always had great contempt for each other; the most money I have ever had in my life at one time is eighty pounds, and that only recently. It may have been Mrs Grant's abnormal regard for thrift which turned me against it. Every week I asked if I might buy sweets; but I had to bring home a stamp, or else! "You'll be glad of it when you are grown up, and thank me for it," she would say. I regret to say that I took to stealing from the baby's money-box, salving my conscience first by saying, "Can Elsie have a penny, Moyra?" Of course Moyra said "yes". She said "yes" to anything I asked her. When this was discovered — Moyra's money box had a pointer on the front like a clock face and registered how much it contained — all my penny stamps were confiscated, and I was given no more for the rest of my stay.

Mrs Grant managed to dress me better than anyone had done before; but I still noticed, at about this time, that people did not take to me, seemed to be ashamed of me, and would find excuses for avoiding me. The realization that I was disliked as a person, not for things I did, came as a shock to me. I thought that if I was well-behaved and helpful people would automatically like me. Objectionable though I was, most people did: but throughout my life I have roused hatred in some people: the nurse at the sanatorium, and Mrs Grant; but although this sickened and discouraged me, I have felt little returning dislike.

Now I am reconciled to not being universally beloved: but there is no reconciling or surrender when one is eleven years old. I was driven into myself; into dreams and fears and morbid fancies.

There were many jobs to be done in the house. Setting the table, washing up, mending, and on Saturdays cleaning the brass and the copper gas geyser. This contraption terrified me, and no power on earth would get me into the bathroom while it was alight. Even when it was quite cold, and all the gas taps turned off, I always stood as far away from it as possible when I was cleaning it, as I was quite certain it would explode one day. It is difficult to clean a geyser at arm's length, and it seldom reached the degree of brightness Mrs Grant demanded. She would send me back to it several times, until I finally had the sense to see that this timidity only prolonged the agony. Thereafter, I rose at six in the morning, and attacked the geyser in the spirit with which St George met the dragon, my ears alert for any sound which might presage an explosion.

As far back as I can remember, I was frightened of things blowing up. Anything containing an engine of any sort was in my mind utterly unreliable. This fear covered objects from railway engines to wireless sets. The London blitz cured me of this particular phobia. Naturally Mrs Grant, to whom a geyser was merely a convenience for heating water, had no sympathy with me. She found my stiff awkwardness in the bath irritating and compared my timidity with the great courage shown by Moyra, who splashed and swam around in the bath like a little seal.

Most of my days and nights were spent being frightened of something. I slept in a room by myself and woke after dreadful nightmares, too terrified to move or speak. It was a vicious circle, for the fear of having nightmares made me afraid to go to sleep, and the longer I kept awake the more frightened I became. Several neighbours kept dogs, and I

129

was convinced that there wasn't a dog living that was not watching for its opportunity to bite me. Then there was the heavy-traffic road to be crossed four times a day on the way to school — the very crossing where someone's small brother had been knocked down and killed by a bus. The accident had happened before I went to the school, but the details, horribly gory ones, were still fresh in the children's minds and as a new-comer I got the lot from several sources. With so many fears, and with no one to understand or sympathize, it is not to be wondered at that I became more sullen and bad-tempered than ever. For the first time in my life I lived in a street, which no doubt helped with my black moods. I would often go walking for miles, pushing Moyra in the pram because "I couldn't breathe". These non-breathing periods were always worse during the weekends when Mr Grant, who normally worked away, was home. I did not like him; looking back I find there are very few men I *have* liked. In this case dislike was mutual. He spoke for one thing with a strong Welsh accent that I found difficult to understand, and I imagine he felt that I was in the way. As he met his wife so infrequently, he must have looked upon my presence as nothing but an intrusion. He was a quiet man, with a habit of making sarcastic remarks, not to me but about me in my hearing. I had but a hazy idea where Wales was, and the only other Welsh person I had met was the nurse at Holt, and they were both as foreign to me as Tibetan lamas.

One such afternoon, when the hot day had made breathing more difficult than usual, I took Moyra for a walk on Mousehold Heath. When she was tired I carried her and she went to sleep in my arms. She was no lightweight, and although in spirit I would have carried her for miles, I had to sit down in a little sandy hollow by one of the paths, until she woke up. I was quite content, day-dreaming there, one hand supporting the baby's head, and the other tracing patterns in the sand. I was wishing I was older and that Moyra and I could live together, alone, in a hut on the heath, when a man walked by, wheeling a bicycle. I pulled myself out of my fancies and asked him the time. He stopped, and stood above me, leaning on his bicycle and looking at me intently. Instinctively, I knew I had been wrong to speak to him.

He made what are known in Law Courts as "certain suggestions" to me, and offered me sixpence for my compliance. I could not understand what he wanted, but I knew he was using bad language, and the alarm bells ringing in my head warned me that he was up to no good. I had heard grown-ups talk darkly of the dangers of Mousehold Heath and now I was face to face with one of them. There was no one in sight and I felt there was no one in the world but me, the baby and a leering man.

"What kind of knickers have you got?" said the man. "Nice lace ones, I bet." He edged his cycle a bit nearer. "Come for a walk, come on. I'll give you a shillin'."

"I can't." I found my voice at last. "I must take my sister home." Snatching up the child I ran and staggered back to the house. Mrs Grant heard my story and then clutched Moyra to her, wailing, "My poor little baby; did the nasty man try to take you away then?" Up to that moment Moyra had been quite unmoved by the whole affair, but now she started to cry and I was nagged at for taking her on the heath where she might have been "killed or worse".

I don't know what could have been worse than killing, unless perhaps the series of inquisitions which followed. I was repeatedly asked to describe the man, and to say again the dreadful things he had asked me to do. Mr Grant accused me of making it up and being dirty-minded.

"It's you that's dirty-minded," I retorted, not sure of the meaning of the phrase. "You keep talking about it, I want to forget it."

He must have taken some action, for not long afterwards, a man, who was I suppose a plain-clothes policeman, came to the house with several photographs of men to see if I could identify my particular villain. He was there all right, but I was so sick and frightened by the whole affair I refused to recognize him. I don't think I ever lost my distrust of men. The man on the heath *looked* respectable enough; just like anyone's father. There was nothing to point him out as a man sick with evil intentions. And how others, outwardly respectable people, seemed to enjoy the dirty details! In childhood one sees grown-ups as straight lines, either nice or nasty, but consistent. Now I discovered that men, at least, were waves and curves and circles; they made no sense at all.

The school at Sprowston was the biggest I had ever been to and I wasn't particularly fond of it. I found the men teachers noisy and over-ready with the cane and we were all, boys and girls, called by our surnames. However, I gained favour in the eyes of the class master by being bright and well-behaved. I was always smugly satisfied when he said at the end of a question, "Burrows, keep your hand down. We know *you* know."

He was a young man, and he roared like a sergeant-major. We had been told to learn by heart some of David's lament for Saul and Jonathan and I have a vivid mental picture of him, scarlet-faced, belabouring a dull witted boy with a Bible, beating out the words, "They were *lovely* and *beautiful* in their *lives*, and in their *deaths* they were not *divided*". Although we did not lightly rouse his anger we did not cringe before him as we did in the Headmaster's presence. Perhaps it was because we seldom saw him that he frightened us so much, or maybe he really was a tyrant, for I find he is still spoken of with dislike by anyone who knew him. One morning he came into our class-room and told all the children who would be eleven years old that year to stand up. I was one of them, and we were due to sit for the scholarship examination. Pointing a finger straight at me — like Kitchener in the poster — he growled, "You can sit down. Who do you think is going to keep you until you're sixteen? The over-taxed ratepayer!" I sat down, and I didn't take the scholarship. It gave me some slight pleasure to learn some years afterwards that this gentleman died of a heart attack — in the lavatory.

As I have said, one of my duties at home was to set the table; a job which I disliked intensely and still do. Only the threat of no meal unless I did would bring me to this irksome task. Mrs Grant had a very nice Wedgwood teapot, which was presumably valuable. To me it was a delightful thing, I loved the blueness of it, and the chaste clean-cut white classic figures following each other in timeless attitudes, from spout to handle, from handle back to spout. It was a foolish thing to use it every day, but perhaps Mrs Grant had the same feelings about it as I did.

She was always warning me to be careful; always declaring I'd break it one day; and if I did!! One dinner-time after loading up the tray, the whole thing slipped from my hands to the pantry floor — the tumblers, the cups and saucers, the thin delicate plates, were all safe — the only thing broken was the teapot. There was fury on both sides. From Mrs Grant naturally for the loss of a treasured possession, and from me because the daily hated chore had brought about the ruin of something I liked.

"You're nothing but a great, lazy, gawking, clumsy good-for-nothing," she yelled, underlining each adjective with a box on the ear.

"I'm going to run away," I screamed back. "You're not supposed to hit me on the head. I'll tell the Pensions." I put my coat on again and went dinnerless to school.

All the afternoon I puzzled over what I should do, for I was determined not to go back without some kind of demonstration. I played with the idea of joining the gipsies on Mousehold Heath; then I considered doorstep-cleaning, but some spark of good sense told me that neither of these plans would work. I then remembered that Miss Cozens-Hardy lived at Sprowston. Some way from the school it is true, but I would go and see her, and ask her to find me another home.

By the time I reached Sprowston Hall a lot of my defiance had evaporated in hunger and tiredness, but I was still determined. I don't know if I should really have plucked up enough courage to ring the bell, but Miss Cozens-Hardy's brother was in the drive, and he was so gentle and sympathetic I did not hesitate to pour out my woes to him. He seemed rather at a loss what to do with me though, for his sister was out, but he rang the bell for the maid who took me to the kitchen to wait.

While the cook gave me some bread and butter, she and the parlourmaid listened to my story.

"And you've no father nor mother?" asked the cook when I'd finished.

"No. Never had any," I replied cheerfully.

"Just fancy. No father, nor mother," the cook repeated. "All alone in the world." She sat in a wide windsor armchair, and tears rolled down her stove-scorched face and splashed on the bib of her apron.

"Poor little thing," whispered the parlourmaid, restraining her tears with difficulty.

Their reaction completely flabbergasted me. Not having parents was simply my condition, one of the hazards of life; I had never considered it in any way pitiable. In fact the attitude of most people seemed rather like that of Lady Bracknell, "To lose one parent is unfortunate: to lose both suggests carelessness." I was always given to understand that I had been almost criminally careless. I was not in the least sorry for myself, but Miss Cozens-Hardy's cook and parlourmaid showed me that I could draw sympathy from other people, and use my unfortunate state to play upon their feelings, and their desire to be charitable. I became an adept at the sob story, and had I been given a few good looks I should never have needed to earn my living at all. To be a successful orphan, however, one must also be beautiful, and have no conscience.

Now, having eaten the bread and butter, I managed to hint that I was still hungry, so the cook heroically dried her tears and produced some cake. A workman came in to

135

draw water at the pump, and he was told my sad story. I felt rather let down that he did not weep, but merely said "Oh-ah. There's a lot like that", and went out.

The bell rang and the cook urged me to hurry up with the cake, for that would mean Miss Mary was home. I was never able to eat quickly so I reluctantly had to leave the cake when the parlourmaid showed me into Miss Cozens-Hardy's small sitting-room. She was still in her outdoor clothes, and I expect her day had been very tiring, but she listened patiently to all my troubles. I was now becoming much more articulate and less afraid of authority; when I had finished she said, "It seems you can't get on with Mrs Grant — or with anyone; we can't keep finding different homes for you."

"I did try to be good with Mrs Grant. But it isn't any good — she just doesn't like me."

"Stealing from her baby's money-box isn't a likeable habit, is it?"

I felt very uncomfortable, and remembering the cook's tears I prayed desperately that she would never hear of my sins.

"Well, is it?" Miss Cozens-Hardy's voice demanded an answer.

"No, it isn't. I didn't mean to. But I always feel like an unpaid servant."

Miss Cozens-Hardy sighed. I thought the phrase "unpaid servant" was entirely my own, but she must have heard it so often from discontented foster-children: and in so many cases this was exactly what they were. The foster-mothers had in their time been brought up to work, and often went into service at ten or twelve.

136

Mum started work at nine years old, emptying chamber-pots and wash basins at the "big house". Because it was economically necessary that they should work, they had been taught that it was morally good for them, in order to make their slavery more palatable. Most of the foster-mothers were a generation older than our mothers would have been, and they tried to instill their precepts into a race of rebels. The country was confronted with the unprecedented task of finding homes for a legion of war-orphans. Never before had a government department had to undertake this work, and with inadequate knowledge, and an even more inadequate Treasury grant, mistakes were bound to occur. They learned as they went along, and we were the guinea pigs for the Children's Charter of 1948.

Guinea pigs don't often have any say in their own fortunes, but after a pause Miss Cozens-Hardy asked, "If you had a choice, what would you like to do?"

"I'd like to go to a boarding-school."

"That, I'm afraid, isn't possible."

"Well, then, I'd rather be in a home where there are other children."

"You'd like company of your own age?"

"Yes," I said, but it wasn't what I meant at all. At Gimingham I had discovered that in a crowd it was possible to be more one's self. This is perhaps a paradox, but I found that where there were numbers, many of my bad habits and silly sayings passed unnoticed. I could read what I liked, and I had a set job every day and one for Saturday mornings. Once done, I was free of housework until the next day, and I was to discover that with a little

137

wheedling and charm one could escape the jobs one really loathed; a possibility where there were thirty other people to share the work. Companionship, too, perhaps I needed; I certainly liked an audience, and other children were more easily amused by me than adults.

Miss Cozens-Hardy turned to her desk.

"I will write a note to Mrs Grant, explaining where you have been. She was wrong to strike you. And don't worry, we'll see what can be done."

I carried the note triumphantly home. Mrs Grant's only remark was that she couldn't think how I'd had the nerve to go to see Miss Cozens-Hardy. In spite of herself I think she grudgingly admired me for taking action on my own behalf, but from then on until I left there was scarcely an unnecessary word spoken between us. She no longer insisted on my doing any work, so most of my spare time was spent with Moyra.

Before I finally left I was taken by Miss Cozens-Hardy for an interview with Miss Lawrence, the superintendent of Anguish's school in Norwich. The square, grey block building of purely utilitarian design overlooked the reservoir in Hospital Lane at the front, allotments down each side, and the backyards of a street of houses at the rear. It was clean and well ordered and so like my idea of a boarding school that I was impatient to live there. There were at that moment no vacancies, and there was also a question as to whether I was eligible for admission.

"Please, please let me come," I yearned inwardly. "Please God. I'll be good if only I can come here."

Miss Lawrence saw none of this holy bargaining, however, for in my anxiety I relapsed to my usual

138

inarticulate inaccessibility. She has told me since that although on paper she was not anxious to have me, there was something so lost and needy about me then that she just *had* to find room for me.

To me she seemed a little severe as she talked in her small sitting-room where the walls were almost papered with the photographs of girls. Pretty girls, plain girls; girls in school uniforms, girls in wedding dresses; all giving the impression that they had been taken for the one specific purpose of adorning Miss Lawrence's sitting-room. I could almost hear them saying, "If you come here, and if you are good, you will be one of us." But it was Miss Lawrence who was saying, "You know, Elsie, if you come here, you mustn't do any stealing."

"No. I won't want to."

"But you did with Miss Gooch, and with Mrs Grant, and yet not with Miss Huntley. Why was that?"

"I couldn't at Miss Huntley's."

"You mean everything was locked up?"

"Yes, and besides I didn't want to."

Miss Lawrence was puzzled, and I couldn't explain. I was so anxious she should take me, I didn't dare say any more in case I should say the wrong thing. At the door I made a desperate effort. "Please let me come here. I will be a good girl."

She had already decided, but then she only said, "We'll see, Elsie."

It cannot have been very pleasant for Mrs Grant to have to feed and care for a child who was longing with all her soul to be somewhere else, but we got through the weeks somehow, and at last the order came to move. She did not

139

tell me, but I saw her packing my box on the hall door mat, and heard her shout to her lodger, "Tomorrow'll see the end of this, thank goodness."

Tomorrow came, and with it an ultimatum that I was "not going out of her house carrying that daft great doll", so I regretfully left "Tommy" for Moyra. It is true I didn't play with him much, but I liked to know he was there. He was a link with what seemed the distant past, and besides he was the biggest doll I'd ever seen anywhere. I regretted giving him away even more when I found that girls older than I at Anguish's played with dolls, not one of them a patch on Tommy.

The car arrived and I kissed Moyra good-bye.

"Elsie come back," she said.

"No," said her mother, "Elsie's not coming back."

Moyra howled, more I think at the tone of voice than an understanding of her mother's words.

"Well," Mrs Grant relented, "perhaps Elsie can come to tea one day."

Now that I was really going she didn't mind the thought of an occasional tea party, and so I left them both, waving cheerfully from the doorstep.

The greatest kindness I did any of my foster-mothers was to leave them.

CHAPTER
SIX

The Thomas Anguish Hospital School of Housecraft for Girls was a very old Norwich charity. Founded in the seventeenth century for "the poor and such as do lye in the streets for want", it trained girls for the highest posts in domestic service. In my time there were thirty-two girls from the age of nine to sixteen. There were one or two Pensions girls training there, but most of them were citizens of Norwich with homes near at hand. Their families might be unusually large, or the parents separated, invalid or in great poverty, but there were few who were complete orphans.

It was a very happy community, headed by Miss Lawrence, of whom we stood in great awe and respect. Miss Hayhurst had now left the Ministry and was her second-in-command. She was still inclined to talk telegraphese, and still had that electric-switch smile. I think she was probably shy of small children and the younger ones found her rather unapproachable. With the older girls she was more at home, and I personally found her kind, if a little uncertain in temper. An under-matron, Miss Bedingfield, later replaced by Miss Fleming, and a daily sewing matron completed the staff. All the work in the large building was done by the girls as part of their training. The work rota was changed every term, so that on leaving school at fourteen the girls were thoroughly trained in every branch of domestic art. It was a proud boast of Miss Lawrence's that none of her girls ever lacked a job — or a husband. There was a great deal of freedom and "rules" were very few. The girls were allowed to go home on Saturday afternoons one week and Sunday the next, so that they did not lose touch with their parents. We joined outside organizations, such as the Girl Guides, and were allowed to bring school friends in to play and to tea. All this is common practice now in children's homes, but then it was very rare.

One of Miss Lawrence's happier innovations was to send us in groups to different schools. In those days, before the phrase "catchment area" was applied to children, one could go to whatever school one fancied, and this made life much more interesting. The largest number from Anguish's went to Lakenham school just across the road, some went to the "Model", a few each to the Blyth and Technical, but I in my solitary glory went to Crook's Place.

I don't know exactly why Miss Lawrence should have sent me there. She probably understood my peculiarity in wanting to be of a crowd, yet separate; anyway, it was my good fortune that I came to Crook's Place and Miss Bill.

Miss Bill was the finest teacher I ever met, and I had a good deal of experience in that matter. She was years ahead in her ideas, and she had the gift of imparting these ideas to her staff. What a splendid staff they were: Miss Adcock, Miss Gaze, Miss Gout, Miss Pye, Miss Rump, Miss Scarlett, as individual as their oddly assorted names, but all welded in loyalty to Miss Bill and her great idea. Miss Bill's aim was education as opposed to schooling.

Someone is supposed to have defined education as "what is left after you've forgotten everything you learnt at school". I can no longer recite the date of the accession of every British king since Egbert I, 827, nor can I do long division, nor find the square root of anything. I could once recite the "Speech of Pitt on Slavery" and dissect a buttercup into all its component parts. Most facts and figures have gone from me, except that in Kidderminster they make carpets and that the Christian names of the Duke of Windsor are Edward Albert Christian George Andrew David Patrick. But if I have ever done anything worth while, and whatever small amount of goodness and decency there is in me, is entirely due to the efforts of Miss Lawrence at home and Miss Bill at school.

My first few days at Crook's Place, however, I found rather confusing. Being eleven I was put in Standard V, Miss Pye's class, but I was surprised to see that after a lesson had finished, some girls would dash out and others rush in. The first time this happened I followed, but was called back. "For the moment," said Miss Pye, "you stay here for all your lessons."

After a week I could understand what all the to-ing and fro-ing meant.

We were placed in classes according to our ages, and these were known as Register classes. There we took handwork, history, geography and other lessons. For arithmetic and English we moved about according to our abilities. In my second year there I was in Standard VI (Miss Rump) for the Register, with Miss Scarlett in

Standard VII for English, but still with Miss Pye for Arithmetic. By this method those who were bright could forge ahead, and those who were not weren't forced to strain at work beyond their capacity. This avoided the chief causes of boredom among the pupils, and is nowadays known as "streaming" and considered to be very new! There were few girls who went below their Register class for long; if they did it was usually through missing school because of sickness — and they soon caught up. There were some of course who remained permanently dull, the word- and figure-blind, and for these Miss Bill held special classes which she took herself.

Apart from helping both the bright and the backward this system had another advantage. Moving from one class to another in most schools involves the child in coping with a fresh teacher, with different methods, voice and habits as well as new work. At Crook's Place we knew all the teachers equally well and the yearly moves did not cause so much upheaval or so many setbacks as they usually do. Most of the teachers were themselves mobile. Miss Gaze taught singing throughout the school, Miss Pye elocution, Miss Scarlett games and Miss Rump a subject known as "Hygiene". Hygiene covered a great deal of ground, from personal cleanliness to compound fractures. She was thorough and bold in her teaching, never afraid to mention the unmentionable, and I don't doubt that she often received protesting notes from prudish mothers. "Don't believe anyone, not even your mother," she would say, "who tells you it isn't safe to bath at certain times of the month. You need a bath then more than ever."

This was an extremely advanced idea in those days, for

the opinion was strongly held that getting the feet wet during menstruation brought on consumption. Even as enlightened a person as Miss Lawrence subscribed to this idea, and was furious with me one day when I paddled in the sea, on an outing, when in that condition.

With ghastly porcelain models, which took to pieces, and lurid coloured charts, Miss Rump taught us all about the action of the heart and lungs, the formation of the ear, the brain and the eye, and I have never forgotten that the *medulla oblongata* connects the spinal column to the brain, and that this is what breaks and causes death when you hang a man. Somehow Miss Rump managed to make the passage of bread and butter from the plate to the w.c. a veritable voyage of discovery. Any Crook's Place girls who became nurses must have found her grounding extremely valuable. No one was ever bored at school, and misbehaviour was extremely rare. The school served one of the slummiest areas in Norwich, and many families were desperately poor, but I cannot remember seeing a dirty or ill-kempt child there. However little the money, the mothers, who had themselves in many cases been Miss Bill's girls, managed to send their daughters to school well shod and tidy. It was not so at all Norwich schools in these years of depression. There were even then school feeding centres for the children of poor parents and Miss Bill saw to it that needy children were fed. She spent a great deal of her time trying to persuade the girls to aim for something higher than factory work, which she considered a "dead-end" job; and where conditions then were very bad. Christmas crackers and chocolates were made in an ugly red brick factory in nearby Chapel Field, and this absorbed most of the juvenile labour of the district. Miss Bill seemed to look on this building as a personal enemy; and even today, though the old red brick building has gone, and a perfect palace risen in its place, I still shudder slightly whenever I pass it, and am thankful I didn't know its old bad days.

A casual visitor to Norwich could easily have missed the slums. They were reached through narrow little archways in the main streets, which led on to filthy courts and tenements. They were known as the Backs (no connection with Cambridge), and the Backs of Ber Street were reputed to be the worst in England. To come from there made one a social outcast, and no one I met would dare go down Ber Street late at night. Among the children it was called "Blood and Guts Street", and if you wanted to really annoy somebody you shouted "Blood and Guts Kid" at them. One of the Anguish girls came from that area. She had won a scholarship to the secondary school and for that reason came to Anguish's. I suppose the authorities thought that her home environment would neutralize any good the secondary school might do. She was unmercifully teased at first, but it had little effect on her; she accepted it as part of life, and she was such a good-natured girl she seldom retaliated. She was, however, fanatically loyal to her family and home, and the nearest I have ever been to murdering anyone was on her behalf.

I didn't particularly like her, she ate noisily, sniffed and was a bit smelly, but that Saturday afternoon I would have hanged for her. We were playing very inferior tennis; this girl, Edna, and I on one side, and two sisters on the other. Tennis was played at Edna's school but not at ours, so she was the expert among us. An argument developed about whether a ball was in or out, and in no time at all a gale of fury was blowing. Edna was definitely right, and neither of us would give in. Connie on the other side was one of those children who hate to lose games, and as she was very good at them, she seldom did. Her sister was more peaceably inclined: "Let's not count it at all," she said. "Let's start again."

"All right," Edna conceded. "But I want my own racquet back" — she had generously lent it to Connie; ours all had broken strings.

"There you are then" — the racquet flew over the net, hitting Edna right in the face and making her nose bleed — "you old Blood and Guts closet-cleaner's daughter!" Fear at the spreading scarlet stain on Edna's white shirt, and guilt; for I had told Connie Edna's secret: that her mother sometimes cleaned the public lavatories — went to my head. Not bothering about obstacles I flew at Connie, bringing down the posts and tearing holes in the rotten netting. I punched her wherever I could find a landing-place for my fists, and finally grabbed a handful of her hair in each hand and battered her head against the ground. Fortunately, we were on the grass, so that I could do little actual damage, but I know that all I could see was a red mist, and all I wanted to do was to blot Connie out. I just didn't want her to be there any more. Finally other girls came out and separated us, and, as suddenly as the storm rose, it fell. We all said we were sorry, and swore on oath not to tell Miss Lawrence or any of the staff. Nearly all Anguish quarrels ended with this oath; not because we were afraid of the staff, but because it was a point of honour with us not to worry them unnecessarily. Connie and I escorted Edna to Miss Fleming, to explain that she had run into a wall, and "please could she have a clean blouse".

That was the end of it for them, but not for me. My own lack of control had terrified me, and the knowledge that I had really wanted to kill Connie haunted me for months. I woke up at nights thinking, "Suppose we had been on the path and not the grass. Suppose the other girls hadn't come, Connie would have been dead." And I? I knew what would have happened to me. I would have been sent to a reformatory for "the rest of my natural life". I saw myself in grey sackcloth, scrubbing endless corridors for ever. Although my bad temper still remains unconquered, and the old barbarian still gets me in trouble, I have never let those red mists gather so thick as to obscure my sight. This incident taught me a little the wisdom of self-discipline and made me realize that most violence springs from fear and guilt.

The Ber Street slums had bred Edna tough. When the Municipal Secondary School moved to its new buildings and was re-named the Blyth, they held a mock election. A real one was taking place at the time, and Edna held the fort very daringly for the Reds. Communism was such a rude word then that it was never uttered. Even Miss Lawrence, who always managed to see thirty-two different points of view at once, was a little perturbed.

"I hope you don't advocate going back to hanging on Castle Plain, Edna," she said.

"No, Miss Lawrence, we'll take 'em down the Backs and shoot 'em."

Although I never dared to venture into Ber Street, so I don't know if it really was as bad as we all believed, I had to go to school down Southwell Road, a narrow little street of mean overcrowded houses. Dirty babies crawled about the pavement, or were penned in the dim front rooms by low gates in the doorways. By the papers in the gutters and the smell in the air the inhabitants seemed to live entirely on chips and boiled cabbage. I could avoid Southwell Road by going down Queen's Road, but I somehow felt duty-bound to go the unpleasant way. Elizabeth Fry, daughter of Norwich, was my heroine, and in my day-dreams I saw myself moving in and out of these houses, shedding light and love as Mrs Fry had done at Newgate. But whatever it was that had helped her to face the shrieking female felons did not come to my aid. I did once summon up what courage I had to ask through an open doorway, "Would you like me to wash your baby for you?"

The woman's reply to that sent me flying up the road as if the devil was at my heels, and I used Queen's Road for some days afterwards. It was a long way from Lakenham to Crook's Place, but I was used to walking and city streets were a novelty to me.

Most of my stories were made up on walks to and from school; I ruled the world in my head. When my own imagination failed, there was poetry, and I frequently bumped into people while I was muttering "The Charge of the Light Brigade". Sometimes I stood at the edge of the pavement declaiming

"Ruin seize thee, ruthless king
Confusion on thy banners wait"

to passing cars. No one appeared to think it odd. Now and again I made up my own poems, and one inspired by Southwell Road began

"Here in my lovely city
Of towers and spires grey.
I break my heart with pity
As I go on my way."

It continued at great length, now mercifully forgotten, and ended:

"But we must build a city
Where more than churches flower."

Interest in local and national elections was particularly fostered by Miss Bill. "People have died," she would say, "so that when you grow up you should have a voice in the way you are governed. *Use* your vote, or those people will have lived, fought and died in vain." At the election feeling ran very high. At Anguish's Miss Ramsay the sewing matron was kept busy for days making rosettes of party colours. Purple and yellow for the Conservatives were much in demand, and because I liked this combination of colours I decided to be Conservative. When I found that one of the candidates was called Geoffrey Shakespeare, and that his colours were blue and white, Liberal, I think, I changed my party. Anyone, I decided, bearing the name of Shakespeare must be right.

On the eve of poll itself some of us asked if we might go out and see the fun. Miss Lawrence was dubious. "It'll be very educational," I said. "If the Reds get in we might never have another election."

Miss Lawrence couldn't believe that, but she was a sucker for education, and so we were allowed out. The whole child population of Norwich seemed to be on the streets. Some from the Backs wore paper highwayman's masks with "Vote for ..." written on them. One group had blackened their faces, and were making rough music with comb and paper, dustbin lids and tins full of pebbles. Their rivals had gathered a large supply of long grass. A blade of this placed between the thumbs and blown through makes the loudest and rudest sound of derision there is. Our nearest polling booth was at St Mark's school, and with others we linked hands and made a barrier across the street, singing "Vote, vote, vote for Mr Shakespeare, shove old 'what's it' in the bin; for he isn't any good, he's like a log of wood, and we won't go voting for him." We jumped on the running boards of cars and yelled "Vote for Shakespeare" through the windows. Miss Lawrence had said we were to go no farther than the end of Hall Road, so we formed up and marched down the middle of it chanting, "Shakespeare, Shakespeare, Shakespeare." Someone had said they were burning him as a guy in Ber Street, and from the end of the road we could see a glow which might have been a bonfire. "Come on," shouted a boy. "Let's go and pee on it and put it out for 'em."

"No, let's go and pee on them," said another.

They streamed across the road, taking the election flame with them, but we from Anguish's turned back as we'd been told and arrived home in good order.

We reported our return to Miss Lawrence in the board room.

"Mr Shakespeare will get in," we told her. "We've got him in," and when we heard of his success next day we were sure he owed it entirely to us.

Most women can look back on their lives and say, "There, on that day I grew up." The process is, I think, more gradual for men; that is if they ever do grow up, which is a debatable point. But for girls; one day you are a child, an equal of other children, boys or girls; the next you are apart — a consciously female person. In spite of all the outspoken books which have been written, in which every intimate detail of sexual intercourse has been described, and in spite too of all the frank radio talks, it is still considered "not done" for women to mention or discuss the suffering menstruation causes them. Consequently a morass of stupidity, superstition and old wives' tales has grown up about this phenomenon; and the average man has no idea what happens to a woman then, not only physically but mentally. More marriages have been wrecked through men's lack of education in this matter than from any other cause; though it is seldom the reason given for a break-up.

If it is still unmentionable today, it was even more so when I was young. It was so unmentionable that I had never heard of it. Once at Gimingham when I had been helping Miss Denny to make beds, we discovered Elizabeth's sheet was stained. My comment was "Oh-er, what's happened to Elizabeth?" Utterly missing her opportunity, Miss Denny muttered that "she had sat upon the article and it had broken". I glanced at the pile of

152

articles, great thick handleless affairs of a pattern compulsory in mental homes (presumably to discourage the inmates from throwing them about) and wondered how even fat Elizabeth could break one. Apart from being very careful about trusting my own weight on them after that I thought no more of the incident, so that when my own periods started at about twelve I was quite unprepared. I was convinced I was suffering from some dread disease. Cancer being the worst thing I had ever heard of, I decided it must be that, and went about in an agony of mind and with a "dying air" for three days. An older girl, noticing the state of my clothing, informed Miss Lawrence. She called me to the infirmary, showed me how to fold a thing like a baby's napkin and without any kind of emotion at all told me that until I was about fifty this catastrophe would fall upon me every month.

"But why?" I asked.

"It's just nature; it's part of growing up." I couldn't understand her matter-of-fact acceptance of such a thing.

"It's the end of my childhood," I wailed, "there won't be any fun any more."

"Good gracious, Elsie, don't make such a fuss; it happens to every woman."

I suppose if I had been prepared it would not have been such a shock to me and I would have been more reconciled. Even when I recognized the fact that Miss Lawrence was right — they did happen every month — I didn't know why, and couldn't connect them in any way with woman's function of reproduction. There are still too many mothers who think this is the sort of thing a girl learns automatically. They don't.

This incident illustrates the way the unwritten Anguish code worked. It was a point of honour for some reason never to report one's own sicknesses. If the illness was a noticeable one, such as a cold, or an outbreak of spots, you hung about and got in the way of various members of the staff hoping they would notice how poorly you were. You used every opportunity for coughing outside the board-room door; asked to be excused from meals, or just wilted around. If the staff continued to be blind then you persuaded a friend to tell Miss Lawrence. There was a formula for this reportage, "Excuse me, please, Miss Lawrence, but have you noticed Elsie's cold"; or spots, or what have you. I don't mean to imply that our health was in any way neglected. When really ill we received every possible attention. To a lazy person like myself, a day or two in the infirmary, with special food and a large supply of books, was very tempting, and as I never really *looked* well, and was an accomplished actress I often managed to get there. No one, in fact, "enjoyed" ill-health more. I loved lying in bed in the infirmary, hearing the bells being rung — but not for me. The "first" bell sounded no warning, and the "second" bell asked for no action. Perhaps I really needed these odd days off; and it may be that Miss Lawrence, realizing this, lent a sympathetic ear to my various aches and undefined "sort of giddy" feelings. These attacked particularly on cold mornings. My favourite trick was to stand at the passage window nearest the board-room door, and lean my supposedly fevered brow against the pane, looking I hoped like the Lady of the Camellias. Once when I was doing this one of the girls appeared in the yard on the other side of the window and

154

said, "You don't half look soft with your snout all flat like that." She pressed her nose against the glass and the result was so comical that my illness for that day vanished in a gale of giggles.

It is a commonplace to speak of an institution running "like a well-oiled machine", but Anguish's really did that, with the added grace of not being boring. There were seldom any rows or upheavals, and panic was unknown. If the staff had arguments or quarrels we knew nothing of them. Except at mealtimes we schoolgirls saw little of them, though they could always be found if needed. They did not supervise our leisure hours and minor worries were dealt with by the house-girls, who were treated with almost as much respect as the staff. As I have said, our quarrels were always settled among ourselves and a tale-bearer was treated like a leper. Such an offender would be "sent to Coventry" for days. The routine held enough momentum to carry us through the bleak days when Miss Lawrence and Miss Hayhurst went on holiday. Then Miss Minnie Bowyer, a relation of hers, took charge. She was extremely strict and forbidding, and reminded me of Miss Murdstone in *David Copperfield*. I gave her this nickname, which in time was corrupted to the totally undeserved one of "Murdering Min". During her visitations we just suspended living, not daring to "play her up", and we only spoke to her whenever it couldn't be avoided. It was when she was on duty that I fell and cut my knee. It wasn't a bad cut, but I must have either got some dye from black woollen stockings or some dirt into the graze, for the knee swelled so much it was a painful weight to carry around. For a week I hobbled to and from school four times a day, gritting my teeth and feeling so sick with pain I couldn't eat. It never occurred to me to report the trouble to Miss Minnie. It would have been the essence of bad taste, causing trouble while Miss Lawrence was away and having anything all to do with "old Murdering Min". It says a lot for my sticking powers, loyalty — and stupidity.

When Miss Lawrence came home the first thing she noticed was my face which she declared was "green as grass". On discovering the reason for it she really lost her temper. "Why on earth didn't you go to Miss Bowyer?" she rampaged. "You might have lost your leg if I hadn't come back. It's a pity I can't go away for a few days and not be able to trust you."

The point was that she *could* trust us, but I was too far gone to argue, I just said I hadn't wanted to stay away from school.

"Well, you'll have to now, and in bed."

Instead of going into the infirmary at the back of the building I was moved into a single room over the front porch. It contained a bed, a locker, cupboards for the Sunday hats, and the entrance to Miss Eileen's bedroom. She was Miss Hayhurst's sister, and lodged but didn't work at the school. I don't think I ever said anything but "Good night, Miss Eileen" to her, and for this I would have to keep awake for hours, but for a while she occupied a high place on my list of adored ones. I became so attached to this room, right in the heart of the house, where I could hear everything that went on, that Miss Lawrence let me stay there always. As I was a great offender against the "silence rule", that is, chatting after "lights out", it no doubt suited her as well as me. For the first time in my life the night held no terrors for me. I always envy those people who say they fall asleep as soon as they touch the pillow. This is something I have never known. Getting to sleep with me is a major operation equalled only by that of waking up in the morning. Lying awake in the dark, a victim of my own imagination, had been a nightly torture. Now in this little room I found lying awake quite pleasant. There was a street lamp in the lane outside which lit the walls and kept away the shadows. I could hear the comforting "ping-ping" of the tram bells in City Road, and the landing night-light shone through the doorway. Sometimes there would be running footsteps along the landing, followed by the ker-lank-swish of the lavatory cistern, comforting me with the knowledge that someone else was awake. Besides, just the other side of the thin partition, snoring, now gently like a dove, now roaring like a lion, lay the beautiful, beloved Miss Eileen, who might with luck need rescuing from a fire or some other nocturnal catastrophe. The fact that she snored endeared her more than ever to me; it was a weakness — making her mortal and thus attainable. On moonlight nights it was possible to read and scribble without being disturbed by the rule-ridden house-girls.

If it hadn't been for growing up I would always have been happy at Anguish's. I managed either by charm or determination to get things mostly as I wanted them. I disliked all housework, and some jobs I loathed. I managed to escape washing up and table-laying by having a long distance to go to school. Fortunately, for one who felt the cold so keenly, I was an excellent fire-lighter and usually managed to wangle this job in the winter. We were allowed two sheets of newspaper, six sticks and three matches per fire, so they had to go first time or there would be trouble. Artificial aids, like paraffin, were strictly taboo; but I discovered a liberal sprinkling of "Brasso", and even unadulterated Jeyes' Fluid had the same effect, so my fires — I lit three every morning — always went. It was a little tricky, because we were each issued with our own cleaning materials, appropriate to the job in hand, and these had to last a certain time. Brass polish was no part of a firelighter's equipment and I regret to say my tin was "swiped". I kept it in the hat cupboard under the "straws", which were not likely to be disturbed in the winter. This cupboard was locked and Miss Hayhurst kept the key, but wonders could be worked with a hair-slide.

We didn't suffer from over-much religious instruction. Prayers were said after breakfast and the text for the day read out. This had to be remembered and the next morning's proceedings were opened by the duty matron asking "the text for yesterday?" We all raised our hands and one of us was selected to repeat it. Anyone not raising her hand was deemed to have forgotten it, and had to write it out five times. It would have been quite easy to raise your hand anyway and risk being called on, but I only remember this happening once, and that was to me. I had been far away dreaming and my hand went up automatically, when I suddenly realized that all eyes were on me, those of Miss Hayhurst boring holes in my thin fabric of honesty.

"Thou God see-est me," I brazened hoping to have made a lucky guess; but I hadn't. "That is the wrong one," Miss Hayhurst's voice crackled like electricity in the cold room. "But it is one to remember when next you want to cheat. I will have ten copies of yesterday's text."

My temper boiled and all discretion evaporated in the steam. "I won't do it ten times," I said.

"No," replied Miss Hayhurst icily. "You will do it twenty."

Most of the girls were on my side. They thought I was either funny or brave in the way I stood up for myself. No doubt their admiration encouraged my insolence. They enjoyed vicarious pleasure from my boldness.

I never did write out that particular text, and Miss Hayhurst didn't mention it again. She had made her point and it was a mistake I didn't repeat. As at Gimingham we learnt the collect on Sundays, which we all said in turn after dinner. I could pick it up from the others, and by the time my turn came I was word perfect, so I had no trouble there. These sessions were very boring to us and must have been more so to the staff.

Sunday was pocket-money day and this was given out at the breakfast-table. Ordinary Anguish girls had two halfpennies each, except the house-girls, who had, I think, sixpence. Ministry of Pensions girls had threepence, two pennies and two halfpennies, and this is the only time in my childhood that I received my due as regards pocket money. One halfpenny was supposed to be put into the church collection, but we discovered that by just giving the bag a little shake and passing it on, it was possible to keep the halfpenny in one's hand. We walked in crocodile to St Andrew's, the other side of the city from us. A rather dreary walk it was, through empty streets and past shuttered shops. Hall Road, Surrey Street, All Saints Plain, Orford Place, Bridewell Alley; here all chattering ceased, while we held our breaths so as not to smell the bad fish in one of the shops. It was me of course who tried to make the walk livelier by crying out "Bring out your dead; Bring out your dead" as we went through a narrow echoing passage, and by giving the brass door bells in All Saints Plain a surreptitious pull. Now and again a ripple went through the crocodile: "Tell Elsie Burrows to keep in line. Pass it up." If I was feeling particularly truculent, I answered "Who said?" and "Who said" danced back behind me. The next wave brought "Miss Hayhurst"; only then would I get in line, for I was a great observer of protocol and took my orders only from the senior member present. On the whole, we were quite a gay cavalcade; especially in summer with our bright thin frocks and straw hats. How heartily we pitied the Catholic orphans whose crocodile we often met. Topped and tailed by a pair of beetle-black nuns, it seemed an incredible length, and every little girl from about five upwards was dressed exactly like every other little girl; in shapeless frocks of butcher blue and plain white hats. We told each other gruesome stories of what went on in the convent, but I must admit the children didn't look as if they suffered much.

There must have been some good reason why we went to St Andrew's Church, when we passed at least three others nearer to us, but I never knew it, and found no favour in St Andrew's. The vicar was the Reverend Baumer, who years before at Gimingham Parish Hall I had seen doing conjuring tricks at a concert; and for this

160

reason I had no faith in him as a clergyman. Not that I considered it wrong for a parson to be a conjurer, but I did think someone so gifted ought to be more interesting in the pulpit. St Andrew's was very well attended, so obviously our elders didn't agree with our view that he was "dull as ditchwater". The twelve youngest schoolgirls, including me, sat on chairs in a corner beside the organ, and at right angles to the rest of the congregation. I have a very low opinion of organs as musical instruments. I think they are clumsy, ugly and the noise they make only fit for raising devils, and this instrument blasted away, turning our insides over and battering our eardrums. We could see nothing of the choir, and the Reverend Baumer was only visible to us when preaching.

These were the days of the chorister Ernest Luff of the Temple Church, and no household was complete without a record of him singing "Oh, for the Wings of a Dove". St Andrew's also possessed a boy soprano, equal to, and we considered better than, the London boy. He was Arnold Miller; and I fell in love with him. So far as I can remember I never saw him, but his "Oh for a Closer Walk with God" and "Lead me, Lord" took me to the very gates of heaven. They told me he was spotty and wore glasses, but still I loved him, spots, spectacles and all. The anthem was announced on a board hanging on the church railings, and one quick glance would send me either to the heights or to the depths. If it read "Soloist: Master A. Miller" my day was made. I have a memory that his voice broke suddenly when he was in full song, and that the twelve youngest schoolgirls, who of course were all in love with him as well, wept through the rest of the service, but that is one of the memories I distrust. There is a road on a housing estate called "Arnold Miller Road", and I have always liked to think it was named after him. I have never investigated — the idea of the City Fathers naming anything as solid as a road after something as ethereal as a boy's voice is too charming to lose.

When this boy stopped singing there seemed to me less reason than ever for going to St Andrew's, and I was constantly hatching schemes to escape church-going. These plots nearly always failed, and made me lose my temper, so Sundays became anything but a day of rest for me. We all went to different Sunday schools in the afternoon, some to Methodists, and some to Baptists, but most of us to St Alban's, Lakenham, then a corrugated-iron building, somewhere around the back of Southwell Road. If I disliked St Andrew's, I loathed St Alban's, and can remember nothing pleasing about it except a sermon preached by the Reverend Newby at a children's service.

I can still hear him thumping the pulpit and urging parents to "stop telling your children the lie about the doctor's bag. Tell them the truth!" "You came from your mother's womb!" The doctor's bag and mother's womb were equally inexplicable to me, but I had a vague feeling the Reverend Newby had sworn in church. The collective astonishment of the congregation at his utterance was as real as the smell of the varnished planks that made the inner walls.

Then I went on strike, declaring I would go to neither St Andrew's nor St Alban's. I would not learn collects or texts or say prayers. I wrote all this down on a piece of paper, gave it to Miss Lawrence and waited for the

162

reformatory doors to open. Although many of the girls were shocked at my declaration, some even deciding to send me "to Coventry", Miss Lawrence merely told me not to be silly! "It's one of our rules you should go to church," she said. "They can't be altered just to suit you." Not for nothing was Elizabeth Fry my heroine, so I replied, "I can't go to church if I'm a Quaker." This idea came to me in a moment; it was a compromise, my original resolution was to have done with religion altogether.

"But you're not a Quaker," Miss Lawrence regarded me over the tops of her spectacles. "Anyone less like a Quaker I have yet to meet."

"I've been converted."

"I haven't noticed it, so you will go to church until I do."

"But I hate St Andrew's, and I loathe St Alban's. If I have to go anywhere I'd rather go to chapel."

This was another compromise and I could see Miss Lawrence searching for a reason to reject it.

"Your father gave his religion as Church of England on his army form; and you have to follow that while in our care. When you grow up you can please yourself."

Argue, argue, argue. Like a terrier I couldn't let go.

"That's years and years ahead; I can't stand St Alban's and St Andrew's all that time. It doesn't seem to have done much good, all those people being burned at the stake."

I flounced out and vented my temper on the window-sills, slapping each one as I passed. This only stung my hand and fed my fury. The real truth was that I had no religious conviction at all. This lack of conviction made me feel guilty and so I blamed the churches where I was bored. I would like to have gone to the meeting-house in Goat Lane, because it would have made me different in the way that going to Crook's Place school made me different; but I suspect, after a while, I should have agreed with the Gurney girls that "Goats was dis". On the other hand, it may have made all the difference. In a Quaker atmosphere, and under the influence of Friends, I might have learned much earlier to exercise self-control and to curb the barbarian side of me. For there must have been a part of me pleasing to others. Some kind of promise that encouraged them to persevere and which kept me out of the ever-threatening reformatory.

My school teachers had nothing but good to say of me, and I can imagine the confusion created in the minds of the Ministry's area officers when they received two such conflicting reports about the same child. They must have wondered if the one who lived at home was identical with the one who arrived at school.

At the end of my first year I was in the top standard for all subjects and my essays were the joy of Miss Scarlett's heart. Each week they were read aloud to the class, while I squirmed in my seat and dug my fingers in and out of the inkwell. I was surprised to find that no one teased me about these readings, but that the girls regarded me with something like awe. They *liked* hearing my essays and eventually insisted on Miss Scarlett reading them, whatever their quality had been. I know that I often wrote bad ones, and then I begged Miss Scarlett not to read them. There were others who could write good, workmanlike compositions, but Miss Scarlett told them, "You don't write like Elsie does; but then I don't expect you to. *She* has a gift." It was the custom to make fair copies of the best compositions into a special thick book, and I would dearly like to have it now. My bedside locker was always stuffed full of notebooks and sheets of paper. I had such an appetite for writing paper that Miss Lawrence, generous though she was with it, could not keep up with me, and I resorted to toilet paper and tearing out the end papers of books in the library. Once when turning out the box room, Miss Hayhurst had unearthed a pile of obsolete hand bills, advertising some long forgotten church bazaar. She met me on the landing and said:

"Would you like these, Elsie; you can write on the backs."

I have never in my life received a present that gave me so much pleasure.

Pens and pencils were my currency. Everything I had I swapped for them, and was often reprimanded for having untidy hair. The hairslide had been exchanged for a pencil. When Miss Lawrence was sent some advertising fountain-pens by the makers of that horrible but no doubt efficacious concoction, Angiers Emulsion, she put them aside to dole out to me. I didn't break them, or lose them, they literally wore out.

The state of my locker became too much for the Junior Matron one day and she brought up a large wastepaper basket and emptied the contents into it. On her way to the boiler house she met the superintendent. "Just look, Miss Lawrence," she cried in righteous indignation. "Look at the rubbish from Elsie Burrows's locker."

"Oh, but that's not rubbish," said Miss Lawrence. "It's her writing. You must put it back. Never destroy anything like that." It is no wonder I was extremely unpopular with the under staff. Getting that mass of still-born literature back into my locker must have taken a lot longer than pulling it out. That evening Miss Lawrence told me that before I did anything else I had to tidy my locker. I was hungry, and tea was waiting. Tea with bananas and apples, which if no one else pinched, might be exchanged for less attractive ones. I bundled the lot, stories, poems and essays, into the boiler, a sacrifice it pleased me to compare with the burning of Byron's memoirs. Somehow after that, though I still had the ability to write, the fiery propelling urge left me. One had as one's first duty to be tidy; and for me the only way to be so was by never getting untidy.

Summer holidays at Anguish's were looked forward to and talked about as soon as Christmas was over. As soon as the last snow faded, and the new grass appeared on the reservoir someone said, "I wonder where we'll go for holidays." That started it; from then on until the wonderful evening in mid-July, when Miss Lawrence came into the dining-room with the holiday list, and read out where each of us would spend the month of August the air was full of gossip, surmise, scandal and counter-scandal. The entire establishment closed down in August, and in little groups or singly we were scattered round the county in private homes.

Thirty-two cases were ranged against the walls of the gym, and thirty-two piles of clothing gradually assembled on the long benches. The correct way to pack these cases was a lesson we learned with joy. Before the final packing the gym was forbidden territory, but intrepid spirits would sometimes make a foray and dash out with the information, "Freda's got a blue spotted dress. New." Or "Elsie's got the coat Olive had last year." Then there would be cries of "Coo-er", or "T'aint fair", according to whether the news was welcome or not. Everyone knows there is nothing so evocative as smells. Even today the smell of new cotton print takes me back to packing night, and the heaven that was to be found in the rectitude of new folded vests, the bold blue lettering on white socks, and the strange joy to be had from running one's finger over new plimsoll soles.

One year I went to Winterton, a small seaside village near Yarmouth, and this became my "golden land". I cannot now remember which girls shared my lodging in the Council house, or what the woman's name was who lived there. I know that her husband was a trawler fisherman and was away with his ship. As the trawlers returned on their way to Yarmouth they would signal on their sirens not only the code of their ship but the number of cran they carried. Then some of the Winterton wives and mothers would relax and clean out the house, for they knew their men were on the way home. The men had been away for weeks, and fishing was never safe. Now and then our landlady would stop our mealtime chatter with "Shush. Listen. That's the so-and-so. Count the pips." Then we sat and counted the blasts, each one standing for ten crans. Her husband's boat didn't return while we were there, and she grew daily more anxious. I hope he came home in the end.

Most of my time, no matter what the weather, I was out

by the sea-shore, helping the fishermen to paint their boats. One or two ran trips out to the Cockle Lightship, and one of them took me free nearly every time he went out. I had to stand in a rather smelly hatch at the front of the boat, but I didn't worry. The coast became a smudge on the horizon, and when there was nothing in sight except the choppy green sea, I could understand a little about eternity and God. I was sure that if I stayed in the boat long enough and went far enough something important would be revealed to me. But the Cockle was only three miles out and the great revelation never came. I must have had more courage then than I possess now for I thought nothing of climbing up the swaying steel ladder to the lantern chamber of the lightship. I was at a loss to understand why the pretty young ladies needed such a lot of help from the crew to make this ascent. Nor why the crew so obviously preferred them with their shrieks and giggles and "Oh, I daren'ts" to me; so sensible, so nimble, and reciting "Roll on thou deep and dark blue waters roll".

If it wasn't fit for the boat to go out I walked and talked with Boy Jimmy. There was something slightly Irish about Jimmy. He had never worked in his life and had no intention of doing so. "Did Adam work?" he would say. "Do dandelions? Do that there beach work? I'm a tellin' you, the world wore all right till some silly bugger thought o' workin'." I, to whom work was also an anathema, had found a kindred spirit. We walked miles — we talked the world inside out, and never once did Boy Jimmy take his hands out of his pockets, or reduce the gap of a foot or so between us. In our companionship there was not one evil

168

thought, nor suggestive word, but there were plenty in the heads of the village women. To them anyone who had looked at life, come to terms with it and made it go his way, as Jimmy had done, was obviously an unfit person. News about us reached Miss Lawrence in her lodgings in the next village of Hemsby, and she forbade me to go out in the boat, or to go alone with Jimmy. I can see now the dangers there were in both these things and that she was quite right to be worried and to exercise her control. If she had pointed out the dangers and given me reasons I might have understood. She gave me none, but just forbade me to do the two things I most liked doing. I thought it was only because I liked walking with Jimmy and riding in the boat that I was stopped; and the holidays ended with me being a martyr and defying the ban whenever I thought I wouldn't be found out. Not long after we returned home Miss Lawrence took me to the doctor for a rather odd examination, which puzzled me, for I had not been ill. Not until years afterwards when I became familiar with the *News of the World* did I realize that she was afraid I might have been "interfered with".

Discontent fell almost like a curtain upon me. It was the Autumn term at Crook's Place, and I realized that I was beginning my last year at school. When I was fourteen, just as I had begun to appreciate learning, and had formed the habit of acquiring it, I should have to leave it. All the poetry, the history and my own written words would be useless to me as an Anguish house-girl. The future held two years of learning to cook, scrub and wash, and then a lifetime of domestic service. Morning dresses, afternoon dresses, white caps and aprons, "Sir" and "Madam" all my days, ending a narrow life with a narrower grave.

"You will get married," they said, "and have a home of your own," but marriage as an escape never entered my imagination. I knew no boys of my own age now. Those I remembered from Tacolneston had been vile and cruel. The only men I met were other beings before they were men, doctors, inspectors, schoolmasters; I couldn't see them as anything else. I remembered the woman who had come crying up Mum's garden path because her husband had beaten her and locked her out. I remembered the girl at school whose father had been sent to prison for petty swindling and whose mother had sold everything they had, even the beds they slept on, to repay his victims. Marriage was certainly no panacea for my troubles. But I had my loves, Miss Scarlett, Miss Eileen, the unseen Arnold Miller, and the long dead Byron and Rupert Brooke. All the usual, sexless passions of adolescence. The love that should have gone to a mother was naturally poured on school teachers and Guide captains; and so long as it didn't show it was all right. The living Byron and Brooke, beloved as they were, never knew such adoration as I gave them. It was not their works, but they themselves I worshipped, because they were beautiful and died young. They were set for all time in their splendour and nothing I could say or do would bring a frown to their faces or a cutting word from their lips. There was safety in loving the dead.

Now everything irritated me. The sight of the secondary-school girls doing their homework and grumbling. How I longed to have homework and be one of them. The daily and Saturday tasks which seemed to take longer and longer to do. The lonely emptiness of

Saturday and Sunday afternoons when the "going out" girls had departed. Miss Lawrence tried to find somewhere for me to go now and then. Once or twice I went to tea at Mrs Grant's but we were awkward together and she didn't ask me often. Sometimes I visited Mum, who had moved to Shotesham six miles away, but this meant a bus journey for which money was needed. One memorable afternoon I was sent to the pictures with a house-girl. I have seen hundreds of films since then but none has lingered with me so long as this first full-length feature I saw then. It was called *Trail of '98* and starred Dolores del Rio and Ralph Forbes. I don't know if by the standards of the time it was a good film and the thread of the story escapes me, but it acted as a spring to my imagination. Now it was in the snowy Klondike wastes that I rescued Miss Eileen or Miss Scarlett from certain death; and it was by the frozen Arctic sea that Miss Burgess, the Guide captain, caught my dying words and raised a monument of rocks above me. How much we lose, when with age, we realize that the impossible exists; it is then we cease to day-dream.

More than ever now I wanted relations, people I could call mine by right, not courtesy. Time and again throughout my childhood I had heard people shrug off my orphan state with the words, "Well, what you've never had, you can't miss." There never was a greater fallacy. The born blind miss the light, the barren woman a child, and to be an orphan is to be an emotional cripple. All my life I had been looked on, either as an object of maudlin sentimentality, or as a nuisance to be borne, like bad weather.

171

I still remembered the two sisters I had seen at Reedham, and the rumours of the sailor brother. Miss Lawrence suggested I wrote to Miss Duff, who, it was thought, knew most about me, to see if they could be traced. She replied that I must have been mistaken, after all I couldn't really remember so far back, and advised me to put up with things as they were. "God has a plan for every man," she ended cheerfully. His plan for me seemed incredibly dreary.

With autumn dying around us, I felt that year a-dying within myself. Everything was being done for me "for the last time". This would be my last Christmas as a school-girl. Next year I wouldn't be able to ask for frivolous things for presents; I should have to write down things likely to be of use to me in my future life — as a domestic servant. There was no law about it — it was just the custom. A list was put up around October and in the blank space beneath our names we were expected to write the three things we wanted from the Christmas tree. We didn't always get exactly what we'd asked for, but usually one of the three came up. This year with something like despair I wrote:

1. a writing book
2. "   "   "
3. "   "   "

What I did get were a fat manuscript book, an address book and a box of stationery; but by then I knew I was going away, and that this was the last Christmas in Norwich, and the presents satisfied me.

Every young girl, if she listens, can at some time hear

disembodied voices calling her. Joan of Arc was in no way unique in this matter, and there is no doubt some scientific and psychological explanation for it. I have never heard of it happening to young boys, and most girls forget in time. It happened to me quite vividly in the garden at Anguish's. It was an autumn day of low treacly sunshine, and I was away from school with a cold. Miss Hayhurst had shooed me into the garden where I sat on all that was left of an old revolving summer house and read the *Girls' Quiver* for 1908. The library had shelves of bound volumes of this magazine and from them I learnt a great deal, mostly about etiquette and the correct attire for young ladies attending balls, Ascot, supper parties and so on. The book was too heavy to hold so I laid it on the boards to read; suddenly, it seemed of its own accord, the book closed, and the gold figures of 1908 spun all over the cover. From near at hand I heard someone say "Elsie". I sat up and looked in the direction of the voice, but there was no one there, only the wall and an overgrown patch of couch grass, and still the voice said, "Elsie, Elsie". Had I been spiritually inclined I ought to have answered the equivalent of "Speak, Lord, for Thy servant heareth", and I might have learned something. Instead I went and looked closely at the grass, decided it was a trick of the wind blowing through it and went indoors. Some years later, in a place where there was no wind or grass, and when I was no longer called Elsie, I heard this voice again. Spiritualists would have it that these voices are warnings and directions from "loved ones who have passed over". If that is so, it is a pity that after taking all that trouble to "get through" they are not more explicit on their arrival.

I was not alone in worrying about my future. It was very clear to Miss Lawrence that housework was definitely not my line. As I had not taken the scholarship at the right time there was nothing the education authorities could do about higher schooling. Office jobs were poorly paid and led nowhere, and besides I was working up an aversion to earning my living in any way. After a series of tempestuous outbursts and flouting of authority Miss Lawrence decided, reluctantly I think, that she could do no more for me. After she had paid a visit to London she called me in to the board room.

"Well, Elsie," she said, "I have found a very nice place for you, where you'll be able to carry on with your schooling. You're to go to Dr Barnardo's after Christmas."

The board room was suddenly full of doors clanging and locks turning.

"Barnado's," I gasped, "but that's a reformatory."

We all believed that. All the worst children we knew went to Barnado's. Magistrates sent bad boys there to train as sailors. Doris from Tacolneston had gone there. No Barnado girl did anything better than kitchen work. Everyone knew that in the strata of orphandom there was nothing lower than Barnado's.

Miss Lawrence was contradicting me. Barnado's was a large organization, they had more scope than Anguish's. I should get learning there, and go to College perhaps.

"I won't go," I said. "I'd rather go to the Catholics."

Knowing how much we all heartily despised the poor Catholic children, Miss Lawrence smiled.

"I assure you Barnado's is much superior to the

174

Catholics, and you are quite wrong about it being a reformatory. Thousands of their children have done very well indeed."

I knew, no matter how I protested, I would have no say in my fate.

"Well I'll try it," I said, "but if it *is* a reformatory, I'll run away."

CHAPTER
SEVEN

The journey from Norwich to Barkingside in Essex was the longest I had made in my life, and the first time I had ever been out of Norfolk. So consumed was I by depression though, it made little mark on me. Miss Lawrence spent the time discussing God with a bearded gentleman who shared our carriage, while I watched the telegraph lines play see-saw past the window. At Liverpool Street I was forcibly reminded of a mediaeval description of Hell as I followed Miss Lawrence like a dumb puppy dog. My luggage must have been sent in advance, for I don't remember carrying any, and this was fortunate for I found my feet so hard to lift. So far from leaping eagerly towards a new life I was just letting it creep towards me like a cold oily sea. All the time Miss Lawrence was searching for a train to Ilford, I wanted to shout, "No, no, let's go back to Norwich", but there was no question of the words being uttered. At Ilford we made a mistake and boarded a bus, which put us down at the side lodge gates.

"Ah now," said the Irish gatekeeper, "you should have got a tram. The tram goes to the main gates you see. I can't let you in this way; but if you follow the fence round you'll come to the main gates. You'll be all right then, but you should have caught a tram."

She omitted to tell us that the main gates were about a mile and a half away as the fence went.

Miss Lawrence, always very lame, was also weary from the journey and every slow step we took added another shade of black to my mood, and I hated myself.

"If you'd been good," I told myself, "you'd just be having dinner at Anguish's. Hot meat and batter pudding, with rice stodge and baked apple." For a moment I wondered who would get the coveted "blanket" from the rice. Not, I hoped fervently, Elsie Button again; if she did — then with another downward drop I realized that the burning questions of rice "blanket" and pork crackling would never concern me again. There would be, I felt with a premonition, no rice blankets or pork crackling here.

"If you'd been good," I said to myself again, "Miss Lawrence wouldn't be crawling round this beastly fence."

"I couldn't help it," my other self said weakly. "I couldn't help it."

"This walk might kill Miss Lawrence, and you'll be to blame," and still my only defence was "I couldn't help it".

At every few yards in the fence were enormous blue enamelled signs, with "Dr Barnardo's Homes" in white letters hideously large. Slightly smaller underneath were the words "Girls' Village Home". We passed a church, "Dr Barnardo's Homes, Girls' Village Home, Children's Church" announced the notice board.

"They have their own church," remarked Miss Lawrence, "and hospitals and library."

"And mortuary too I suppose," I muttered, refusing to be impressed.

"Yes, I expect they have," Miss Lawrence didn't rise to the bait. I found out later that they really did have a mortuary, and needed it too in those terrible depression years.

A great water-tower now came into view; with Dr Barnardo's Homes on its four sides it must have been an excellent guide to aircraft. We reached the main gates at last; the porter, after scrutinizing the letter Miss Lawrence showed him, even turning it over and apparently reading it from back to front, grudgingly let us through and waved a hand in the direction of the Governor's house.

Before going in Miss Lawrence paused and leaned on her stick. "The ladies in charge here are called Governors. One is the daughter of a Lord, and the other the sister of a member of Parliament. Most important people."

Undoubtedly Miss Lawrence was impressed by the Governor's connections; which was no doubt why, without a word of protest, she had put up with the off-hand treatment of both gatekeepers. I tried to be impressed too, but failed.

We waited in a small office, where a crippled girl worked a telephone switchboard. Every time she plugged in she said in a refined and beautiful voice "Dr Barnardo's Homes, G.V.H." There was no doubt about it, I had arrived at Dr Barnardo's Homes.

Conditions prevailing at Barnardo's over thirty years ago were very different from those of today. Like all other institutions they have moved with the times and most of the unpleasant aspects of my day have disappeared. But even then, they were, as they still are, in the forefront of child care. Particularly, they have pioneered work among

178

what are now known as juvenile delinquents, cripples, spastics and the subnormal. After Anguish's I found the superficial conditions terrible, but I had to admire the organization, planning and the love which went into the work. I cannot but tell the truth about the place as I found it; but I am always proud to write "educated at Dr Barnardo's Homes" for anyone who wants to know. Such an admission has usually done me no good; so great still is snobbery in this country. I believe firmly that it is better to have been well educated at Barnardo's than badly at an expensive school.

Barnardo the man and the saint has not been enough appreciated by his countrymen — or rather by his adopted countrymen, for he was Irish, from Dublin. This may be because in an age of enormous wealth, when Britain is really supposed to have ruled the waves, he became her conscience. Opening up the sores in her cities and countryside, and bringing the smell right into her drawing-rooms. The man had no tact or taste; he wasn't particularly likeable, even to the waifs he rescued, but he was a saint nevertheless. He believed, not only that the homeless should be housed, but that all school-children should be given a mid-day meal by the state; and that the old should be cared for by the state. Both outrageous propositions in his time, and one with which he was able to make little headway. Apart from his Empire-wide organization for "Nobody's children", he started clubs for boys, continuation schools for old and young and clubs for the aged. He was *the* greatest social reformer in this land of social reformers, and his story has never been adequately told. The enormous village home in which I found myself on a drizzling January day in 1930 was started by him on prayer alone. It became his favourite residence and is now his final resting-place.

He dreamt of a complete community; of cottages surrounding a village green, each cottage containing about a dozen children in the charge of a "mother". In 1930 it was the only open space in the area, for ribbon development had brought houses right to the gates. Old cottage mothers could still remember when they left the village by a stile leading into cornfields. There were now over seventy cottages, crammed to bursting-point with about twenty-five children apiece, for the promise "No destitute child ever refused admission" was strictly kept to. The 1930s saw such an influx of destitute children as never before. There were within these two square miles 1,400 children and about 300 staff. As Miss Lawrence said, they had their own church, hospitals, massage department, laundry, schools and library. It ran like clockwork, it was magnificent; and I loathed it, with a loathing that could, had I been less well balanced, have embittered all my after years.

At thirteen I was perhaps too old to fit into that enclosed life. Most of the girls in the village had been there since babyhood, and had grown up into its traditions and customs. They absorbed its prejudices and taboos as easily as they spoke its nasal drawling accent; inherited no doubt from the beggars' whine of earlier generations of children. It took me a long time before I could understand my fellows, they might have been foreigners, and they on their part found my ironed-out Norfolk highly jeerable.

Miss Lawrence and I sat in the ante-room for what

seemed hours, listening to the telephone operator's chant "Dr Barnardo's Homes, G.V.H." Eventually we were shown into the presence of the Governor.

She was standing, centre, to receive us; the Honourable Ann MacNaghton; short, stout and low-voiced, with a face that would have been beautiful but for the cold eyes and hard, straight mouth. I was to meet her but rarely in the next three years, but every time I was repelled by this inner hardness. I was in a minority; for most of the village adored Miss MacNaghton, and feared her co-Governor Miss Picton-Turbervill. I of course had to be different, and although I never spoke to Miss Picton-Turbervill, who dealt mainly with staff matters, it was to her I gave my loyalty.

The Holy Trinity at Barkingside were the Governors, the Doctor, and God, in that order. To be "sent to the Governor" was equivalent to facing the last judgement. To criticize any aspect of the Doctor was sacrilege, and God would punish us for all affronts to these super deities.

After a brief welcome, trusting I "would be happy", Miss MacNaghton passed me on to a girl who was to escort me to my cottage. I turned to Miss Lawrence; now that the end had come I wanted to have done with it quickly, but she said she would see me later at the cottage. My escort was full of information, she was called a "Guide Messenger", and was dressed in what I considered an apology for a Girl Guide uniform, obviously home-made, of coarse denim, with a belt and hat of the same material. I looked at the dress with distaste: "Do you *have* to wear that if you're a Girl Guide here?" I asked.

"Yes, unless you bring your own."

I made a mental note to ask Miss Lawrence for my Guide uniform, with a proper leather belt and the latest soft felt hat. I would at least shine at something, for already I was determined not to be utterly swamped by "Dr Barnardo's Homes".

The Guide Messengers had left school and were usually the brighter girls, who sorted post, delivered messages, escorted visitors and so on. These jobs were highly coveted, because they usually led to office jobs, either at the Stepney headquarters or elsewhere. Also, although I believe it was forbidden, tips could sometimes be earned. Only the hospitals and staff houses were on the extension telephone, and as no one thought of providing bicycles for these girls they must have tramped miles every day.

The weather brightened a little as we walked through the village. The girl beside me kept up a running commentary, first asking the ritual questions.

"Did you come from boarding out?"

"No."

"Did you come from your own home?"

"No."

"Did you come from a Branch Home?"

"No."

There were apparently no other sources for the supply of village girls.

"Where *did* you come from then?"

Angry as usual at being questioned I snapped, "East Anglia."

"Oh, you're a foreigner then?"

"Yes," I answered, and it was the truth. A foreigner I

182

came there, an alien remained, and was an outcast in the end.

The Guide Messenger considered my foreignness for a minute or two and then continued her commentary in a somewhat louder voice.

"That's Pussy Cottage, where the wet beds go. You don't wet the bed, I suppose. That's John Sands — that cottage mother has all black children. If you were black you'd go there. She's ever so nice. Not black herself, of course. That's the library — you can have two books a week. It's not allowed to walk across the green, only for mothers and cripples. That's the hospital, you'll have to go there tomorrow to see the doctor — and the dentist on Thursday. He's horrible — a great big German; nearly pulls your head off. This is the cripples' home and over there is the babies' home" — and so on, until — "this is Reckitt cottage where you are going to live. The food is horrible, and the house-girls are horrible, you'll hate it at first, especially being a foreigner, but you'll get used to it." She lifted the knocker: "Miss Lewis wallops with a hairbrush." I found she was wrong in every particular save one — the food *was* horrible.

The door was opened by an exceedingly untidy girl of fourteen or so, who swung it back and then hid behind it. Into the opening walked a small elderly woman, with a shock of white shingled hair and large horn-rimmed glasses. She wore a pale blue dress covered by a flowered overall. The Guide Messenger snapped to attention, held out at arm's length a green envelope and said:

"New girl please, Miss Lewis. Will you sign please, Miss Lewis."

The woman looked me up and down, a smile twitching round her lips. She took a slip from the envelope, signed it and returned it to the messenger.

"New girl received, apparently in good order," her eyes danced with humour. The Guide saluted again, then added in a confidential whisper, "She's a foreigner, Miss Lewis."

Miss Lewis shut the door, revealing the hidden opener; with nothing more than a jerk of the head she sent her scuttling to the back quarters.

"What sort of foreigner are you?" asked Miss Lewis.

"I'm not. I told the girl I came from East Anglia. The foreigner idea is hers."

This Miss Lewis found highly amusing and she roared with laughter.

"Well, then you'll be in good company; we've got another girl from your country. Olive!"

A voice from somewhere shouted back, "If you please, mother, she's in the bath, mother."

"To me when she's finished," roared Miss Lewis — then turning to me she asked, "Would you like an egg?"

This hardly seemed promising. I was ravenously hungry. Seeing my hesitation Miss Lewis added, "There's nothing else, we've had dinner."

So an egg it had to be, and I sat on a backless form in the dining-room to wait for it. The room was grubby from the recent meal, cold and smelly. The smell came from the brown umber powder which was mixed with Ronuk to make the floor boards darker. Apart from a rag mat by the fireplace these boards were bare. Three tables were covered with white American cloth. It was easy to see where the fidgets sat, by the patches where the surface had been picked off. These tables were served by forms down the side, and chairs at each end. A high close-meshed guard, padlocked to the wooden surround of the fireplace, successfully prevented any heat escaping into the room. Just in case it should the guard was draped with damp washing. A pile of hymn books, Bibles and prayer books decorated the mantelpiece, and above them hung the usual large stern portrait of the Doctor. Over the floor crawled the dirtiest baby I had ever seen. It approached me on all fours and to my horror tried to climb on my lap. A big heavy girl in coarse blue working dress came in and picked up the creature.

"Isn't she lovely? She's Eleanor. Do you like babies?"

My answer was such an uncompromising "No" that the girl was startled.

"Not like babies!" Then after a pause: "You're potty."

Miss Lewis's voice roared out from the sitting-room, "Isobel! Have you done that baby yet?"

"Just going please, mother," and she went, with the baby, to my great relief.

The egg was Polish, underdone and slightly "off". The bread was scraped with bright yellow margarine. It took me right back to the day when Cissie and I had experimented with cart grease. She had managed to be sick straight away, but my cast-iron stomach held, and I only *felt* sick for days. Pushing this obnoxious meal away from me, I realized with a rush that never in my life before had I been so truly miserable. I wished I could cry, but as I had grown older the ability to shed tears, except over books, had left me. In a temper, I would rage and shout and bang things, but very seldom weep. Now I realized this ache I carried had to be put up with.

Coming from one institution to another should not on the surface have seemed such a great change. To the powers that were, there could have been little difference between life at Anguish's and that at Barnardo's. But they were worlds apart. At Anguish's within limits we had a great deal of freedom, and lived as near as possible a normal life. At Barnardo's drawing breath was our only freedom; and then it had to be drawn silently. Now things are very much altered, and the gates are completely removed. Gone too are the great tin signs; but it took the war to do that. I am speaking of the only Barnardo Home I knew at that time, and only one part of that home. Beside this village, and the Boys' Garden City close by at Woodford, run on similar lines, there were many smaller Branch Homes. Practically every large town had one, and they were all to a certain extent autonomous. In 1930 8,500 children were in the care of the Homes. No doubt some homes and cottages were better run than ours; and some, I know, were much worse. The fault of my misery was in me; the system, for the time, was a very good one, but its faults and cruelties were glaring to an outsider.

It was impressed upon me that I was fortunate to be in Reckitt Cottage with Mother Lewis. She has been written about elsewhere, and was certainly a great character, but by the time we met she was old and not many years from her retirement. For a time she and I were at loggerheads and could only see each other's faults, but eventually respect, and even a spark of love, grew between us. She was full of idiosyncrasies, accepted by the other children in the same way as they accepted rain from heaven. She ruled the cottage from either her bedroom or her sitting-

186

room. She frequently suffered from "bad heads" and considering the way she roared, as loud as any sergeant-major, I don't wonder at it. But she was the only one in the house allowed to shout; even the babies had to go outdoors to yell.

The day began at 6.30; we had to rise in silence and dress by the landing light only. Mother professed to be able to tell whenever an unauthorized light was turned on. Each of us, from eight years old upwards, had a household task to complete before breakfast. Some of these jobs were of the army "bull" variety. The baking-tins had to be polished with emery paper, and the floor underneath the bath hearth-stoned. The window-sills, doorsteps and surrounds of the drains were whitened daily, whatever the weather. When all the jobs were reported to Isobel, the eldest girl, as being done, breakfast was put on the table — tin bowls filled with a grey mess called porridge. In the raw it looked exactly like chicken food, and should have taken twenty-four hours to cook properly. It never had that, and was more often than not burnt and lumpy. Sometimes as sloppy as tea, at others so stiff that the spoon stood up unaided. Its consistency depended on the state of the monthly stores. Apart from the porridge there was one round of white and one round of brown bread, and margarine for each child. There was no difference in the food allowance for a year-old baby or a fifteen-year-old house-girl.

When we were all silently assembled, each standing behind her place, and the baby in her high chair, Mary, who was really the eldest girl, but who didn't count because she still went to school, would stand at the bottom of the stairs and call, "If you please, mother, we are ready, mother". If mother was in the mood she would come down straight away, if not she would call down "Sing", and we would have to sing hymns and choruses until she arrived. As she entered we all chanted in unison, "Please mother, may we have sugar *on* our porridge". Sometimes it was yes, sometimes no, there was no way of telling what we had to do to earn this privilege; but sugared or not, by the time we came to eat it, the porridge was stone cold.

I don't ever remember seeing mother herself eat. She had all her meals in her own room, with Auntie Dolly and Ella. They must have had different fare from us; and I find it difficult to reconcile mother's fastidiousness and our awful meals. It was also strictly rationed; dry stores came monthly, and perishables weekly, and there would be no more if these ran out before time. It was cooked by the house-girls as part of their training. Mother never wasted time standing over them. After each stage had been completed — assembling the ingredients, mixing them together and so on — the bowl was taken to mother's sitting-room for approval. Sometimes she forgot what the menu was and would order sugar and currants for what should have been a first-course batter pudding. Only the bravest dare put mother right, and it was soon discovered that I would do *anything* to get a decent meal; so that I was often deputed to wait on mother, "If you please, mother, excuse me, mother, but have you forgotten —" Sometimes these reminders were taken in good part — frequently not.

The twenty-five girls were divided into sections — little ones, mediums, big girls, house-girls. At thirteen I was from the start a "big girl", which carried a few slight privileges. The lot of a medium was very hard indeed. They had all the worst jobs, and were blamed for everything. Mother's shout "Who's that talking?" brought an automatic response, "If you please, mother — mediums, mother." I used to wonder why there was never a revolt of mediums at Barkingside, but of course, it was a state with a definite end. On one's twelfth birthday one became a "big girl". Likewise on one's fourteenth birthday one was a house-girl. The hair had to be put up in a bun, and life began in earnest.

Auntie Dolly was a cripple and as a child she had been used as a model by Frampton on his Barnardo memorial. She worked in the massage department and lived at Reckitt's, which was the only home she had known. She was now on the staff, and I don't know if she ever went into the outside world. The function of Ella I never could discover. Most of her time she spent on a footstool in mother's sitting-room; she was only galvanized into activity in the evening, when she stripped and scrubbed herself all over with a nail brush and cold water. She didn't seem particularly abnormal; but she was the cause of much unhappiness through her tale-bearing. As I see it now, she was probably a girl who could not cope with living and needed shelter and protection. Psychology and psychiatry were being studied by the Homes, but apart from a visiting "head doctor" these sciences were still mysteries. No one bothered to explain Ella to us, she was just one of those hazards of life. Every cottage had its drawbacks and she was ours. Miss Lewis was quite shameless about having favourites; all the mothers did —

189

in fact "mother's pet" was a recognized status. One would hear that a certain cottage was losing its mother's pet, and speculate on her successor. To be our mother's pet was not enviable, for she never ceased to find fault and make demands on her favourites, whereas the children she disliked she ignored as far as possible. To say that this was wrong is to expect too much of human nature; to love in equal measure twenty-five children of varying ages from different backgrounds, some of whom were extremely unattractive, would only be possible to God. So far I have found no proof that even He is impartial.

The units were of course too big, and the staff over-worked and underpaid. Many in my time worked for no salary at all. But what could be done? The living motto of the Homes was "No destitute child ever refused admission", and the year was 1930. Children poured in, many from hitherto well-to-do homes. The beds were set head to foot with scarcely room to stand between them; and for a time at Reckitt's we had two cots on the landing. Fortunately, due to rigid quarantine rules, and lack of outside contact, there was little infectious disease. There were many deaths while I was there, but these were mostly of children newly admitted, usually babies. Their condition was so bad when they came in that no care on earth could have saved them. The debt the nation as a whole owes to Barnardo workers during the depression years cannot be calculated. The sorrows of the outside world — the follies of statesmen and the futilities of war — reached us in the tears of children's partings; in the cruelties done to them and in the deaths of babies. The task of finding jobs for the hundreds of yearly leavers and fitting them into a workless world must at times have seemed hopeless, so it is no wonder that here and there Ellas were allowed to remain quiescent. Even so, with all these problems the authorities had enough courage to embark in a small way on another venture, the higher education of girls.

Except in very few cases, Barnardo girls went into service, as housemaids, nursemaids and anything domestic. As such they were famous. Certain titled families always had Barnardo girls "below stairs" as a matter of custom, and the nursery maids in royal households often came from the Homes. It was, and still is, a boast of theirs that no one unfit to earn a living would be sent into the world, and many crippled, deformed and abnormal people lived and died in the care of the Homes.

Some cripples graduated from the village embroidery school to the Royal School of Needlework; others did the dressmaking and upholstering necessary for the village. All the much-scorned Guide uniforms were made by them; in fact anything that could be stitched on the premises was, not only for the village, but also for the Garden City. The Homes were so organized as to be almost self-supporting. The technical school at Goldings supplied brushes, basket-ware and for some reason black stockings; and did all the printing. The village did the laundry and sewing, and the Garden City grew vegetables and made the bread. Shoe repairs were done by crippled boys; also at Goldings.

I don't think I was ever so miserable as on my first day at the village, but it was not in my nature to mope for long. My chief trouble was getting on with the other girls, to whom I felt superior, and in conforming to what I considered silly rules and customs. The speech was not only different, but many phrases and expressions had evolved which were quite unintelligible to an outsider. The other girls could tell by the way mother said "Sing" whether she meant hymns or choruses. Then there were "pass-ons", messages from the Governor sent to be read and signed by the cottage mother and passed on to the next. When making a request, or merely a statement, you began and ended with "please, mother". Most things, I discovered, were "not allowed". It was not allowed to walk on the green, to bounce balls on the road or to go outside the gates unless in crocodile, or with another big girl, and only then with a pass. Running away, so far from being an act of daring, was considered a disgrace, and one avoided a girl with such a reputation.

In spite of her oddities we considered Mother Lewis to be the prettiest, cleverest and best-dressed mother in the village. At regular intervals, I believe once a month, mothers went to tea with the Governors, and Mother Lewis always asked us what she should wear. We all advised this and that, and when the clamour had died down she would twinkle at me, "What do you say, Elsie? The grey silk or the flowered voile?" "You can't wear the voile, please, mother. Angas is all over flowers; Bessie said she bought it new last week."

The mother of Angas Cottage being very large, the idea of her being "all over flowers" brought forth a scarcely suppressed giggle from everyone, which mother would silence sternly, though laughter flickered round her mouth.

"I am sure Angas will look very nice," she snapped, which somehow made us want to giggle more.

Although cottage mothers naturally had names of their own, it was very unusual to use them. Some I never knew; they were always referred to by the name of the cottage. Mother Lewis was an exception.

Whatever dress she wore for the Governors' tea, the most important thing was the hat, which must not in any way resemble another mother's. We tried at school to find out how many hats our rivals possessed, which she had worn last and so on, but as everyone else was playing this game it wasn't easy. I was very well informed about Angas, because my best friend Bessie was also mother's pet; but in the matter of hats Angas was very conservative, having it seemed only one for summer and another for winter. Our great rival was "Dorothy". "Dorothy" was kept by an "honourable", reputed to be fabulously rich, who clothed not only herself in fine raiment, but most of her children too. "Dorothy" was opposite us across the green, and we could spy from our playroom window.

"She's coming out, the door's open," the watcher at the window would cry.

"She's coming out, the door's open, please, mother," the intermediary relayed.

"It's the red, the red straw."

"Please, mother, it's the red straw," excitement would now be intense. Mother who never dreamt of buying a red hat, sighed thankfully and put on the white one. Once, however, "Dorothy" cheated. She stood on the doorsteps in her fawn felt "coal scuttle" talking to her house-girl, and our mother set off gaily across the green in a jaunty, black, violet-adorned toque. When she was half-way across and no retreat possible "Dorothy" darted indoors

193

to emerge again in an almost identical toque. Where our mother had violets, she sported a large red rose. "Dorothy" had a fine Scots humour, and was a great flouter of conventions, but until we forgot the incident, she and all hers were beyond the pale. She had betrayed our mother "in the middle of the green".

Barnardo's dream had been to found a village community and he was successful, even to founding with it, though unwittingly, all the faults of a village. Prejudice, quaint customs, wild rumour and gossip. Some of the mothers had worked with the Doctor himself; they were now very old, but still followed his decrees and kept their bastions firm against the new-fangled ways of the younger mothers like "Dorothy". In these cottages the girls still wore their hair long, appeared on Sundays in white frilled pinafores, and curtsied to the Governors. Barnardo had made the rule that no girl should have her hair cut except for medical reasons. This was in revolt against the prevalent custom in his day of shaving the heads of orphans, whatever their sex. Gradually, as children entered the homes with hair already bobbed, the long tresses were dying out; and only the little boys under seven were close cropped; and now this has died out too. Gossip flew naturally from cottage to cottage, and Mother Lewis was as avid as the next one. Having listened to some new tit-bit, she would say, "Don't come to me with those tales", but not until she had heard the last word.

Rumours, such as the one about the wealth of "Dorothy", abounded. A Russian lady, an exiled duchess of course, was housekeeper at Mossford Lodge, the staff house. She was called Miss Putiatin; in Barnardoese, Miss

Put-your-heart-in-a-tin, and the stories about her were legion. When I was sent to her with a note one day I went with some trepidation, quite expecting to see a dragon. The grey-haired, soft-spoken old gentlewoman I met was both a relief and a let-down. It was the same with the dentist, who was a German. There could not have been a kinder man living, but one had only to mention his office to send small children screaming with terror. It is a pity that authority did nothing to discount this poor man's reputation; his work would have been much easier.

There were traditional stories and jokes. The stories always had a moral like the one about the little girl in "Dr Truell", who during the First World War got into bed without saying her prayers. After a struggle with her conscience she hopped out again and knelt down; as she did so a piece of shrapnel came through the roof and landed on the bed, where, if she had not been praying, she would have been killed. Sometimes this child was in another cottage, sometimes in a Branch Home, but the essentials were the same.

One of the jokes was about a woman who was so impressed with the work of Barnardo that she promised when she died she would leave him all she had. She died and left him six children. Another concerned a child who was asked what she knew about Jesus Christ and replied, "It's a swear word". Quite recently I heard this on the radio as something new, illustrating the Godlessness of the present generation, but it was an old story thirty years ago.

Mentioning new-old things reminds me of the Brownie Band. The establishment from the beginning shamelessly exploited the natural charm of children in order to get money. In fact singing for one's supper meant more than a line in a nursery rhyme. Great displays were given at the Albert Hall every year, by Barnardo children from all over the British Isles, and similar things went on in the village on Founder's Day. A feature of these displays was always the Brownie Band, and the great ambition of every eight-year-old was to be a Brownie Band conductor. For the rest of one's life at the village one could live on the glory of it. Dressed in a smart new "*shop bought*" uniform, with a scarlet sash and a Field Marshal's baton, the current partaker of glory, chosen more for good looks than musical appreciation, strutted to the rostrum, tapped the music stand and conducted her cacophony. And the instruments — wash boards, wooden spoons, sand trays and empty soft soap barrels. I firmly believe that we owe Rock an' Roll to a frustrated Brownie Band conductor. *We* all thought the noise was awful, but the general public loved the precocious airs and charming bows of the band leader.

The displays were masterpieces of organization. With scarcely any rehearsal on the spot the items from the various homes dove-tailed perfectly, and I never heard of a hitch. The Children's Choir, girls from the village in white dresses and red sashes, and boys from Woodford in grey suits, were banked around the organ, and in the arena the Bell Boys from Goldings performed, and the sailors from Watts and Russell Coates. Scottish reels were danced by Epsom to pipes played by MacCall. Not even the Baby Drillers put a foot wrong, and these were toddlers of two and three years old playing singing games with the gravity of very old politicians.

196

These were the only times when boys were seen by girls; one cannot say they met. There have been no Albert Hall displays since the war, and in theory it is a good thing that small children of misfortune should cease to be public spectacles, but I think the children of the day enjoyed these affairs; particularly the ones from the Branch Homes, as it gave them their only chance of a London visit.

There was in the village a prescribed order for everything; even going to church. To avoid confusion at the church door we had to arrive there behind our right-hand neighbours and before our left; this meant either a tearing rush or a crawl, and grumbling either way. If a cottage was in quarantine it was courtesy to inform your neighbours, but sometimes this was overlooked, and the whole schedule would be put out. I disliked everything about that church; the tinny bells, the flat choir and snuffling coughing children. No matter what the temperature outside, the inside was like a refrigerator. Singing was a great pastime among Barnardo children, so I do not know why the choir was so tuneless. It may have been the acoustics, or the fact that there were more adults than children. Certain offices seemed to hold an automatic right to a choir stall. They wore an extraordinarily unattractive outfit, of blue serge overalls and dustcaps. The blue, I was told, was supposed to be Madonna, but it missed it by several shades, and even the most dignified lady only managed to resemble a superior charwoman.

The prayers and responses were given in the usual nasal whine which angered me out of all proportion. After all it was, I suppose, worshipping God. I refused to be a party to any of it and my silence in church was the cause of many scenes with mother. In the end, to keep out of trouble, I mouthed the words, but would lend no volume to the whine. When the children were not ruining Cranmer's English they were coughing. After a positive gale of coughs, of every timbre from the churchyard to the hack, Miss Picton-Turbervill once rose from her stall, a black granite pillar in the robes of a deaconess and announced:

"If you must corf, corf during the singing of the hymns, not during the reading of the prayers or the ser-r-mon. Will mothers kindly see that children with corfs do not come to chur-rch."

Naturally "if you want to corf — corf now" became a catch phrase and mothers were more worried than ever. So many children who showed no signs of a cough at home became veritable "Dames aux Caméllias" once through the church door.

Everything in the village had its due season. There was Doctor's Night, when we had a film show on Barnardo's birthday. Under cover of darkness the naughty laundry girls (for the laundry was a kind of approved school) would hoot and whistle at the least sign of love-making. Once during a performance of the *King's Highway* starring Matheson Lang, the love-making was so passionate and the sound effects by the laundry girls so noisy that Miss Picton-Turbervill once more made a pronouncement. Stopping the film she delivered a lecture on the beauty and wonder of being in love. The laundry girls were not impressed.

After Doctor's Night, came Christmas. Each cottage

was allowed a small sum for decorations; something like half a crown, but in those days a great deal of crêpe paper could be bought for this amount. Some cottages would buy made-up decorations and keep them from year to year, but we in Reckitt's scorned this method. Mother Lewis always had a scheme. We only decorated the dining-room, and each year the scheme was changed. Once it was summer flowers, and many evenings were spent turning bare twigs into flowering rose bushes, peonies and sweet peas. The next year the whole half-crown went on blue crepe paper and we were all told to collect silver paper wherever we could. Greatly daring I asked the librarian for some, as it was whispered that she smoked, and I was twice a heroine — for confirming the rumour and for getting a good supply of tinfoil. We cut out tiny silver stars and stuck them on the blue streamers which radiated from a large magazine print of Raphael's Madonna. We had to temporarily cover up the Doctor, take him down we dare not, and "next door" accused Mother Lewis of vandalism, and although it was hardly breathed, *Romanism.* Mother was very sarcastic and whispered with a naughty twinkle in her eye, "If *she* kept her windows a bit cleaner, we might see what she was up to", and we had the Governor's word that our decorations were "tasteful".

On Christmas Eve the staff came round singing carols. They carried lanterns and sang to the librarian's violin and a portable harmonium. This choir had one deep bass voice and there were always arguments as to whether this belonged to the only man, the electrician, or to Miss B., a massive lady, who, it was rumoured, had served disguised as a captain in the Scots Guards during the First World War. I have heard of several such women and it is always in the *Scots* Guards they are supposed to have served; never in the Grenadiers or Coldstream. I don't think we ever settled the argument, but I am certain the electrician was a tenor. As soon as the group of carols had finished and the choir prepared to depart for their next stand, a small procession of Eldest Girls converged upon them; and each in turn would say, "Mother says thank you very much, and a happy Christmas from all at Reckitt's", or whichever cottage they represented. As soon as the staff choir had gone, all of us were sent to bed, except for the house-girls, who helped mother to fill the pillow-cases; we called them sacks. We were allowed to keep our Christmas things in our sacks until next laundry day, for I recall one heartbroken little girl, who had spent her first Christmas with us. She had been inseparable from her sack, though she hardly ever took anything out of it; but sat hugging it for hours on end, stroking the little attached card that bore her name. But Isobel in her usual bossy manner had emptied out the pillow-case to be sent with the next day's laundry, and the child sat weeping beside her pile of toys.

We tried hard to comfort her, showing her the locker where she could stow her belongings, but still she wept for her "sack and her own name". We retrieved the card, but Isobel was adamant about the pillow-case, because having been handled so much it was very dirty.

"I can't see that it matters," I stormed.

"Well go and ask mother," this was always Isobel's trump card; for no one dared to bother mother over trifles; but I was roused.

"All right, I will." I took the child by the hand to mother's door and knocked. I scarcely waited for her to say "come in" (she didn't always; she was just as likely to say "go away") before I entered.

"If you please, mother, she's crying."

Mother laid down the wireless magazine she had been reading and took the child on her lap.

"Do you know why?" she asked me.

"If you please, mother, she wants her sack. She doesn't want her things by themselves, she wants them in a sack. Isobel put it in the wash."

I knew very well why the girl wanted the sack, and mother knew that I knew. It was something we both understood, but neither of us could explain.

"Send Isobel to me," and so the incident ended. The child kept her toys in a pillow-case, until she was fully integrated into the cottage life, and into life itself, for the first time. Without anyone noticing, the pillow-case was eventually discarded.

Each of the big girls was responsible for a little one. We had to wash and dress our charges, do their mending, and, the worst part, be responsible for their behaviour. This was known as "doing" a little one. I started off with an absolute horror named Zena, but with a certain amount of artfulness *offered* to change her for Wilhelmina, whom nobody else wanted to "do". Wilhelmina was not very naughty, but she had few other points in her favour. The treatment for ringworm in those days entailed the removal of all the hair by X-ray. It grew again eventually, and was very curly, but there was a long bald period to live through, and Wilhelmina was very bald indeed, having no eyebrows or eyelashes, as well as no hair on her head. Then, to straighten her rickety legs, she had to wear padded splints which added to the time it took to dress and undress her. My motives in volunteering to do Wilhelmina were anything but noble. For one thing it gave me a pleasant martyred feeling to take on a job no one else wanted, and for another Wilhelmina had to be taken to the massage department every day, a very slow journey because of her splints. All this took so much time that I was able to avoid the jobs I hated, such as washing-up. Walking was such an effort for Wilhelmina that she did not talk much and I was able to day-dream. I was also able to read while waiting for her, until Sister Lane discovered that I was not only very round-shouldered but also lop-sided. Then I cursed Wilhelmina as I hung on wall bars, and did energetic exercises under Sister's eagle eye and the whip lash of her tongue. Many women walking about now only do so through the hard work of Sister Lane, but I am still round-shouldered.

On my first Christmas morning at Reckitt's I decided that bald and splinted though she might be Wilhelmina should look as nice as possible, and I grabbed the prettiest dress in the cupboard from under the nose of Jessica, who had designs on it for her Mollie. In the ensuing fight the dress was almost torn apart, but neither of us would give in. Strictly speaking Jessica had right on her side, as she was three days older than I. The two little ones stood shivering in their combinations, while we pulled and tugged, now the dress, and now each other's hair. When mother arrived at the scene Jessica asserted her rights of seniority. "Mollie," I declared, "is pretty and it doesn't matter what sort of dress she wears. Wilhelmina needs a pretty dress more than she does."

Mother probably saw my point, but she could not, for the sake of law and order, ignore Jessica's three days.

"The dress isn't suitable for either of them," she said, and Solomon-wise gave out identical skirts and jerseys.

When the little ones were all dressed they were paraded before mother, who then distributed new hair ribbons. Jessica was still sore at not winning the battle outright.

"Wilhelmina hasn't any hair," she hissed.

"She has a head," I snapped. Mother cut off the length of ribbon from the roll, and handed it to me with what I am sure was a wink.

The highlight of Christmas Day came after church when we lined up on the front concrete for the Governor's visit. Miss Picton-Turbervill, carrying her pekingese dog like a muff on her arm, and Miss MacNaghton were driven round the village in an open car. They stopped at every cottage, wished us a happy Christmas, kissed the baby, inspected the decorations and moved on. I don't know when they, or the last visitors had their dinner, for there were over sixty cottages besides other buildings to be seen. It is possible that a different set of cottages were visited each year and the rest probably had to content themselves with a regal wave as the car went past. Behind the Governors came Father Christmas in a lorry, its "Dr Barnardo's Homes" sign partly hidden by streamers and holly, with a sack of toys for each cottage. He was followed by the delivery man and his horse and cart. Today he delivered the red mail bags, filled with parcels which had come for individual children by post, from parents and friends. These were held back at the office for this day. Ordinarily we were afraid of the delivery man, who had a name something like Panks. He rang his bell impatiently when handing out groceries, meat or fish, and "Panks won't wait" was one of our beliefs. There was a theory that if the girl was not waiting with the tray or bowl to receive his goods he would go straight by. It didn't work, because we tried it once on boiled-fish day when mother was out. Two great cod came hurtling up the passage, apparently of their own volition.

On Christmas Day he was all smiles, in his best blue suit, and his horse was gay with ribbons. Finally, triumphantly, came the Salvation Army band.

In the afternoon we went for a walk, in a crocodile once round the village. Past the library, through the Old Village, down the New Village, round the back of the hospital, by the Extension and home. We did not go outside on this day for fear the general public should embarrass us by offering gifts. The best part of the day for me came in the evening, when the little ones and troublesome "mediums" were in bed, and we few bigger ones went into mother's sitting-room. She brought out ginger wine and biscuits, and we talked and played harmless card games. Actually playing cards were strictly forbidden in the rules so that mother, an ardent patience player, always kept a cloth handy to throw over the game, if anyone knocked at the door.

"Some rules," she would say, "are meant to be broken, but mind you, _I_ am the one to say which rules."

The day ended with mother reading from the Bible, and prayers.

204

With approaching spring came "Hats". Each cottage in turn on a certain date, and at a particular time, would have to present itself at the clothing store, to be equipped with summer hats. I don't think we went every year, for I only remember one nearly disastrous occasion when we from Reckitt's sallied out. Twenty-one of us walking, with four babies in two prams. Pram-pushing was the right of the two eldest girls, but as a special favour this right could be delegated; so, because Isobel wanted to borrow my Guide belt, I was pushing one and she the other. She also carried the green envelope containing our names and style. House-girl, big girl, medium, etc.

Arrived at the stores we lined up in ascending order of age and faced Miss Thomas, who was seated on a kind of dais. Myrtle, her Filipino assistant, who for some reason always wore Red Cross uniform, stood by her side.

Isobel presented the envelope, saying, "Good afternoon, Miss Thomas. If you please, Miss Thomas, Reckitt's — with mother's compliments."

Miss Thomas took the envelope, inclining her head and replied "Thank you, girl, return my compliments to mother." It savoured of India under the British Raj.

When Miss Thomas opened the envelope the business of "hats" began, while we stood in a silent unmoving line. Not even the babies murmured, so awe-inspiring were the clothing stores. All sound was absorbed by mountains of vests, pyramids of combinations and walls of boots and shoes. Dotted here and there were smaller dunes of jerseys, skirts, knickers and so forth all no doubt plain and clear to Miss Thomas and her Myrtle.

"Two baby boys." Miss Thomas's voice, though hardly raised, bounced round the room.

Myrtle scuttled away, and reappeared almost instantly with two paddy hats, which she plonk-plonked on to the heads of the boys. Now they couldn't see, but made no complaint.

"Six little ones"; now Myrtle brought forth six straw bonnets and the same plonking procedure went on.

In this fashion we were all hatted in a few minutes and Miss Thomas hadn't moved from her chair.

"Turn round," she ordered.

We all did an about turn, and faced her again after a brief inspection.

"Now," she said, "do you like your hats?"

Everyone said, "Yes, Miss Thomas, thank you, Miss Thomas." Everyone except me, and I said "No."

There was a sharp intake of air, and for a split second the earth stood still. Miss Thomas was graved for ever, pencil poised above *Summer hat issue. Sir Francis Reckitt*, eyebrows raised and face struck with astonishment. No orphan since Oliver Twist had made such an outrageous statement.

"You don't like your hat! What's wrong with your hat?"

Miss Thomas, now on her feet, was as awesome as a tree about to walk, but I clung to my rag of courage.

"It's too — fussy."

"Fussy! It's exactly the same style as that worn by Princess Elizabeth."

"But she's only a little girl, and she's pretty. I'm not, I just look daft."

Some of the truth of this statement must have convinced Miss Thomas, for she asked:

"And what kind of hat *would* you like?"

"Somethin' plain, like a panama."

"Myrtle, that white straw, and a glass."

Myrtle returned with the nearest thing to a chamber-pot ever meant to adorn the female head, but it was plain. It was also very large, and I almost disappeared under it. Miss Thomas jerked it off my eyes, and ordered me to look in the glass, which Myrtle was holding at an angle so as not to turn her back on Miss Thomas. I turned my head, but the hat stayed where it was. As I surveyed my silly face beneath the cock-eyed brim I was seized with an irrepressible giggling fit, and I almost burst in an effort to control it.

Miss Thomas's face was twitching with what looked like towering anger and she raised her hand, I thought to box my ears, but instead she whipped the hat from my head and disappeared into a smaller room. She was gone for some time, and when a strange spluttering noise came from that room Myrtle stunned us by shouting, "Miss Thomas 'ave got a suffin awful cold, poor dear lady." Eventually Miss Thomas returned with a real standard panama hat, not quite new, but which fitted perfectly. Finally, we were dismissed and Isobel almost ran us home in her eagerness to tell mother how I had argued with Miss Thomas. I had expected an explosion of wrath, but instead I only received a token telling off, quite nullified by the look of wondering admiration in mother's eyes. Miss Thomas's duty was to clothe 1,400 children of all ages. This was not a static population either. Children were constantly being fitted out, for boarding out, holidays and transfers, but whenever after this I appeared before her she would call, "Myrtle, see this girl gets what she wants. She's the one who didn't like her hat. Remember?"

The baby boys were an innovation during my time at the village. There were more boys being admitted than the nursery homes could accommodate, so it was decided to try one or two in each cottage. We in Reckitt's were the first to have them, and there was great excitement the day the boys arrived. Two bewildered visitors from another planet almost. We all crowded round to watch them bathed, both screaming like tortured pigs. In a lull while they regrouped their forces one of the "mediums" asked:

"Whatever are those little bits dangling down?" She had lived in the village since babyhood, and was scarcely aware that there were two sexes.

I never fitted into the routine of cottage life. I have read how my contemporaries found the caring for the babies, the tenderness towards their weaker sisters and the abiding love that flowed through and around the village a wonderful thing. Looking back now I can see that there was all this and much more, but it did not touch me at thirteen. Babies I found nerve-racking creatures, and I only felt irritation towards the "potties", those who were not mentally very bright. I did not think that anyone loved me, not even mother, who seemed angered every time I looked at her. Many years after I had grown up she told me I had been one of her favourites, and of all the hundreds of children who had passed through her hands in nearly forty years, it was me she remembered shortly before she died. It would have made so much difference if

I had known it sooner. As it was I could only see the petty things about the village where everything I wanted to do was "not allowed".

One of the worst customs in my opinion, and I have not changed my mind about that, was the opening and reading of all letters to the children. If money was enclosed it was removed and the amount pencilled on the envelope. If letters were considered not suitable or were from some relative the Homes disapproved of, they were not delivered. I scarcely ever had a letter and was quite sure that the office destroyed my post. I did not like to face the fact that there were very few people interested enough to write to me. Outgoing mail had to be delivered to the office unsealed. The amount of time wasted over this business must have been appalling, and it has long since been done away with. Many children came from bad homes, of course, and in a lot of cases the parents were criminals; it is a fact that the Homes often changed a child's name and age so that it could not be traced again by worthless relations. This was done in an honest attempt to protect the child, but no one will now admit that it ever was done; although in my time there were several instances of it. It took an Act of Parliament to make Barnardo's change its attitude towards adoption, and the idea that "you never get out of the Homes" had some basis in fact. Quite the most cruel practice was that of "returning boarding outs". These were children who, often from earliest infancy, were boarded out with foster-parents, who frequently brought them up as their own children. At the age of twelve, they were torn out of these surroundings and brought back into the Homes for training. Even to me

209

as a young girl it seemed an utterly wasteful way of breaking hearts. This custom too is a thing of the past, but it was stopped too late for me, always affected by the miseries of others.

I cannot deny that I was difficult. I had gone into the Homes in a mutinous mood, and very little I had met with had pleased me. I put on superior airs, flaunted my rather better clothes; I was lazy, cheeky and quarrelsome. Without being ill, I was never particularly well, and confinement bored me. Mother ranted and dealt out punishment, and the other girls disliked me, so in a fit of despair I wrote a note to the Governor. I complained about mother, said the food was uneatable and asked to be moved to Angas. But I never delivered it; the next day I expect the sun shone, mother smiled and perhaps we had sugar *on* our porridge; I didn't give the note another thought. Somehow the wily Isobel found it and took it, in high glee, to mother. I expected torrents of wrath, and I got it. "How dare you," stormed mother, "How dare you have the impertinence to write to the Governor in PENCIL!!" Later she said more kindly: "Don't let little things worry you too much. There are changes abroad, things will be different soon."

Things were to be so different that we never really caught up with them. My life with mother was ending; not altogether, but the cottage atmosphere was finishing. I don't think she ever really approved of the change, and always looked a little lost and unsure in her new situation.

She was in many ways like Mum. She always had to find out. How many letters in the Russian alphabet? A note to Miss Putiatin would settle that. Are there such things as yellow sweet peas? — the gardener who was the lodge-keeper's husband would know. How long do horses live? Ask Panks in the morning. Wireless was her passion in life. She took sets to pieces; re-made them — adapted them for electricity and back again to accumulators. She ate wireless magazines of which at that time there were many; and she knew the name of every component of a radio set.

To most people in the village this hobby of Miss Lewis's seemed crazy; but to me who had met so many odd people the idea of a woman in her sixties becoming a radio mechanic appeared quite normal.

There was one problem however she never solved; or at least I don't think she ever did. One Easter some benefactor had presented each cottage with about half a dozen little fern-like plants in pots. After a few weeks everybody else's were dead, but not Reckitt's. Ours flourished and grew out of their pots and had to be transferred to larger ones. Miss Lewis received many congratulations but was unable to give a satisfactory explanation, and she would often gaze at the plants, and then turn them round and round as if trying to read their secrets in their leaves. My explanation may be the wrong one; but it so happened that I was supposed to be taking a particularly horrible tonic. A bottle was meant to last a fortnight and loud were the complaints of the hospital sister if the bottle was not emptied by the right day. By pretending I liked the stuff, I was trusted to take it without supervision. Each dose went in turn to the plants which certainly flourished, and according to sister, so did I.

CHAPTER
EIGHT

Unlike most of my less fortunate companions, I did not have to attend the large village elementary school. Very slowly the authorities were beginning to recognize the need for higher education for girls. What started as a class for school leavers who had never mastered reading and writing, was gradually turning into one for the very bright. I don't quite know how this came about, but when I arrived the "Continuation School" had become the Meadow School, and was shortly to be the Meadow High School. With the nursery school for two- to five-year olds, we were housed in a hut seemingly made of cardboard, and the whole outfit was in charge of Miss Julian, assisted by Miss Blandford.

Even after thirty years I find it difficult to be unbiased about these two women, to whom I owe so much, both good and bad. Some of my happiest, and certainly my bitterest days, were spent under their tutelage. The Ministry was still nominally in charge of me, and presumably had to pay for my support. Now and again I was inspected by one of their officers, but that was all.

While the school was small and Miss Julian and Miss Blandford lived outside the village, things went very well. There were only school hours in which to adore them, and

I think without exception we all worshipped them. Children, particularly deprived children, must love. It is more essential to them than being loved. A cottage mother had to be shared with twenty-four others, the Governors were too remote, so it only left the school teachers. Miss Julian was in her fifties, delicately fragile like china, and with a classical Grecian nose. Her teaching qualifications were of the highest order, and she had the ability to share her love of knowledge with others. She had a sense of humour, but it was edged with ice. Miss Blandford had lived since early babyhood in the village, and had only native intelligence behind her. She had learned well from Miss Julian, whose adopted daughter she was. She was about twenty when we first met, heavy-figured and green-eyed. She had been our mother's pet and had run the gamut of Barnado privilege from Brownie Band leader upwards.

Although there was no denying her Barnardo background, because so many of her contemporaries were still in the village, she was never anxious for outsiders to know about it — a form of snobbery which is unfortunately common among Barnardo men and women who have done well. A certain film star who spent his boyhood at Woodford puts "educated privately" in theatrical reference books.

Miss Blandford however could teach, particularly history and English, and on her I pinned my star. Bessie favoured Miss Julian, so there was nothing to spoil our friendship.

After having for generations refused to face the fact that girls should be educated for things other than the kitchen and parlour, the Homes now went mad. The few remaining "Continuation School" girls were either given up as hopeless or went somewhere else; and the largest room of the little cardboard hut was filled with about ten of us; the bright pioneer lights of higher education! There was still the nursery school, racketing away on the other side of the partition. The noise made by these infants, compounded of hammering, chair throwing and screams of every timbre was unbelievable. Against it we did our examinations; and in that atmosphere Mary learned enough to pass School Certificate and gain a place in a teaching college; the first village girl ever to do so; and on her the fate of us all had depended.

We were fitted out with expensive uniforms, not from the village workshops but from the Educational Supply Association. No queen ever donned her regalia with as much pride as we put on our dark green gym slips, cream blouses and green blazers. Is there anything like the smell of new blazer cloth to bring back schooldays? Thus gloriously adorned we peacocked through the village, to be met with sour looks from the staff, hisses and boos from the daring, and rude, very rude comments from the laundry girls. Our talents, we discovered, were not appreciated!

It was decided to turn two cottages into boarding-houses. For weeks much whispering went on. "Bad head" cottage was to be closed and fumigated together with "bad head" school and we were to move there. I don't know if ringworm and all the other complaints which came under the title of "bad heads" had declined, or if other treatments were now used, but the rumours proved true and the two cottages and the wooden hut were now renovated for the high school. The greatest wonder of all was that Miss Julian and Miss Blandfort left their home and came to live inside the village.

Bessie and I agreed that this was "more than ever we dared dream about". But after a few weeks we found that the reality did not reach up to the dream. As school teachers Miss Julian and Miss Blandford could not be bettered, but as managers they completely failed. We still had to do the housework, but as it wasn't supervised, the cottage soon became a crumby muddle. Clothing was unmended, and as it was often unmarked as well it failed to return from the laundry The rations ran out and we began to understand why our cottage mothers had been so strict about the daily routine. There is nothing so worrying to children as disorder and a few of us elder ones took things in hand; if we hadn't the whole scheme might have fallen through in the first six months. I recall a humiliating visit paid by Olive and me to the laundry in search of unmarked sanitary towels, always referred to as "those things". Bold as the laundry girls might be out of working hours (their favourite name for us was the Meadow Muck School), they were silent under the eye of their supervisor but their faces spoke volumes and we well knew how the tale would fly how the Meadow Muck School had to come crawling to the laundry for "those things". A house matron was appointed to keep things in order; and our household chores became "Domestic Science".

My school work progressed favourably towards my goal, which was a librarianship. At fifteen I sat for the Junior Oxford; a blissful long desired week, for exams held no terror for me; travelling to and from the centre at the Wanstead Royal Orphanage, alone with Miss Blandford. It is true Agnes sat as well; but she was an unobtrusive child I found easy to forget. The Wanstead Royal is to the orphanage world what Eton is to public schools. Agnes and I looked at the small section of it we saw with a critical eye, and decided we would rather have Barnado's. True, the children were better dressed, and looked very content, but we gathered from one or two candidates we spoke to that they saw less of the outside world than we did. Just before the history paper Miss Blandford urged us to make sure of some dates; but I refused. "We shall have the steps in Henry VIII's breach with Rome," I said, "and I know them all."

"There are dozens of other questions you might have," insisted Miss Blandford.

"We shall have *that*."

The first question on the paper was about Henry VIII and his separation from Rome.

I gained a distinction in history; and now I have no idea how or why that fat Tudor King left Rome, but it meant all the world to me then.

No one I have met has had the power to make me wretched as did Miss Blandford. In her presence it was impossible for me to be natural, or to retain my individuality. I studied and worked like a slave for her, and for the most part was treated like a slave; to be petted or spurned as the fancy took her.

Then suddenly I grew out of it all. Work and books became all-important. Because of a fit of temper I had been taken off the bedroom work, and I found I didn't really care. I could listen to Miss Blandford singing, and allow myself to wonder if she really wasn't after all something like a crow. If she went out at night, I could fall asleep before she returned and I couldn't care less if she said "good morning" to me first or to Agnes.

We had a visiting French mistress, a Belgian, who brought a breath of wordly wisdom into our stronghold twice a week. She taught French from the books of M. Chardenal; one book really *does* contain the sentence "the pen of my aunt is in the pocket of the gardener". Her methods and M. Chardenal were perhaps out of date, but it is odd that I still remember her French, and not Miss Blandford's history.

I was not her brightest pupil, but I was one of her favourites; and she warned me: "Your heart, little Elise, will be your fall down. You should listen to the head. When you get old and ugly like me, *pouf*, what is the heart? If I did not have a head I should now be singing with the angels. Now, *un*, *deux*, *trois*, *quatre*," and so on, through the numbers, the days of the week, the months and seasons of the year and half a dozen verbs we romped; then after a pause for breath, Mademoiselle would say "My cheque. You will ask Dr Barnardo for my cheque."

"But Dr Barnardo is dead, Mademoiselle."

"So? Then Miss Julian. She will pay me the cheque."

Every month or so this question of the belated cheque cropped up. Vainly we explained that cheques came from Stepney, and neither Miss Julian nor the office could speed them up. One day I helped her carry her books to the bus; this was allowed, because Mademoiselle was elderly and a hunchback. I did not often volunteer, having formerly been too anxious to get back to the sight of my beloved Miss Blandford.

"Ah," said Mademoiselle as we closed the lodge gates. "We can now breathe. It is not good Elise to live so much with women. How old are you?"

"Sixteen, Mademoiselle."

"And you have no sweethearts?"

"There aren't any to be had, unless you count the boiler man, the electrician and Panks."

"When I was sixteen I had many," she sighed. "It is so different this country; he's with he's and she's with she's. You know, Elise, I believe that is why the Englishmen conquered the world. They went into far places to get away from their own sex."

Just then the bus came, so there was no time to follow up this fascinating theme. I took my time getting back to school, for the French lessons were held in a disused building at the other end of the village, and was met by an infuriated Miss Blandford, who I had unwittingly kept waiting to begin an English lesson.

"Five hundred lines!" adding threateningly, "by tonight."

As I had passed the Junior Oxford and Agnes hadn't, I was in a class by myself, ostensibly studying for the School Certificate. Most of the time I worked on my own and as one of the set books was *Jane Eyre* I counted out five hundred lines of foolscap paper, and proceeded to fill them with an extract from that novel. Seeing myself as the ill-treated misunderstood Jane, I read on and on after the five hundred lines were written, and finished the book. At the end I announced that I had changed my name to

"Janet", for that was what Rochester called his Jane in his fondest moments. By steadfastly refusing to answer to anything else, Janet I became, and am still.

Although in many ways I welcomed my release from loving, the fact that I seemed to be so shallow and devoid of loyalty worried me, and I felt now and then obliged to sting myself into championing Miss Blandford's cause. Once, a new house matron had arrived and had captured some of her admirers.

"I thought you cared for me" — wearing the air of a tragedy queen Miss Blandford met me on the stairs.

"I do," I answered, out of old habit.

"Miss C. is bathing in *my* water," she swept past me and down. (The bath water was always a bone of contention between staff and children.) Perhaps she was really angry; or perhaps she was giggling at my discomfiture. I failed to see how I could prevent the amazonian Miss C. from bathing if the inclination took her. Great events do not hang on great beginnings, but depend upon the "want of a horseshoe nail". My kingdom was lost on bathwater, for the next time Miss C. wanted to bath I treated her with such insolence that she threatened to resign.

She was a very good house matron, quite the most efficient we had yet been blessed with. Miss Julian certainly did not want to lose her; and I had long been a nuisance. I could not be got rid of on the grounds of lack of intelligence. Every term two or more girls were turned out through not being up to standard The school had grown, and so great was the pressure on places that only the very best could be kept on, especially after normal school-leaving age. The wails and sobs of those unlucky ones, who now had to resign themselves to being "service girls", had haunted my dreams, and not even my adoration of Miss Blandford had caused me to neglect my school work. I could, however, be removed as an "upsetting influence". My temper was still uncontrolled at times, and I had little respect for rules. I had often been warned that this state of affairs could not last, and since the summer I considered I had been very good. It had been easier to behave, now that I was growing out of adolescent "pashes", and had I been left alone I should have developed quite normally

In the summer I had defied the whole school and received a "last and final" warning. It had been appallingly hot, and the crowded bedrooms were like furnaces. It must have been the summer of the yo-yo craze, for I was idly spinning one over the railings of the school steps when we were ordered to bring our mattresses and blankets on to "the back concrete". The cottages were separated by fences and small asphalt yards; these yards in spite of their composition were always known as "the back concrete"; and the path from the front door, which really was concrete, was called "the front concrete". Most of the girls thought sleeping out was a terrific idea, but I considered it a fag and not worth the effort. With bad grace I stuck my yo-yo in my garter; the securest place to keep anything of value. (The other garter kept safe a photograph of Miss Blandford, top half only. I had won it by force from another girl, who treasured her half — of a pair of black stockinged legs.) I lugged my bedding outside muttering about the daftness of sleeping next to the drains. Actually I was frightened, not of anything in particular but of all the thing that could get at me much more easily outside than in. I crawled down underneath the blankets, covering myself completely; and I dreamt I was in front of a firing squad. There were others with me, and we were lined up with the tallest (me) at the back. The soldiers raised their rifles and shot the first one, who dropped revealing the next until it came to my turn. As the man was about to fire I woke up, and my first feeling was one of relief, "I was about to die — and I *wasn't afraid.*" My next one was of panic, because although my eyes were open I could see nothing; also I had a violent pain in the middle of my back — the bullet obviously. Convinced now that the dream had been real, but that I was buried alive, I twisted and struggled in my grave of darkness; smelling what I was sure was the corruption of the others who had died. I tore at the blackness above my head, and there, leering and mocking, hung the full moon, dragging up to himself the smell from the drains. The tightly wrapped blankets, the full moon, and, I discovered, the yo-yo on which I had been lying, had all combined to produce a nightmare; which had left me wet and jittering with fear. I had had enough; rolling up my bedding I went indoors, determined that no power on earth would get me camping out again. The next evening which was just as hot, there was a scene because I refused to take out my bed. Afraid of Miss Blandford's mockery I dare not give my reason, but resorted to being rude about the drains. If I had been able to explain to Miss Julian no doubt she would have understood, for there was no reason why I should sleep outside, except that she had ordered it. With an ominous "I'll deal with you in the morning", Miss

Julian retired, and so did I, praying 250 times "Oh God let it rain". I slept, to be awakened about midnight by everyone rushing in out of a thunderstorm. Murmuring "Thank you, God", I rolled over to sleep again.

The next day Miss Julian gave me a solemn warning that I had been given my last chance. "One more outburst," she promised, "and you shall go."

After that for three months, until the bath-water incident, I managed to keep out of trouble. Now with something like triumph Miss Julian declared I had overstepped the mark; she would report me to the Governor at once.

Another month went by, and I was hopeful that the matter had been overlooked. I still went to school, and although notice was taken of me, I put it down to the need for concentration on the next lot of school certificate candidates. Then I was called in to see a lady from the Ministry of Pensions, Miss Hayes.

"I'm sorry to hear you are no longer happy at school," she said.

"But I am."

"I understand you have been giving trouble."

"Not so much as all that." This approach puzzled me.

"Have you decided what you want to be?"

"Of course, years ago. I'm going to be a librarian."

"That needs training and a degree."

"I shall get that all right. I'm starting the school certificate in July."

It had all been so plain. School certificate, college, a degree and then librarianship.

Miss Hayes fumbled for her words.

"But I'm afraid you have spoiled all that. Barnado's won't keep you any longer, and *we* haven't any funds. Now it means a job."

"You mean I have to leave school?"

"We have been asked to remove you."

"But I can't leave school. I've *got* to be a librarian, there isn't anything else I can be."

"We must — think of something."

I went out of the room as from a death sentence. Nothing, I felt, could be more unjust. It had never occurred to me that this was what Miss Julian had been threatening. I thought the worst that could happen would be that I should be moved to another cottage. That I should have to give up everything I wanted, and have to leave the village in shame like any laundry girl — this I had never thought possible.

I went to see mother, who had moved next door and was in charge of the junior girls. She was sympathetic. In the old days she would have be-hatted herself and been across the green to the Governor. But now, since the changes had come, she seemed to have lost some of her old spirit. "I miss the babies," she had said once. Now she said, almost to herself:

"I knew no good would come of this school. They've run beyond themselves."

"But I haven't been all that bad," I sobbed. "Gertrude is much worse than I am, but *she* keeps at school."

"Why not go and apologize to Miss Julian? Perhaps things will be all right again, and you can live here with me."

Cheered and comforted, pathetically certain that mother

would make everything right, I knocked on Miss Julian's door, my apology beautifully poised in my mind. She eyed me over the tops of her spectacles, her small straight mouth almost invisible. Miss Blandford stood by the window.

Before I could speak Miss Julian began, "We shall want your uniform for another girl, so collect it together. For the few days you will be here, you can wear play clothes."

I did not speak a word, but went out already undoing the buttons of my tunic. I wanted to tear it to pieces, anything for action; anything to stop someone else wearing it. Miss Blandford followed me out.

"I'm sorry it's like this," and as if she read my thoughts; "don't do any damage to that uniform. There might be a chance, just a chance, you may need it again."

"Why should I have to leave?" I burst out "Why me? What have I done that Gertrude hasn't done worse?"

"It isn't your fault. We pleaded, but the Ministry insisted you left."

This was a lie, as I was later to learn.

The Ministry, at a loss to know what to do with a half-trained girl, had wanted me to stay. It was they who pleaded; and Miss Julian who insisted. This lie was to colour my attitude to the Ministry for several years, until I learned the truth.

Another fortnight dragged by and Miss Hayes came again.

"It has been decided to give you another chance — but not here," she added hastily. "You are going to board with a lady; and will go to Clark's College, where you will study for a Civil Service examination."

224

This didn't sound so bad, and I cheered up for a little while, until Miss Blandford sneered, "Civil Service! A nice safe job with a pension! When you could have done — anything!"

Like a somnambulist I got through the days of outfitting. I was surprised to find that other people were not concerned with my failure; they seemed to think I had done quite well. Miss Thomas went out of her way to give me the best clothes she had in the store; and, moreover, produced a suitcase to carry them in. Service girls had boxes, and boarders-out blue canvas sacks; but drowned in shame and selfish misery, I did not then appreciate her kindness.

The last day came; and I stood in my brand-new clothes, underneath which a full-size pair of corsets creaked like a suit of armour; restraining a concave stomach and two little knobs above. I had not cried until the moment of parting. Up till now, deep within me, I had believed that something, someone would save me.

"Don't forget," whispered Miss Blandford diabolically. "In about six months write to Miss MacNaghton and ask if you can come back."

Bessie carried my suitcase for me to the Governor's House. My tears made me almost blind. Many eyes were on me as I went through the village, and there were loud comments on my clothes and suitcase. My tears were unremarked for everyone cried when leaving the village, even if they had been miserable there.

The Governor, cold as at my reception, bade me a short farewell. I wanted to fling myself at her feet and beg to be allowed to stay, but this was real life, not the stage; I just dumbly joined the anonymous Ministry officer, and went through the main gates to the tram. Leaving behind me that small closed world, that had for three years held all my dreams, and shown me visions of life as it might be; even "poor little, plain" as I was. Leaving the library and the cool picture gallery behind it — the cups marked "Beta Café" and "Royal Zoological Society"; the phrases "Lick your spoon and keep it" after soup; "Governor's notice — pass it on" — "Look at the Meadow Muck School, Coo-er —" and the babies, babies, babies.

The tram conductor reversed the power arm; sending out bright blue electric flashes The driver walked through the vehicle turning the back into the front. We mounted the platform; a whistle shrieked and we clattered towards the City.

CHAPTER
NINE

I don't know what the Misses Tansley thought they were getting on that foggy All Souls' Day in 1932; and it is one of those unsolved mysteries of my life how they ever thought the presence of a miserable adolescent orphan in their home would be a good thing. I am certain of the date, because Miss Tansley, being the headmistress of All Souls' School, Langham Place, had a holiday. Miss Winifred kept house and did the cooking; up in the attic slept Miss Tyrell, the almost invisible lodger, who worked in the Post Office in the Archway Road; for we had come to Highgate. I believe the road was called Cromwell Avenue, and the wall of the cemetery formed part of it. The house was the kind that a respectable murderer might have chosen to live in. Tall and narrow, of blood-red brick, with a few parched shrubs in the front, and a small garden at the back. It had everything necessary for a gloomy Victorian setting. The tiny conservatory with its coloured glass insets; the french windows leading from the dining-room to the garden; gas; and dark, antler-infested hall and stairway. Here Smith might have drowned his cleanly wives, or Crippen poisoned his Bella, but instead the house sheltered the kindly, ageing Misses Tansley. They were thrilled with me — at first. I spoke so nicely and was much better-mannered than they had first expected.

I had a room to myself in the attic next to Miss Tyrell's. I sat on the bed and thought, "Now I am not a child any more, tomorrow I shall be a student at College."

They had taken great pains to explain at the Pensions Office in City Road that this was my last chance; it would never come again. In January, less than three months away, I should take the examination for Postal Sorters; if I was successful, and I had better be, I should have a permanent job at Mount Pleasant. A pensionable, Civil Service appointment — sorting letters. Then they added as an afterthought that there were only twenty-five vacancies, for which about 700 girls and boys would be competing. I was congratulated on my good fortune in finding a home with the Misses Tansley. All Souls' was one of the foremost churches in London and All Souls' School consequently very important. On the tram to Highgate I made up a rhyme

> "The bell tolls
> There are doles
> For all souls"

which didn't mean anything, but sounded mournful.

Somebody took me to Clark's College at Finchley the next day. I was certainly let down to find no shady lawns or quiet quadrangles. "College" to me meant Cambridge, Rupert Brooke and high gaiety — but I was used to let-downs and accepted the converted suburban villa as my College. I believe this institution still flourishes in its various branches all over the country, and at nowhere better could one learn shorthand and typing, book-keeping and other business techniques; and it would have been more far-seeing of the Ministry if they had entered me for the "commercial" course. Shorthand typists can always earn a living somewhere; but instead I took the equivalent of a "Classics" course with Postal Sorting as my goal. The students were all "young ladies and gentlemen", and the young ladies in particular were very sophisticated.

In my black woollen stockings and unmade-up face I looked exactly what I was. I don't remember that anyone was unkind to me on account of my odd appearance or for any other reason. The Principal was a Mr Savage, and his voice matched his name. Being very lame he relied on its volume to save his legs and for a time his sudden bursts of bellowing frightened me. I believe he thought me an utter fool, if he considered me at all, but was very flattered, for his branch's sake, when an essay of mine was printed in the college magazine. No one at Finchley had achieved that honour before. I must say too that I considered I had "arrived" for this was the first time anything of mine had been printed. It pleased the Misses Tansley for one of them cut it out of the magazine and I never saw it again, and now haven't the slightest idea what the essay was about. When not moaning to be back at Barnardo's I was quite lively, and my innocence and unworldliness caused amusement to others. As all the exercise paper had to be bought and paid for by the sheet this was quite a drain on some parents' pockets. Mine was booked to the Ministry of Pensions and I gained quite a lot of popularity by being free with it. Our tutor was a rackety Irishman with a fantastic memory. "Go to the source books!" he urged us in history lessons, "consult the fountain 'ead." Following him to the "source books" has ruined my taste for historical novels.

It did not take long for the Tansley ladies to get on my nerves, and less time still for me to get on theirs. I was not the little lady they had hoped for. My charm and good manners were only a veneer. Underneath I was as much a savage as any barbarian dweller below the Archway Bridge, where respectability ended and the slums took over. I cannot remember that I ever did anything particularly dreadful. The constant nag, nag, "Do your homework!" "Don't bite your nails!" "Brush your hair!" "Did you go to the lavatory?" — would cause me to explode with irritation. I wanted to be left alone; to do as I liked; to go back to school. Back to school. It was to take the best part of a year for that dream to die.

Something else which did nothing to help my temper was the constant state of jitters I was in about the traffic. I went back and forth to Finchley four times a day, suffering torture. I was terrified of a street accident. This terror was fed by Miss Tansley's constant warnings, and the accounts she read out of the newspaper of dreadful accidents which seemed to happen every moment of the day.

The Archway Road was thick with all kinds of traffic — trams, trolley buses, petrol buses, anything on wheels. Miss Winifred doled out the fare to me for each journey, but I would sometimes walk all the way rather than entrust myself to a public vehicle. Accidents haunted me day and night, and I would dread the ending of school hours. I kept this fear to myself and was well on the way to being a nervous wreck. Then it happened, of course — the accident. I was walking along the Archway Road, when a man on a motor bicycle slewed across the tram tracks, was knocked off by a car and finished up in front of a bus. My first impulse was to shut my eyes and run in the opposite direction, as I did years before at Tacolneston; but a voice, clear as the one that arrested Saul on the Damascus Road, sounded inside my head. "Stop! If you run now you will go on running. Look your fear in the face."

The man had been laid on the pavement. Once he had had a nondescript, ordinary face; now one side was black and shapeless. Blood trickled down his nostrils and from one corner of his mouth. One hand below a leather sleeve twitched; he had lost his shoes and his socks had been darned with ill-matching wools.

I looked at my fear, red blood, blue bruises, a twitching hand and a bundle of clothes. This was *all* that could happen; even if he had been in several pieces, it would have been no worse. Crying for that unknown man, shouldering my load of fear, I went home.

Later in the week Miss Tansley read an account of the accident in the local paper.

"I saw it happen," I said.

"But you didn't tell us," both ladies spoke in chorus.

"You," I said, loftily and bitterly, "*enjoy* accidents. I don't."

It was an unkind and untrue thing to say, and very rude into the bargain. Probably fear walked with the Misses Tansley too, and they met it by collecting newspaper reports of ghastly tragedies; thankful that this time at any rate they were not the victims. But this psychological aspect did not occur to me then.

They did their best for me. I was well fed, and part of my wardrobe was replaced with clothes more suitable for the times. All their lecturing, all their worrying was for my own good, and from me they had *nothing* in return. Not one spark of affection and scarcely a word of thanks. The cold kiss on their plushy cheeks, my nightly duty, was enough to freeze an angel. Dodging their enfolding arms and lavender-watered virgin bosoms, I mourned away to the attic to dream and scheme of Miss Blandford. No one had taught me that one had a duty to *receive* affection. I showed no interest in the Civil Service and its pension; and only did my homework because it was more interesting than sitting with the ladies.

When the results of the examination came out I was not among the first twenty-five. I came 333rd — which was in the top half, at any rate. There came an unpleasant interview at the Ministry, where for once I exerted myself and asked to be taken away from Highgate. The Miss Tansleys, I declared snootily, were too old-fashioned, they didn't understand a young person like me. It was pointed out that the elder Miss Tansley was a headmistress of high standing, dealing daily with young people. I could only counter with, "Living with them is different."

The high narrow house was left behind, and now remains in my memory only as a dark impression. It is true that I only knew it in dripping winter, and I never went back again. The only modern thing in it was a photograph of the handsome rector of All Souls', Arthur Buxton, who had in years gone by graced Miss Huntley's garden fêtes, and sent her feather-boa streaming with excitement. One of those senseless coincidences which keep happening in my life. I was to live for years in the parish of All Souls', but I only saw Miss Tansley once again. It was shortly before she died, in the Middlesex Hospital. She was scarcely conscious of my presence as I sat awkwardly beside her bed, clutching the few marguerites I had been able to afford from the stall in the hospital courtyard. All around were chattering patients and their visitors, while she and I in separate worlds formed two concentric circles of silence. Finding the tension unbearable I laid the drooping flowers on her locker and crept out. Her name was Marguerite.

Hyde House was one of a group of "Christian and Homelike Hostels for Working Girls" situated in various parts of the west side of London. They were more Christian in the narrow sense of the word than homelike, but they filled an urgent need. Their clientèle was made up of apprentices, students, shop assistants and office workers. One or two were blind and quite a few disabled; they came from all over the British Isles and occasionally beyond. Most of them came to London either to learn a trade or to earn more money than they could at home. For some, these hostels were their only home. Most were between seventeen and thirty. Some were older. The turnover was rapid; but as in hotels, there was a hard core of permanents.

Hyde House, in Bulstrode Street, bounded by Welbeck Street, Marylebone Lane, Wigmore and New Cavendish Streets, was within easy reach of everything metropolitan; which made it the most popular of the hostels; there were seldom any vacancies. Full board and lodging cost 18*s.* 3*d.* a week, and it is not surprising that at such a price the board was somewhat bare.

The girls and women came mostly from good middle-class homes and there were very few of the "fast" type. Rebels there were who kicked against the rules and defied the "no smoking" ban by every possible means. One woman locked herself in her wardrobe, another hung perilously from the bathroom window, puffing out such clouds of smoke that it is a wonder passers-by did not call the fire brigade. For me a more trying regulation was the night curfew. The door was locked at 10.30 p.m. and at 11 on Saturdays. Late-comers had to ring the bell, so there was no way of getting in without the superintendent knowing. No matter how deeply one plotted with accomplices, and thought out ways of silent entry, Miss Leake was always there, disappointed and long suffering. It was no good making excuses — she knew them all. She was not very witty, but on the day the London Passenger Transport Board came into being she was heard hoping that the bus and Underground systems would now be more efficient, particularly in the late evening. She was a very mild, meek kind of woman, easily given to tears, and it might be wondered how she managed to keep control of eighty-two assorted girls and women; but underneath the outer shell was a core of rock stubbornness, and a single-mindedness that in earlier days would have led her to the stake for her principles. Her strongest threat was "I shall make a note for the office", but I doubt if these notes were ever made or delivered.

I was so relieved to get away from Highgate that I quite

welcomed Hyde House. I had a cubicle in a dormitory three floors up. It contained a bed, a bookshelf, chair, chest of drawers and a wardrobe; as much as anyone ever really needs. The partitions were of wood, painted green, with white curtains on to the central corridor.

This little box, and others like it in other hostels, was to be my world for the next six years. There was nothing left for me to do now except to earn my living — a task that has proved so difficult and frustrating that I wonder why I bothered at all. I was naturally endowed with only two gifts; a phenomenal memory, and fantastically long eyesight. Neither of these gifts are of any commercial value, and both are now not so good as they were. I was also blessed with optimism. Is blessed the right word? I am inclined to think that in the long run an optimist suffers more than a pessimist.

The first stage in earning one's living was to find a job, and day after day Miss Hayes from the Ministry of Pensions presented me, a plain, mulish lump, to her opposite number at the Ministry of Labour, Great Marlborough Street.

"If only," sighed this lady through her wire grille, "we could bring out her charm — which I am sure — I *know* — she has, we could get her suited." She was an optimist too. At last, I don't know how, unless it was at gun-point, I was taken on by Debenham and Company as a Parcels Dispatch Clerk. A relieved Miss Hayes delivered me at the staff entrance, with a promise that if I did well I should be sure to rise; and that Debenham's was an excellent firm to be with — they provided pensions for their staff.

A rise, in more ways than one, soon became an urgent

235

necessity, if an early burial was to be avoided. I did my parcel dispatching two floors below ground in a room full of machinery. Chutes from all the departments vomited parcels on to a revolving table, from which they had to be snatched and sorted according to the colour of their attached tickets. Some of them contained bolts of cloth, and a bolt is usually sixty yards. I worked from 8.30 in the morning until 6 at night and earned 17*s.* a week. Out of this 1*s.* 6*d.* went for insurances, and 12*s.* 3*d.* to the hostel, the Ministry making up the balance. So 3*s.* 3*d.* was mine; my very own with which to buy clothes, soap, toothpaste, writing paper and go to the pictures. And all the time this silly longing to go back to school. It stayed with me like a sickness while I laboured with parcels among miles of cotton belting. I woke with it in the morning, giving substance to my dreams. It revived my old passion for sweets, and somewhere in the parcels' labyrinth was an unfrocked Father Christmas who sold bars of chocolate, so that my 3*s.* 3*d.* was mortgaged from week to week.

I suppose if I had had any guts at all, I would have gone to evening school and pulled myself up by my own efforts, instead of maundering about the doornail-dead past. But I was only conscious of the desire to eat and sleep when working hours were over. Eating, to supplement the prison-like hostel fare, was expensive, but sleeping cost nothing and passed the time. I suppose it sounds a shocking thing for a seventeen-year-old girl to spend all her spare time asleep; but there it is; I was waiting for something to happen, enduring the dust and noise of the dispatch room in a kind of coma, until somebody noticed I was quietly dying. Then with a flurry I was moved up to

236

first floor level, where there was a window of opaque glass facing a white-tiled wall, and at the top "that little tent of blue which prisoners call the sky". Blown-up silhouettes of pigeons marched up and down the window-sill, for ever scandal-mongering.

I was now in "Wholesale Tweeds and Suitings", and my particular job was to paste snippets of cloth against their catalogue numbers which were typed on the travellers' order sheets. I was never quite certain about the ultimate destination of my handiwork, but it seemed to be important. When there were no sheets to hand I cut up samples of cloth ranges with pinking shears. We had a little office partitioned off one corner of the vast show-room; there were three of us, a middle-aged woman clerk, whose name I forget but who was infinitely kind to me, and a girl a year or two older called Olive. In a similar office in the opposite corner was the head of Wholesale Tweeds, a fearsome six-footer, Mr Colenut. He flew round the department like Strewel Peter's Big Tall Tailor; he went upstairs three at a time and down them with his body leaning forward at a right angle to the steps. On the night of the departmental dinner he recited comic verse of his own composing, all about Debenham personalities and customs. That was the only time anyone ever laughed at him. Even the most brash and hardened commercial traveller jittered when his order book showed too many blanks. All except Mr Cohen. Mr Cohen was just about five feet high and almost as broad. He was an aristocrat of commercial travelling. It was said that no rival traveller dared follow the footsteps of Mr Cohen. He must have sold miles of material in a week and I dreaded getting his sheets, which he always wrote out himself in a firm slanting hand, but so crowding the paper that sticking on the samples was a tricky business. I asked him once how he managed it; with an Hebraic gesture as old as Genesis he said, "I know *cloth* — from the back of the sheep, to the back of the she." I didn't learn cloth that well, but I did take from Debenham's the ability to tell good cloth from bad, and match colours in my head.

The showroom outside our partitions was crowded with bales — lightweights, heavyweights, stripes, diagonals and fancies. Each little section was presided over by a salesman and an apprentice. The place was full of men. The salesmen and their college-boy apprentices upstairs, and little gnomes downstairs, wheezing, sneezing and choking in the dusty, fibrous atmosphere. All day long they cut off cloth, calling out the lengths from one end of the basement to the other. "Fifti — thirti — fourti." They used the "ti" sound to prevent confusion with "teens" and they always called the digit before the tens, thus — "seven-and-fifti".

Early in the morning came the matchers — the English equivalent of "midinettes". They were gay and heavily made-up, and they clicked on stilted heels, waving their cottons, ribbons and wisps of material from the dressmaking firms, matching up samples. Their laughter could be heard ringing from "Wholesale Silks", but as befitted a more sombre department they were wary and well-behaved in "Wholesale Tweeds". Should a giggle escape from behind the baffle wall of fancy checks then Mr Colenut's small round head on its long neck would rear up like a dinosaur's above his partition, and thunder

238

"Clarke!" at the offending apprentice. Salesmen were all given a "Mr" but not apprentices or travellers, save Mr Cohen. Olive whispered to me that the matchers were "street-walkers" by night. I said "Oh," very knowingly, but was puzzled, as I could see nothing wrong in walking streets; I did it myself.

Win Summerhayes was my oracle at Hyde House. She was older than most of us, and I was quite sure imbued with all worldly wisdom. In spite of being heavily crippled she managed to do a great deal of walking. She was a heavy smoker, and every evening, dead on nine o'clock, no matter the weather, she stomped up Marylebone High Street, round the Inner Circle, Regent's Park, and home again, about three miles, puffing furiously all the way. She used one match and about ten cigarettes. Most nights I went with her. I liked her hard astringent wit; she thought me a fool and said so, but from her I didn't mind. We talked the world over, tearing to pieces all the residents of Hyde House, and Win's workmates at Madame Schiaparelli's. Men, according to Win, were "filthy beggars" with only one thought in their heads, to get a girl in the family way. "Run up and tacked down for life." I was sure Win would know about street-walkers. She did.

"They're women who go with men for money."

"Go with men where?"

Savagely Win lit another cigarette from the stub of the old one, which she sent golden-raining over the bridge into the lake. "To bed, you nincompoop. They commit adultery with them."

"Oh, you mean harlots."

"That's right, harlots. You're not so soft as you make out."

I wasn't soft at all; just plain ignorant. Although I knew a harlot was an illicit partner for the bed, I had no idea what she did there.

Practically all the girls in the hostel had steady boy friends, and the ones who hadn't were always telling tales of being accosted in the street or the park. One reason Win gave for always carrying a lighted cigarette was to ward off would-be rapers, who were likely to haunt every doorway of Marylebone High Street. Many were the stories of "getting-off" in the cinema, and being "picked up" in tea-shops —

"He said, 'Excuse me, may I have the mustard?' I said, 'Sure — but aren't you hot enough?' Of course I didn't mean anything, just making a joke, but he took me up and said, 'Do you want a demonstration?' Well, we went to the pictures, had some supper, he bought me some chocolates and brought me home. We're going to *Fresh Fields* on Saturday." It all sounded so easy; cinema, supper, chocolates and theatre, just for passing the mustard.

I tramped London from end to end, spent whole afternoons in the park, lingered over a cup of tea for half an hour, went to the cinema whenever I could, but like the lady in the revue sketch, I remained un-insulted. No man ever asked me to pass the salt, let alone the mustard. So far as I remember no man ever made the slightest immoral suggestion to me. I say "so far as I remember" because I don't think I would have recognized an immoral suggestion if there had been one. I was extremely plain, unmade-up in a decade of heavy cosmetics, and most unfashionably dressed. But I was young, and it is a wonder that in 1933 London apparently contained no depraved men at all. It is possible that innocence is its own protection; but that doesn't sound like common sense.

With 3s. 3d. to spend, week-ends were anything but riotous. Directly after lunch, and sometimes without it, if the programme began early, I tore along to Madame Tussaud's cinema which had the longest showing in one sitting of any picture house. For a shilling it was possible to see two full length films, shorts, news, trailers and to be blasted by an organ. I had seen very few films until I left school, but now they "got me" like a disease. I began to live in a film world; the real world was a shadow, and films the reality. Fortunately for my education I lived in the era of classic film-making. Magazine pictures of Garbo, Clark Gable, Norma Shearer and hundreds of other stars and starlets covered the walls of my cubicle. But it soon passed. While it lasted I could have found the way blindfold about New York, merely from seeing it so often on the screen. American films led naturally to American books and Hemingway, Dos Passos and Steinbeck were gone through with indigestible speed. I swallowed them whole, and then attacked Runyon and Thurber.

I grew in love with London, and my Sunday afternoons were spent walking its streets, particularly the quiet City ways. I once discovered a pair of cottages with gardens and lilac trees somewhere behind Fleet Street. There was no question of taking a bus or Underground train — I walked. From Shoreditch, where I nearly got killed by a flying dustbin lid in a Communist–Fascist brawl, to Piccadilly — where again I was nearly killed, by suffocation this time, one New Year's Eve.

I was well known to all the door keepers at the Art Galleries, Museums, police and law courts. Those forms of entertainment cost nothing, and I suppose I should have learnt a great deal from them. I am afraid for the most part I was so tired that I found them boring. The exceptions were the London Museum and the Divorce Court; but maybe a little culture did stick in spite of all. Most of the time I was hungry, but tried to forget it by dreaming. I don't think anyone could have dreamed so much to so little purpose. Dictators were the fashion and I dictated to marvellous purpose in my fantasy world. I solved single-handed the problem of the unemployed. It was quite easy; you started with an oasis in the Sahara, and gradually planted more and more palm trees, whose roots eventually held the soil. Gradually, by manuring and irrigating from the oasis you tamed the desert, and it "blossomed like the rose". While half the unemployed were doing this the rest were on the coast pumping sea water into irrigation channels. By some means, I skipped exactly how, the salt was taken out in the pumping process, and was formed into gleaming white blocks which made excellent building material for the unemployed. It was very satisfying to gaze on those acres of palm trees and fields of rice; the legion of happy unemployed all living in gleaming white saltrock houses. In those days Mr St Barbe Baker and his "Men of the Trees" were but a whisper in the wind that didn't reach me. Not long ago I was reading a geographical magazine in the doctor's waiting-room, and an article in it described a scheme for irrigating deserts with salt-freed sea water. But I still hold the monopoly on the gleaming white houses.

242

The unemployed were the chief worry of my teens. I was so often one of them; and the fear of unemployment stood like a spectre at the elbows of all my companions at work and in the hostel. The seamstresses were frequently "stood off" in the spring and autumn and I remember how thankfully they heard the news of the engagement of Prince George and Princess Marina. Such public affairs meant not only work for the big names like Schiaparelli and Molyneux, but for buttonholers, finishers, alteration hands, trimmers and even the matchers. Everyone saw the hunger marchers, and heard the Welsh choirs, and the ex-service men's bands, and these indeed were pitiable, but the little hunchbacked gown hands, darning over the darns in their stockings, filling their shoes with cardboard, and ironing over and over their one decent dress — they broke the heart. Not only could they not work, but they had to spend their idle hours in the soulless atmosphere of the hostel and the barren courts of the Ministry of Labour. For the crippled and deformed there was not even the final hope of the streets. I only remember one young girl openly taking to that life from Hyde House, after several weeks of unemployment.

Nobody annoys me more than people who will hark back to the "good old days", when cigarettes were ten for sixpence and you could buy a shirt for 2s. 11d. The people who made these 2s. 11d. shirts were paid fivepence a dozen! — and they weren't tee-shirts either. People who say we haven't progressed never attended Labour Exchanges in the old days. "Signing on" had to be done every day, and it often took as long as two hours to reach the head of the queue. The officers had only three words to say, "Next", and "Nothing Today". Nowhere — in the buildings, the clerks or the signatories — was there a shred of human dignity.

When not solving the problem of the unemployed, I was taking author's calls at the first nights of my plays. I'd no sooner think of a plot and a few lines of dialogue, than there I'd be, in a scarlet, tight-fitting Plantagenet dress making a curtain speech as memorable as any the play had contained. I did finish one or two plays, and even had a one-act drama produced by a religious play festival. It earned me two guineas and won the prize, but its title and content have faded from my memory. I wrote one about Byron for Ivor Novello, who sent it back with apologies; on his or on my behalf I don't know. I wrote another Byron play for Hugh Williams, who bore in those days a remarkable likeness to the poet. I also cast Marius Goring as Shelley and Alec Guinness as Leigh Hunt. Perfect casting, but not I'm afraid a good play. I always meant to rewrite it, but now we are all too old! I had my greatest near-success with the story of Boadicea, my fellow East Anglian. It was specially done for Phyllis Neilson-Terry. She was very kind and though she liked the idea she suggested I write it again. In my innocence I had given stage directions for the ravishing of Boadicea in the full view of the audience. Miss Neilson-Terry thought it wouldn't do.

Influenced by Ivor Novello I embarked upon a great musical. The fact that I was unable to read or recognize a single note of music left me quite undeterred. I would write the book — Novello could see to the music. The setting was the Botanical Gardens, Regent's Park, where

244

spies chased each other in and out of the grottoes and rose-garden.

The railings of the Inner Circle walk had a distinct list inwards, caused, I was sure, by the generations of leaning lovers, so I opened the musical with a "revolve" of couples propping up those railings, and the only chorus I can remember of dozens the script contained was:

> We can't make love as the rich folk do
> With curtains drawn and the doors shut to,
> Soft-hued lights in a smart boudoir,
> And a butler trained as an expert liar.
>
> So we cuddle up in our Paradise
> Though you may say, sir, it's not quite nice.
> But love is love you can't deny,
> Wherever it's made by lowly or high.

It's a pity I didn't finish it; it might have been as funny as "Young England".

On my eighteenth birthday I was solemnly called to the office of the head of Debenham's staff department.

He was a little Robertson Hare of a man. "I hear," he said, "that you are now eighteen years of age. In which case your wages will be raised from 17s. to —" a long pause: "18s. per week. Eighteen shillings for eighteen years. Ha! ha! ha!" I dutifully smiled and went out. Life was a shilling's worth brighter. The Ministry, however, were soon on its track, and I was told that this shilling

245

must now be paid towards my board and lodging. I was furious, and threatened to leave Debenham's, where it seemed that the only prospect before me was to retire at sixty with 60s. a week! I was tired too of Hyde House. Passionately I wanted to *live* — to do as I liked. I did not know what I meant by living; but I did know what I wanted to do. I wanted to go on the stage or the films, and I suggested to the Ministry officer that they should send me to R.A.D.A. She would have given the same pitying smile to an imbecile and for the same reasons.

"You must realize," she said, "that the money spent on you comes from rates and taxes. Every person in the country contributes in some way to your upkeep. You have had many chances and you haven't taken advantage —"

"I've only had chances," I interrupted, "to do what you want. Never what I want. If I went on the stage I should be able to pay the money back."

"You have the wrong ideas about the stage. It isn't all glamour and bright lights. It's . . ."

"Hard work, and that's what I want. Hard work at the job I want. I don't care if I spend my life carrying on banners. It'll be the banner I *want* to carry."

"There are no funds available. You have now been helped two years longer than you should have been. The Minister would not hear of such a proposition. You must stay on at Debenham's and work your way up. Find a young man who will love and care for you. That is the best thing you could do."

"What do I want with young men? I hate them. I'll never get married. You only want that to relieve you of

246

responsibility. This building's full of women who've never found young men. What hope have I got?"

The officer was retreating behind her files.

"You could make yourself more attractive," she ventured.

"On 3*s*. 3*d*. a week! I'm still wearing the clothes I left Barnardo's in. They're schoolgirls' clothes, and I've had them for nearly two years."

She scribbled on her pad.

"I'll ask for a clothing grant, but that will be the utmost we can do. If you leave Debenham's or Hyde House we will have to finish with you."

New clothes were provided, but even these failed to attract young men. I left Debenham's and Hyde House, and I was completely on my own.

From the distance of a quarter of a century I can sympathize with the Ministry's point of view, though I still think a lot of people would have been saved trouble if they had let me try for a R.A.D.A. scholarship. Being under twenty-one I could not do it without their consent.

It is difficult to remember the exact sequence of my ups and downs from the time I left Debenham's until I married. They were not interesting, anyway; a series of failing at this job and that; and of moving from drab hostels to drabber furnished rooms.

I worked as a drudge in a boys' home at Brighton for £25 a year; when I took the job, I mistakenly thought the figure was 25*s*. a week. I was a nursemaid to a woman in Shenfield who had four boys under six. When I arrived they *all* had whooping cough, and after eight weeks of sleepless nights and mopping up sick, I was sacked because "I read more than was necessary for a nursery maid".

Back at Hyde House I was sent by the Labour Exchange to a hand-bag manufacturer in Oxford Street. Twenty-five shillings a week was the agreed wage, but at the end of my first week, spent incidentally in the filthiest workshop imaginable, the proprietor considered I was not worth so much and gave me £1, promising 2s. 6d. more if I would clean his flat, attached to the workroom, on Sundays. Now I had to pay the full 18s. 3d. for board and lodgings, I *had* to have that 2s. 6d.

Win Summerhayes was highly suspicious. "If he starts anything, kick him in the balls — hard," she warned me. I didn't quite know what she meant, but I put on my heaviest shoes and proceeded to Oxford Street. No sooner had the unshaven, dressing-gowned bag-maker let me in, than I knew I shouldn't have come. The whole block of offices and workrooms was empty and silent. Oxford Street itself was becalmed by Sunday. There was no one in the world but me and a fat continental Jew. He showed me the kitchen and told me to make coffee. He then asked, incongruously I thought, if I was a good girl. Foolishly, taking a line from some film I had seen I parried, "It depends what you mean by good."

This seemed to amuse him and he retired to the bathroom, while I swept the floor. Presently he called to me to get him a towel from a drawer. I looked up and he was standing in the doorway, stark naked. Apart from small boys, I had never seen an unclothed male before, and no Victorian maiden aunt could possibly have been more shocked than I was. He was like a white marble frog, framed in the aquarium green of the bathroom. I put down the broom and without a word fetched the towel, gave it to him, grabbed my coat, and, with what I always considered was classic presence of mind, my insurance cards from the desk, and almost threw myself down the stairs and into the street. In my panic I tore up the dead end of Stratford Place and had to tear down again. I didn't stop running until I reached the dormitory at Hyde — panting like a steam train. Win shot out of her cubicle.

"I knew it," she cried in triumph. "He tried it on. I knew he would. What did he do?"

"Nothing. He didn't have any clothes on. I came away."

"You were lucky to get away," someone said, for now I had an audience.

"Lucky," Win scorned. "She's got sense. I shall tell Miss Leake." I shall never know if the gentleman was behaving according to the custom of his homeland, or if he really had designs on my honour.

The upshot was that after a private note from Miss Leake to the manager of the Labour Exchange, I landed a nice easy job with Corot's of Bond Street. I learnt to work a telephone switchboard, which meant that at least I was qualified as something. It was a happy all-female office, full of gossip and bawdy talk. It was presided over by Mrs Reynolds, smart, kind and easily touched by a sad story — except when it came from a non-paying customer. She was irreverently referred to as Old Flo, and took a little more than motherly interest in the love affairs of her "girls".

Corot's sold fashionable gowns and outer wear on the

hire-purchase system, one of the few firms then in that line of business. They prided themselves on the personal touch and they traded all over the world. Many ambassadors' wives kept the flag of empire flying in Corot "exclusive" evening gowns. Mayfair hostesses and film stars were photographed for the *Tatler* in sportswear obtained on a deposit and eight instalments. The Sadie Oglethorpes of Oldham could grace the works dance in exactly the same models for the same price, but the Sadies were usually more regular with their payments. When I wasn't on the switchboard or addressing envelopes I worked the lift, squeezed into a tight brown uniform meant for a fourteen-year-old. If the lift palled, as it did quite quickly, for there were only four floors in the building, it was easy to make it go wrong by pressing the buttons in a certain sequence. Then the "out of order" notice was hung up and the dowagers had to walk the stairs until an engineer arrived. I usually read a good book, and there is no more peaceful place for reading than in a lift stuck between two floors.

On and off I learnt quite a lot at Corot's. About Jewish customs from Gert, who always shared her lunch with me, strange un-English meats in oddly flavoured bread, motzas and halva, and sticky spiced buns. Gert's mum's idea of an elevenses snack filled a fair-sized shopping-bag, and every day as she unwrapped it Gert would say, "Just look at that! Honestly my Mum is potty. She must think I'm a navvy," and the surplus would be passed to me. I never refused anything; there were others at Hyde with empty belly space. I suppose now that Gert and her Mum concocted this little tale to keep me fed. Sometimes I envied Gert her Jewishness, so welded with love she was into her family. I envied her too when she had holidays for her own religious festivals as well as ours; and she never worked of course on Saturday mornings, and left early on Fridays so as to be home by the beginning of the Sabbath. Gert shared her family with us and so warmly and vividly that we too basked in the light of the Menorah, and rejoiced at her brother's barmitzvor. In those days, with Hitler persecuting her race abroad, and Mosley's blackshirts trying to at home, and when many Jews were understandably changing their names, she carried her nose and eyes like a proud banner for her people.

Most of all at Corot's I liked being a messenger girl. Often a customer needed a dress in a hurry and I would be sent flying across London to one of the railway termini, to dispatch it by passenger train. I learned the Underground system by heart. Imagining myself as the bearer of important despatches, urgently required medicine or a last minute reprieve, I followed the "blue for Waterloo" or the "green for Victoria" with the speed of a bolting rabbit. I never missed a train, though I once had to throw the dress box to the guard as one moved out. Then, the urgency over, I could wander back on foot and spend the fare on something to eat. I was always hungry in those days, for food, for the theatre and for love. It was my hunger for the theatre that drove me from Hyde House and its strict night curfew to shabby little furnished rooms and real starvation. I was frustrated by missing so many last acts of plays and the most desirable thing in the world was my own latch-key and freedom. I got it for 10s. a week in a Chelsea basement, and with it went mice and a diet of bread and condensed milk. Now and again I managed a sixpenny lunch-box from Lyons. London's starvelings owe a tremendous debt to J. Lyons and Company; their cafés filled a great social need. They were warm, clean and cheap, and no one minded how long you lingered. There were of course coffee stalls and shelters for the down and outs, but for the hidden destitutes still holding pride and nursing hope it was J. Lyons who saved us from the river. One day perhaps some professor of sociology will produce a book showing that the effect on our development of such commercial enterprises as Lyons, Woolworths and Marks and Spencer was more important than is generally realized.

It was silly and risky to leave Hyde House; for in spite of the irksomeness of its regulations and the oddity of some of its people, it offered a certain safety. There was also comradeship and kindliness, and although at the time I may not have acknowledged this kindness at least I have never forgotten it. There was a Miss Hoste, so recognizably a lady, with her dark hair parted in the centre and fastened with a bun at the back; her high colour and quaint clothes. She wore either all white or all purple, and this included shoes and stockings. These ensembles were irreverently referred to as her "Indian white" or "passionate purple". One hot Saturday afternoon she suddenly asked me to go out with her; and she took me to St Paul's, and we climbed to the ball, and descended to the crypt, a feat to stagger the stoutest heart, but leaving Miss Hoste as calm, and her Indian white as spotless, as when we started. Naturally we had walked all the way there from the hostel. As we were leaving she casually pointed to a large monument to Admiral Hoste, whom she claimed for an ancestor. Then we went to tea at a select club off Piccadilly. The tea service was silver and the steward ablaze with gold braid. I don't know what he thought as he served us; the strange ageing woman in white, and a weird unkempt nymph in a 2s. 11d. washed-out cotton frock and dusty plimsolls, but whatever his thoughts they detracted not one iota from his perfect service. I did not feel in the least uncomfortable, and I realized for a short while what it is in the past that some old people still long for, and what is meant by good breeding.

All the time my longing for the theatre persisted. I forsook the films and made the Old Vic my place of worship. If ever a wild plain ghost haunts its gallery and stage door it belongs to me. Every Saturday afternoon saw me hurrying over the planks of the temporary Waterloo Bridge; running down the hill past the Union Jack Club to join Miss Fremaut in the queue for the Early Doors. The "Early Doors" for the gallery was 6d., "Late Doors" 9d. There was no music to me sweeter than the ring of the metal discs which were given instead of tickets, and the clink of change; and then the mad rush up the stone stairs where the imperturbable sergeant known as "move up a little, please" took the disc and dropped it over a wire. An eminently simple form of box-office keeping, as the discs could be checked against the till, no doubt now superseded by something much more complicated. The sergeant won his name by the way on crowded nights he went round row by row begging the sitters to "move up a little, please", to make room for "just one more". In the end the only difference between the gallery and a gigantic tin of sardines was that the galleryites were not arranged top to tail. Having surrendered the disc I streaked ahead to bag our favourite seats in the front row of the gallery facing O.P. corner, while Miss Fremaut bought the programme and followed at a more ladylike pace. I never met Miss Fremaut anywhere but at the Old Vic. She was a maiden lady in every sense of the word, living with her widowed mother in north-west London. We had little in common except a passion for the Old Vic; this was one of the few friendships my bad temper and selfishness did not spoil. For some reason she admired me and was angel enough to show it. She told me I had "so much courage". I hadn't, but her certainty gave me a little. As she did not go out to work she was able to get a forward place in the "early doors" queue, where I joined her as soon as I could. Together we saw great things. Redgrave in *The Country Wife*, Olivier in a full-length five-hour *Hamlet* and Guinness in a modern one. The giants of today were all young men, rough-edged but vital, and with their own hair atop. The star was always Olivier, the "darling of the gods", whether he played Henry V or the "Button Moulder" in *Peer Gynt*. He was anything but a mature actor; he sometimes gave an appalling performance, but never an uninteresting one.

The Old Vic gallery at Saturday matinées had the air of a club. You could always be sure of meeting the man in the oily boiler suit; the grey-haired woman who knitted all through the performance and the intervals; the wild-looking coloured man, and Miss Pilgrim. I don't know if this ardent galleryite survived the war, but she was an almost built-in fitting at any theatre where Shakespeare was played. She always sang the National Anthem in a loud, harsh contralto, much to the consternation of new-comers to the Vic. It was the custom in most theatres then only to play the first three lines of the anthem, but this was impossible with Miss Pilgrim in the audience; the orchestra was obliged to accompany her to the end. She always carried a large string bag and at least one paper parcel. She had a very low opinion of Tyrone Guthrie and his new group of actors; but she never failed to turn up for his productions, if only to find fault all the way through. She would grab any helpless-looking individual by the lapel and emphasize her remarks with prods in the victim's chest from a large forefinger.

"That's all right for the halls, dear; *there* you reckon to get laughs; but it isn't Shakespeare"; or "Guthrie, Olivier, Redgrave, who are they? They don't do *Shakespeare*."

She held strongly to the opinion that Laurence Olivier's *Macbeth* killed Lilian Bayliss. As everyone knows, there is a "hoodoo" on *Macbeth* and this particular production was certainly one of the unluckiest on record.

Miss Fremaut always brought some cake or biscuits, neatly wrapped in a paper napkin. We shared the price of the programme, and I am sure at a great sacrifice, she always allowed me to keep it. I hope she had some enjoyment from our meetings, for my part I could not have lived in those days without her encouragement. "No man is an island." At all points our lives are interwoven with other people's. Nowhere can we say this person was of no consequence to me; it hasn't mattered at all whether I met him or not. If we try to pull out one thread from the weave of our lives the whole fabric falls apart; so Miss Fremaut, met only at the Old Vic on Saturday afternoons, made my life as much as anyone I knew better or more intimately. At the end of the performance we would say goodbye and she, bending to the wind over Waterloo Bridge, went back to her mother in the suburbs.

Although I admired the stars, it was not they who lived with my dream-haunted days. I was torn between Leo Genn and Marius Goring, and with both of them I was passionately in love. Leo Genn has the most beautiful speaking voice of any living actor, and it was this which attracted me. Marius Goring's fire-red hair and bright blue eyes I would have followed over the edge of the world. As it was I followed both these young men around London, and did not consider it odd that they were no more given to taxis and buses than I was. They were probably almost as poor, for top salaries at the Vic in those days scarcely reached double figures, and my two heroes were only beginners, scarcely out of the "Rosencrantz and Guildenstern" stage. It was to Genn I gave most of my allegiance; plodding behind him all along the Embankment to Pump Court in the Temple. He was actually a barrister, and I had looked him up in the Law List at the Public Library. I don't suppose he was once aware of me, but as I followed him like a shadow I imagined myself rescuing him from all kinds of dangers, pickpockets, cutthroats, road accidents, or more reasonably, of retrieving his lost wallet or dropped handkerchief. But he was a most careful young man, with apparently no enemies. I racked my brains to think of something more reasonable to say than, "Mr Genn, you were wonderful tonight." I usually said that outside the stage door, and if he heard he smiled and said "Thank you" in a rich golden way. There were limits to the number of times this could be said, and anyway was it ever strictly true of Rosencrantz — or Guildenstern? What I wanted to say of course was, "Mr Genn, I love you to distraction." Had I done so, he would no doubt have been surprised, but not, I am sure, ruffled. These cerebral love affairs were completely pure. There were no tiffs, no awkward suggestions, no heart-breaking at all. In fact they were much more satisfying than any of the real affairs I had later on.

When the Old Vic closed for the season there was a blankness over everything until the Open Air Theatre opened in Regent's Park, with new heroes — Jack Hawkins, Leslie French, Robert Eddison, but none of them replaced Leo Genn in my heart. Here with her bundles and her singing came Miss Pilgrim, declaring with satisfaction that *"This* was Shakespeare". I thought so too until I read James Agate's criticism about "fairies disappearing down paths, which in public parks lead to private places". That one sentence somehow took away all the depth from the Open Air, and although I went religiously every week, and enjoyed it immensely, it was never more than a grand charade for me. Except for *The Tempest.* This in that setting became magic, and it was the one play in which the noises from the nearby Zoo didn't matter. No one has ever surpassed Leslie French as Ariel, or looked more majestical as Prospero than the poet John Drinkwater. Of course he couldn't act, but Prospero is actor-proof. A good actor can improve it, but so long as the man can speak he can't ruin the play. *A Midsummer*

Night's Dream was very successful, with lit-up fairies popping up from behind bushes and swinging from tree-tops, but I was never one for fairies and find the Titania–Oberon business tiresome. Actually I preferred to go to the Open Air on wet nights when performances took place in a tent.

I wrote letters to practically every producer and leading actor in London begging for a chance in the theatre. Most of them didn't answer, but the rest without exception advised me not to bother, but I felt I had nothing to lose by trying, and was quite sure that the stage had everything to gain. Only Phyllis Neilson-Terry asked me to go to see her. She was then playing Queen Katherine in *Henry VIII* at the Open Air. This was in the early days and the dressing-rooms were temporary affairs constructed of canvas with a few duck-boards for flooring. This particular night the rain was lashing down, and she, in all Queen Katherine's regalia, sat in a canvas garden chair, holding her skirts up from the puddles, revealing some kind of woollen garments and goloshes. Water poured down her mirror and made puddles among the greasepaint. Rivers drabbled down the canvas walls and the ceiling bellied like a pregnant woman about to deliver. The duck-boards were hidden under thick coaly mud. Miss Neilson-Terry, the most beautiful woman in England, looked at me with sorrowing eyes. "Don't, dear child," she pleaded, "go on the stage. It is a *dreadful* profession," and my word, how right she was.

There were quite a few acting establishments dotted around London, for then everyone wanted to act.

It hadn't occurred to us before the war that you could

make money without learning a little bit about the trade, so we flocked to Drama Schools in Victorian sitting-rooms and sat at the feet of elderly actors, who had all "been with Irving". Irving must have carried an enormous company of hams and it is not to be wondered at that he died almost penniless.

The Clifton-Cooke School of Drama operated from Pimlico and advertised a yearly scholarship. I entered for this and rendered the set piece "Gone to be married" from King John. Recited "Loveliest of trees" very nicely and pretended to be a burglar (a) seriously and (b) funnily. After some weeks I received a letter saying I had been awarded a scholarship worth £80 a year. Being ignorant and having no advisers I thought this meant that I had to *pay* £80, so I refused the scholarship.

After all my struggles and longings it happened ridiculously easily. I went to a repertory producer and he said, "Start on Monday, £3 10*s*. a week, four if you play," and there I was, an assistant stage manager. The theatre was the Coliseum, Oldham, one of the oldest in the provinces. The stage had at some time been sliced right off to make a car park, so a pocket-sized one was made in the auditorium, and the former boxes became the artists' dressing-rooms; and more cramped and smellier places could hardly have been devised in the "sweat shop" age. The box fronts had been boarded in, but as they overlooked the wings the performers on stage were frequently put off by the chattering of their companions in the dressing-rooms. I was once told by a member of the audience that she had found the dressing-room argument much more interesting than the play. It is almost impossible to keep actors from talking; it is *quite* impossible to stop "coffee girls" from rattling teaspoons.

Looking back at my two-and-a-half years at Oldham, they seem to have been spent in waging a losing battle for quiet. But there were of course wars in other fields; the long-odds battle was won every Monday night, to start again every Tuesday morning. Oldham gave a play a week for fifty weeks in the year, and staged everything from *Hamlet* to *White Cargo*. Better productions were difficult to find anywhere. When one considered that in those days leading juveniles were as difficult to find as boxes of matches, our pride and wonder at ourselves can be understood.

Because the building was considered dangerous, the company had to run as a club, which in some legal way made it safer. The popularity of a play was judged by the number of times the queue wound round the car park. I believe the record was held by *Pride and Prejudice*, when the tail of the queue was right in the centre and the whole thing looked like a catherine wheel.

Men, particularly juveniles, were definitely on the odd side. All the most handsome army rejects preferred an easy chorus boy's life in the West End — once the bombs had stopped. The halt, the lame and the blind came offering their services to Oldham. One young man arrived with twelve pieces of matching luggage (anyone with a "good wardrobe" was more than welcome); each piece bore his full name, "Moses Abram Bronzite". He had never in his life been on the stage before, but he didn't turn out too badly, particularly after he changed his name.

He at least had all his faculties, which was more than could be said of poor Mr X, who declaring himself a "young forty-five" arrived on two sticks — with a flaming red wig and one spare shirt. But even he proved useful and was retained at a microscopic salary to play walk-ons, and butlers. This relieved me considerably, because before that the butlers had had to be changed to maids; maids, unless comic, are always played by A.S.Ms. Oldham was luckier than many companies in having two good solid actors, who, although over military age, could step into almost any breach — Malcolm Russell, the quickest "study" in the business, and the late Maurice Hansard. The women's side was very strong; there are always many more good actresses than jobs. A good deal of my time was spent trying to keep the youngest member of the company in order — a local blonde called Dora Broadbent, who had joined the Rep. straight from school at fourteen. She had a gift for forgetting rehearsal times, mislaying properties, losing play copies — all the things good artists do *not* do. Careless, tantalizing, maddening — she could still act everyone else off the stage. As Dora Bryan, she still entrances but no longer maddens.

Stage history, except to theatre people, is intensely boring, so I shall not bother with the details of my undistinguished theatrical career. I became a stage manager, with a reputation as a prompter. It was hard, satisfying work, with no room for any kind of private life. Once a show is on the artists have only their performances to worry about. A stage manager can never relax, and quite frequently works right through the night. Everything connected with a play — performers, understudies, stage staff, setting, lighting, décor, wardrobe, allocation of dressing-rooms; every duty, down to feeding the cat — are his concern. Everyone blames him if something goes wrong, but no one ever thinks to thank him for the hundreds of things that go right. His pay is lower than a scene shifter's, but as his status is above, he cannot be tipped. My salary was £10 a week.

A "walking understudy" could get £9 then (more nowadays), that is, an understudy who covers one or more principals but is not expected to appear either in small parts or in the crowd. There are men and women who do nothing else but "walk". Very rarely do they have to play, for no artist will lose a day's pay if he can possibly crawl or croak. Others understudy one person whom they may superficially resemble, so that their livelihood depends on the fortunes of the star; they are rather like Peter Pan's shadows. These people, of all sexes, are usually excellent knitters and embroiderers. I always found their dressing-rooms, with their unused make-up kit, and litterings of tapestry and half-finished socks, arid repositories of dead dreams. The occupants reminded me of ghouls waiting for disaster, for nothing short of the sudden murder of their principals would give them an opportunity to play. Many managements, to save a salary, make stage managers understudy instead of carrying "walkers". It was my refusal to do this which eventually led to my being ousted from the theatre. "Good at her job, but she won't understudy", was the damning reference that went round the bars and bedrooms where most theatrical business is done.

Stage idols were eclipsed by a real boy friend, a

mysterious young man called John who was a Green Line bus conductor. I don't know how he came by bus conducting, he certainly hated it, and considered the uniform degrading. He seemed to have no home and no past, except some vague service in Egypt, but he kissed in the approved film star fashion and wrote passionate letters. We met at King George V's Jubilee; or rather after the procession. I was wearing shorts and he jodhpurs, so maybe it was just the unusual nether garments which drew us together. It is odd to consider now that a man actually spat at me for what he considered my immodesty, and I heard several cries of "put your skirt on". I think I must have been the first woman ever to appear in the streets of London wearing shorts, which were incidentally of sober khaki and reached to the knee.

Jubilee Day was scorching hot and there was some sense in my shorts, but why John's jodhpurs? He said he'd got so used to wearing them in Egypt where it seemed he dealt with camels! I believed every word he said then and later, but he was the first and last man I ever did believe.

We courted, for there is no other word for it, for the whole of that glorious summer, and then — he disappeared. There were no quarrels, no warnings, he just ceased to be; leaving his Amersham lodgings and the London Transport employ without a trace. He was the first person who had ever professed to love me, and I was heartbroken; not so much for what I had lost, as for what I had dreamed of having. In my usual balmy way I had day-dreamed a home, children and everything else my heart desired. There was too the terrible loss of face before the girls in the hostel and the office. For a time I had held my own with them and lived life at their level. Now I had to make the most humiliating of all admissions, I had been "chucked over", for I was unable to sustain the usual fiction, "He tried it on, so I gave him the go by." Contrary to popular fiction, broken hearts are not incurable and I recovered, but the distrust of men has never left me.

I ambled uncertainly from one underpaid job to another, but however small the wage I'm sure I wasn't worth it. I was a copy-typist in a government office typing pool, presided over by a she-dragon. These she-dragons are born fully armed from eggs laid on the island of the lake in St James's Park. It is impossible that they ever had mothers and fathers, or were once little helpless babies. If there is anything in the popular theory that Civil Servants do nothing but drink tea all day it certainly does not apply to the typing pools. For one thing the tea is bought by the typists themselves, and is not provided by a benevolent government out of taxpayers' money; and in my day only ten minutes' break was allowed each morning and afternoon. If the pressure of work was high these could be arbitrarily cut out. Not so long ago I saw a letter in a newspaper from an outraged citizen who had belatedly discovered that Civil Servants were issued with hand towels. This he considered useless pandering to an idle race, another extravagance of the Socialist regime. The towels we had were often stamped with a V.R. monogram and this lady was never called upon to be unamused by a Socialist Prime Minister. No one had told the irate letter writer that soap is also individually issued, but to get a new piece the remnants of the old one have to be surrendered. This went also for such things as pencils and india rubbers.

It always seems odd that a nation which prides itself on fair play should continually abuse a body of people who cannot hit back — the Civil Servants. They are for the most part ordinary hard-working men and women, working harder than most (the dragonry see to that) — some are bumbly-jumblies, but some are great administrators, and a few are poets. They have made politics unnecessary in this country, and parliament merely a tub-thumping ground for bad actors. The permanent Civil Servants govern us — for which the Lord be praised. America is governed by politicians — and look at it! There may be sumptuous government offices, but the ones I saw, and they were many, were drab, cold and smelly. As one went up the promotion scale the room got smaller, but smellier too.

It was the method of paying which roused my rabble instincts. An infernal machine containing columns of coins of all denominations was brought in by a messenger and plonked on a table; behind the machine-like priests followed three accountants, all male, and at a respectful distance the female departmental supervisor. She carried a list of payees in order of seniority and took her place at the end of the table. The first accountant opened an enormous ledger, the second stood poised before the machine as if about to play a "mighty Wurlitzer", and the third arranged two stacks of bank notes before him. The messenger, now joined by another, stood behind the cash, as if daring any of us to make a smash and grab. We in the meantime had lined up in the same order as our names appeared on the list. Without looking up the man with the ledger shouted "Smith, J. L. P. Two pounds, sixteen and ninepence." The wurlitzer player brought his hands crashing down on the keys which produced the odd change; this he scooped into one hand and slapped on the table. He didn't look up either; neither did the third man to whom "Smith, J. L. P." presented herself, but merely thrust forward the required notes, first clicking them savagely, as if his one desire was to tear them in half. The next stop was at the supervisor's forefinger, beside which the now amply rewarded "Smith, J. L. P." signed her name on the form. This system was quick, accurate and efficient, but from the humanity point of view absolutely bloody. It is to be hoped that nowadays, when even domestic servants dare to be people, their sisters in typing pools have followed suit, and have by pressure brought into being some method which raises their status a little higher than machine parts.

The wages of a copy typist were about 35s. a week, and with that I lived in a hostel in Pimlico. The rate was higher, but there was more freedom, fewer women and we each had a latch-key. The hostel was named after the journalist W. T. Stead, and had been founded with money collected by his admirers at the time of his imprisonment. It will be remembered that he was much concerned with the plight of young business girls in London, who for lack of decent homes often landed in the hands of procurers and pimps. To prove his point, and to show how easy it was, he procured a young woman himself, and landed in gaol for his pains. The house that bore his name stood cornerways to Lupus Street and St George's Drive. Like the whole neighbourhood it was a relic of more gracious days, but it was a nice friendly house to live in. The last time I saw it the walls were gaping to the road after an air raid; the only room above street level that was fairly intact was the drawing-room. I once wrote a play set in this room and using the hostel dwellers for characters. Fat, wheezy, great-hearted Ethel, who ran the place almost single handed, for the matron had a "heart" and could do little more than clerical work. Miss Maclean, a Scottish mountain of a woman. She had been in San Sebastian the day the Civil War broke out. It so happened that it was also the day her holiday ended, so she packed her bags and carried them through the cross-fire of the public square to the station, where naturally she was going to catch a train. At one point she was confronted by a soldier who raised a revolver at her. Putting down her bags she stared at the little man and thundered, "If ye no put that thing away I'll knock yer block off." Miss Maclean reached home at the hour she said she would, Civil War or no. This is the master race, if ever there was one.

There were Miss Baines and Miss Beer, who were never mentioned separately, and were the aristocracy. Both were very gentle, and infinitely kind. There were others, all rich characters with which to make a play, but somewhere I lost the script and could never recapture the spirit in which it was written.

If this room was haunted it was by the slightly sinister spirit of The Cat. He had no name, he was too remote to be called Tiddles, or Pussy, or anything but plain Cat. He had a passion for the grand piano. He would sit on the stool and dab at the notes with his paw and now and then walk solemnly up and down the keyboard. If the lid was shut, then he thumped the keys from underneath. As a variation he jumped on to the strings and played them like a harp. He would often perform in the middle of the night, and would scare new-comers out of their wits. He was an extremely ugly and malevolent cat, but all the women loved him. Ethel was the only person to whom he showed any kind of affection, and that was natural enough — she fed him. When the war seemed imminent it was decided that The Cat, now about nine or ten, must be put to sleep; a tear-streaked Ethel brought us the news and declared she couldn't possibly take him, "He'd know you see, and he'd turn on me", so Miss Baines and I volunteered for the dirty deed. The Cat, who was as big as a terrier dog, was fastened down in a basket and carried between us. His wails and squawks were unbelievable, and as we walked down St George's Drive to the P.D.S.A. clinic we could feel eyes at every window and fancied that muttered curses were being flung at us. Every time we rested the basket Miss Baines said, "He *knows*." Her conscience was smiting her mightily.

"Some people say cats have souls," she said rather fearfully.

"He wasn't a particularly nice cat." I wanted to lessen her guilt, *I* wasn't worried at all.

"No, but he played the piano."

"And when it was windy he went mad and ran up the curtains."

"He was a bit more than an ordinary cat." When the vet pronounced The Cat dead Miss Baines wept all the way home, declaring she'd never forgive herself. When I think of her genuine concern and sorrow for The Cat I find it difficult to remember that she belongs to the same order of animals as those who, without a qualm, gassed thousands of women and children and dropped atom bombs on helpless cities.

I reached the end of my tether where office jobs were concerned, when, becoming redundant at the Ministry of whatever it was, I went as a temporary copy-typist to the London County Council. There the Supervisor was the Arch-dragon of them all, with, it seemed, a special spite against young girls. The rumour was that she had been embittered by a love affair that had gone wrong. If it was not true, that is certainly how she behaved.

After a few weeks I was asked to produce my birth certificate, and I obtained a brand new copy from Somerset House. The birth certificate of an illegitimate child bears no particulars of the father even if these are known. A positive gleam came into the Supervisor's eye.

"This certificate is worthless to us," she said.

"Why? It's my certificate."

"That may be, but who was your father?"

I told her. "That doesn't mean anything," she went on, "what we want is proof that you are a British subject. This is no proof. Your father might have been a Pole, or a German."

Had she jumped on my chest with hob-nailed boots she could not have winded me more. When I recovered I became insolent: "The Ministry of Pensions kept me for years; they wouldn't have done if they hadn't been sure that he was my father."

"The Ministry are more easily satisfied than we are. You cannot become a permanent member of the Council unless you can prove you are a British subject."

"Then I'll go," I shouted at her.

"We can't give you a reference."

"I don't need a reference — *to get married*."

In fairness to the L.C.C. I am sure this woman was overstepping by a long way the limits of her authority; but she was responsible for a great deal of unhappiness, and should have been flung out years before.

So then there was nothing for it but to get married.

EPILOGUE

This is a story of childhood, and I don't propose to go into great detail now as to "what happened next". I must after all save something for my old age! It doesn't do to write of one's life too close to the events. If I had written this book at twenty-five it would have been a very "angry" one indeed — but if growing older brings nothing else, it does bring understanding and charity of thought. It should bring self-knowledge too, but it can so often bring self-deception instead.

Childhood, of course, decides what kind of adults we shall be, but a deprived childhood such as mine need not necessarily lead to misery and delinquency. It has its advantages, especially for one's husband — no mother-in-law, and in matters of love one can always please oneself, if it goes wrong there is no one else to blame.

All my life I had been looking for love, but had been so deluded by films and novels as to what really was love, that I didn't recognize it when it was there.

Michael was nothing like Gary Cooper or Clark Gable. He was a quiet amateur actor at the Tavistock Little Theatre, that place where you could have all the thrills of the real theatre, and none of the risks. He also happened to work at the L.C.C. as a clerk in the welfare department, so at two angles our lives met. We married within three months of our first meeting, on his wage of £4 a week, and we furnished a flat on the £10 he had saved. I married him out of my loneliness, security didn't enter into it. I wanted to belong to someone, to be able to say "*my* husband" and "*our* home", and many happy marriages have been made for less reason than this. No one else ever wanted to marry me, and Michael did because he loved me, why I shall never understand. We were desperately poor, but our marriage survived the "Blitz", his imprisonment as a conscientious objector, his early precarious years as a professional actor — but it foundered in the peace and the first glimpse of prosperity. He was a good man and I failed him. He is dead and there is nothing more I can say.

At thirty I found myself right back to the beginning again. With no home, no money, but with a baby. I regretted then all the time I had spent mooning around theatres instead of getting myself trained for some well-paid trade. One thing I was determined on, to keep the baby. She was, after all, the only relation I had ever had, and although well-meaning friends gave me reams of good advice about adoption or fostering, I knew, irrationally but with certainty, that if we parted we would both die, not physically, but in spirit. The only gate opened to us was that of resident domestic service — the one thing that as a child I was determined *not* to do. Many people were able to offer quite good accommodation in return for domestic help; but most people are more fortunate with their help than were my employers. For I was quite disastrously bad at the job. One after another these long-suffering ladies would come into the kitchen, fiddle awkwardly with something on the table and begin "Mrs Hitchman, I'm very sorry, but I'm afraid . . ." and off we'd go again. Quite an undertaking with a cot, pram and two trunks. Once all these things temporarily went astray and I arrived at a mansion in Kent carrying one infant daughter and a chamber-pot decorated with Peter Rabbit. Perhaps it was the pot that started things off so badly, for we were out again before the luggage had time to catch us up. Throughout all these upheavals my daughter remained extremely healthy, sweet tempered, and beautiful, which seems to contradict all those books about bringing up children written by weighty American psychiatrists. In fact she always made such a good impression that she usually got the job for me. It was my inefficiency that lost them. My trouble was that in my heart I considered myself too good for domestic work. This was just arrogance, no job is "beneath" anyone if they do it well. There are still snobbish and overbearing employers. I met quite a few, but domestic service nowadays can be comfortable and well paid.

Over the years I have attained a certain amount of cunning and worked out one or two essential rules. Never, if you have a child of your own, take a job where there are other children. They are usually so badly behaved that they make most undesirable companions. Never take a job which has been frequently advertised, or because you are sorry for the advertisers; and never, never, live "as family". You can hold your own in the kitchen but not at your employer's table. Never go to people who want "lady cooks", or "lady housekeepers". Like "gentleman far-mers", these are contradictory terms.

Domestic service in fact is an excellent profession, *provided* you can identify yourself entirely with the family for whom you are working. I never could. Always I have been fighting for the rags of my own identity. These years were in many ways a waste and torment, but I learnt something from them. I became a quite passable cook, a good car driver, and attained just a little patience.

Life has been much easier since I faced the fact that I am not a very nice or likeable person, and accepted my own limitations. The great thing is not to be dependent on other people, or try to hoist your personality to their patterns and standards. There are things which other people consider important, which I cannot bring myself to bother about. Clothes, for instance. I am comfortable in slacks, shirts and jerseys, and these I wear practically all the time.

I lose my temper more than somewhat. Child cruelty, race discrimination, bullying policemen, adulation of royalty, litter louts, there are plenty of things to make me boil over! That a country which calls itself the most enlightened on earth should *need* a Society for the Prevention of Cruelty to Children I take as a personal disgrace. I deplore the modern tendency to look on children as a separate race; they are merely younger people. Much money and time was spent on me as a child, I probably cost the country thousands of pounds one way or another; but I would have given it all for my own mother's love in a slum. It is not bad conditions but bad parents who make bad children. Many problem children today come from so-called "good homes", where they are only looked on as extensions of their parents' vanity, and where they are slaves to "convenience". It is convenient for mum that Johnnie should use his pot each day at 8.30 a.m. and not dirty his knickers at 9 o'clock just as she

274

wants to go shopping. So every morning mother and Johnnie join battle, and this battle continues long after Johnnie has grown out of pots. This asserting of a parent's will over a child is more cruel than physical violence. In everyday life, though, I have become a calmer and more balanced person. This may be due to the normal process of growing older, or to a more realistic facing of the facts. I have had to learn to be patient not only with other people but with myself. I have not become the person I had hoped to be; now I know I never shall and must accept myself as I am. One cannot reach this plateau of beatitude without faith.

Religion has always been prominent in my life. Orphans were considered to be more in need of it than others. In my early childhood it frightened me, and later bored me. In my 'teens it worried me because it didn't seem to matter at all. I went regularly to church and the service was no more than words. I studied the Bible, but it was nothing more than a hackneyed story. Religion did not *touch* me at all. I could not understand how people had been willing to die for their faith. I wanted to be "saved" or "changed" or "converted", but no uplifting spiritual experience came my way. Why was it some people were so certain about the will of God, without apparently taking any trouble at all? When I was at Highgate I attended a Baptist chapel at the end of the road, twice each Sunday, and dreamed of the minister all the week; he closely resembled Clark Gable. I thought there could be no higher bliss than to be ducked by him in the miniature swimming pool under the rostrum. I was all set for being a Baptist when one Sunday my minister was away and his place was filled by a nondescript layman. The service was as flat and meaningless as hundreds of others I had been to in other churches, and I realized it wasn't the Baptist God I was worshipping, but the Baptist minister.

At Hyde House, I went to church for much the same reasons, only this time I knew it was the parson I went to see and not God revealed. Arthur Buxton of All Souls' was the most beautiful man I have ever met, on or off the stage. He was a great loss to the theatre, for he wasn't much of a preacher. He had a great gift for finding curates who could shine in the pulpit, and between them they produced a service worthy of Drury Lane. All Souls' has no east window, instead there is a large oil painting of Christ on his way to the cross. This was lit by a spotlight from the roof, and for the Benediction all other lights were dimmed; one's attention was focused on the tragic eyes of the painting, and the silver curls and Greek profile of Buxton kneeling at the altar, while the sevenfold Amen rose, and rolled and died away. It was theatrically beautiful, and the ecstasy would carry me home on a wave of holiness. But the ecstasy was not enough to cope with the poisonous supper in the drab basement dining-room at Hyde. I knew that for me faith was necessary for my survival, but I set about things in the wrong way. I expected faith to give me something; to clothe me from without as it were, and for me not to make any effort at all. One has first to believe, then to serve, and then *maybe* to receive.

At the back of my mind throughout the years was the knowledge that the right faith for me was Quakerism. For a long time I would not make the final decision because it

276

involved so much responsibility. Every member of the Society of Friends is "his brother's keeper". He is also his own keeper, which is often the hardest thing to be. There are no priests, no intermediaries to interpret God, no canon laws or books of rules. Nothing, in fact, stands between the Quaker and the Almighty. This may sound arrogant but it is in fact very humbling. There are principles that all Quakers must believe. That God is revealed in *every* man. That *all* war is futile and sinful, and that whatever is the honest thing is the right thing.

I have often been asked what advice I'd give to young people. Actually I think advising the young is fairly useless, and to give advice to the present competent generation somewhat impertinent. One does learn a thing or two going through life, but one learns it for oneself. You can never pass on to your children those truths you have learned out of bitterness and blasting experience. Each generation has to re-learn; make its own mistakes, feel and fight for itself. If one generation could take experience from another, human life would cease — for what need would there be to be born? And really what have I learned that would be of any use to a young person of today? Perhaps the most valuable thing is that nothing is for ever. Everything passes.

As for my special knowledge of being a deprived child, I have gained much of value from that; although at times to have been born an ugly bastard is just one degree in hell above the black man and the Jew, at least one knows what it is like to *be* a black man or a Jew. Nowadays there are many organizations to help and advise children who have no families of their own; it should be impossible for anyone to be left as I was, utterly alone at sixteen in London. But even that taught me to be independent, to think and fight for myself. Through this thinking and fighting I am now able to earn a living as a writer. It is a meagre living, but at least I have fulfilled one of my earliest ambitions. I can now "do as I like".

Sometimes when I see my name in print, in a newspaper or magazine, I can hear Mum's exasperated "Gal, you'll never come to nothin'." I like to think that for once she was wrong. That I have come any way at all is to me a never-failing wonder.

"Count your blessings" [we used to sing at Barnado's]
"Name them one by one
And it will surprise you what the Lord hath done."

It will too!

ACKNOWLEDGEMENTS

This book has been written from memory only. I never kept a diary or letters, or even photographs. At times no doubt my memory has erred. Since I began I have discovered that Granfa's name was actually Alfred Sparkes, but I have always thought of him as Sam, and have left it so. Some other names I have changed deliberately.

I owe so much to so many people that a list would look like a telephone directory. Many I never knew by name and a few I may have forgotten. To all I am thankful. Such misfortunes and unkindnesses as I have met have only served to make me resilient. From everyone I have gained something starting with the stoic patience of Granfa to the tolerance of Uncle George; from Mum's humour and determination to Miss Huntley's thoroughness and high principles; from Miss Lawrence and Miss Bill who thought I was worth bothering about, to the enfolding love of Barnardo's. If I have offended anybody I am sorry. The institutions I have criticized have since improved out of knowledge; perhaps people like myself, who were articulate enough to complain and barbaric enough to make nuisances of themselves, brought about some of the improvements.

ISIS publish a wide range of books in large print, from fiction to biography. A full list of titles is available free of charge from the address below. Alternatively, contact your local library for details of their collection of ISIS large print books.

Details of ISIS complete and unabridged audio books are also available.

Any suggestions for books you would like to see in large print or audio are always welcome.

ISIS

7 Centremead
Osney Mead
Oxford OX2 0ES
(01865) 250333

ISIS REMINISCENCE SERIES

The ISIS Reminiscence Series has been developed with the older reader in mind. Well-loved in their own right, these titles have been chosen for their memory-evoking content.

FRED ARCHER
The Cuckoo Pen
The Distant Scene
The Village Doctor

BRENDA BULLOCK
A Pocket With A Hole

WILLIAM COOPER
From Early Life

KATHLEEN DAYUS
All My Days
The Best of Times
Her People

DENIS FARRIER
Country Vet

WINIFRED FOLEY
Back to the Forest
No Pipe Dreams for Father

PEGGY GRAYSON
Buttercup Jill

JACK HARGREAVES
The Old Country

ISIS REMINISCENCE SERIES